HIS CURVY EX

A SMALL TOWN CURVY GIRL ROMANCE

BOOK BOYFRIENDS WANTED
BOOK EIGHT

MARY E THOMPSON

 BluEyed Press

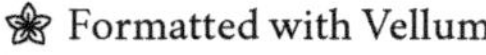 Formatted with Vellum

BOOK BOYFRIENDS WANTED

Welcome back, my friend. It's always nice to see you. I'm glad you could drop by MacKellar Cove for a visit. Hudson has a drink ready for you. Finley's got some cake and a new book. And the whole crew wants to say hi.

Romancing the Curves comes with subscriber exclusive freebies, sneak peeks, and a first look at everything Mary has to offer. Be the first to know about new releases and sales and all the curves ahead!

SUBSCRIBE NOW AT MARYETHOMPSON.COM

Happy reading!

For anyone hoping for a second chance...

ZOEY

*I*t was just a summer. One summer. I repeated the words to myself as I pulled away from the only home my kids had ever known, the only home I'd truly known. Pittsburgh was a great city, but it no longer held anything that made me want to stay. My marriage was over, my family was gone, and I was out of reasons to stick around.

But we would be back. It was just a summer. One summer I could give my kids that was full of fun and family instead of fighting. A summer where I would help my brother and his soon-to-be wife finish a few projects on MacKellar Cove Inn, the inn my aunt ran until my brother and his girlfriend took over. At the end of summer, Gavin and Piper were getting married, if he ever got up the nerve to ask her. Then I'd pack my kids up and go back to Pittsburgh and back to the life I had there.

Because I had nowhere else to go.

The tinny sounds of the iPads that kept my kids entertained reached my ears and told me they would be fine for the drive through New York to MacKellar Cove in the Thousand Islands. That was unofficial home to me, and it always had been, but I ruined the chance to make it permanent years ago. That was why going back could only be for the summer. And why I'd return to my sad, lonely rental in Pittsburgh at the end of it.

I crossed the state line into New York and breathed a sigh of relief. So far, the kids hadn't said a word. No fights, no bathroom breaks, nothing. I knew it wouldn't last long, but with a six-and-a-half hour drive, I'd take what I could get.

Less than an hour later, my luck ran out. Thirty miles south of Buffalo, my six year old daughter announced she had to pee.

"Really bad, Mommy. Now!"

I swallowed my groan and told Alexis I'd get her to a bathroom as soon as possible. It had been a few miles since I passed an exit, and I was fairly sure a sign said there wasn't another one for nearly twenty miles.

Minute by minute, the miles ticked by. The video played through her headphones, but I knew the end of the line was coming quickly.

A service exit sign told me five miles. I stepped a little harder on the gas and prayed I'd make it those five miles without an accident in the backseat.

"Mommy, I really need to go," Alexis whimpered a minute later.

"We're almost there," I promised, pushing it a little more. Twelve over the speed limit wasn't going to be a problem, right?

I finally saw the exit sign. We were good. We made it without an accident or an incident.

Then I heard the siren.

"Shit," I breathed.

"Mommy, you're not supposed to stay that!" Cameron, my eight year old, said.

"I know, honey. I'm sorry." I pulled to the side at the exit, hoping it would be a quick stop when he saw the kids and heard the pleas from Alexis about the bathroom.

"I really need to go, Mommy," Alexis said, almost as if on cue.

"I know."

The officer came to the window and knocked. I was paying attention to the kids and jumped. I rolled down the window and plastered a smile on my face. "Hello, officer."

"License and registration, please."

"I'm sorry, officer. I know I was going a little fast, but my daughter really needed to use the restroom and I was trying to get her here."

"License and registration, ma'am."

I sighed and accepted that I'd be pulling in to clean up pee after she had an accident in her seat. He was not willing to let me go with a warning. I handed over the documents, and he carried them back to his vehicle.

"Mommy, I don't think I can hold it anymore," Alexis whined, sounding pained. She was good. She hadn't had an accident in months. She knew having one was bad, but I was fairly sure the streak was over.

"I know, baby. I'm sorry. I tried. Hopefully he's fast and we can get you to the bathroom. Do you see that building right there?"

"Uh huh."

"That's where we need to go. If you can hold on just a few minutes longer, we'll run, run, run over there and you can use the bathroom. Okay?"

"I'll try."

"Sounds good, baby girl."

I stared at the officer still in his car. I wanted to get out and yell at him to hurry the hell up, but that would have only made the stop longer. When he finally returned with my license, registration, and a ticket, I had to stop myself from laying into him.

"Mommy, I couldn't hold it," Alexis said as the officer started to walk away. She started to cry.

He looked at her and looked at me, his eyes admitting he thought I was lying, but the damage was done. The ticket was mine, and we both knew there was nothing else he could do.

"That's okay, baby. Now that we can go, we'll get you changed and do what we can to dry off your seat." I glared at the officer and turned the car back on. I didn't wait for him to get back in his car before I took off up the ramp toward the service exit.

Alexis cried until I got her out of her seat. Her shorts and underwear were soaked. And so was her entire carseat. I dug through her suitcase while she stood next to the car crying until I found a change of clothes for her and a blanket I could put over the seat.

I took Alexis's change of clothes and both kids to the bathroom. I made both of them use the bathroom, changed Alexis into her clean clothes, and headed back to the car. I laid a blanket on the seat for Alexis and covered that with a trash bag I found stuffed in a side pocket. It wasn't perfect, but it was mostly dry.

Great start to our trip.

I got gas while we were there and got back on the road. It was almost halfway, so I hoped we would make it the rest of the way before we had to stop again.

The closer we got to MacKellar Cove, the harder my heart pounded. I was anxious when we left Pittsburgh, but that was nothing compared to how I felt when I passed the sign saying *Welcome to MacKellar Cove*.

Home to Sebastian Parks, I added in my head.

Sebastian Parks was supposed to be the man I spent the rest of my life with. I fell in love with him when I was too young to really know what love was, and I broke his heart before I learned. I mistreated him worse than anyone I'd ever known, and I deserved to be miserable because of it.

I hated that my kids paid the same price.

We pulled into the driveway for MacKellar Cove Inn, and I was torn between relief that we were there and anxiety over seeing Sebastian again. I knew he wasn't far, and even though I was also sure Aunt Gina had told him when we were arriving, it was still very possible that he would be around.

"Is Sebastian going to be here?" Alexis asked. Was she reading my mind? She met him when we visited at Christmas and fell for him as hard and fast as I had when I was young.

"I'm not sure. Probably not tonight."

"But I want to see him," she pouted.

"I know," I said, trying hard not to be frustrated by her. She had no idea how tough it was for me to see Sebastian, but he'd imprinted on her and she adored him.

"Maybe Aunt Gina can call him for me."

"I'm sure she'd be happy to," I told her, knowing Aunt Gina would do anything for either of my kids.

I parked the car and made sure no one else was in the parking lot before telling the kids to run to the door and go inside. I knew someone in there would entertain them while I took the carseat apart so it could be washed and dried and ready to use again whenever we had to go out.

"Need some help?" Gavin asked a minute later.

I stepped back and hugged my big brother. It was embarrassing to admit hugging him was the most physical contact I'd had with another adult since I hugged him goodbye almost six months earlier.

"Whoa, are you okay?" he asked, pulling back when he realized I was crying.

I shook my head at myself and said, "Yeah. I just really missed you."

"That's why you should just move here. Then you won't have to miss me."

"You know why I can't."

Gavin nodded, but the tempting smile on his face did not fade. He had something up his sleeve.

"What did you do?"

"I didn't do anything. Let's get you unpacked. What's first?"

"Grab the bags from the trunk. I need to take care of Alexis's seat. She had an accident, and I got a ticket."

"Seriously?"

"Yeah. Fun stuff. I'm really happy to be here."

Gavin beamed. "Me, too, sis."

I WAS hot and sweaty and feeling even more gross by the time I finished cleaning up the carseat and the back of the car. I took the entire seat apart and threw the padding in the wash along with the blanket and the clothes Alexis was wearing, then sat down for just a minute. The air conditioning felt good, and the heat outside was enough to warrant it.

"I heard you had an exciting drive up," Aunt Gina said, joining me in the sitting room with a glass of lemonade. "Drink up."

"Thank you, Aunt Gina." I took the glass from her and enjoyed a sip. It was sour and cold and delicious.

She took a seat across from me, her assessing gaze running over me. I knew it wouldn't be long before I got her judgement, although from Aunt Gina, it was always gentle and constructive. Designed to help, with a subtle encourage-ment that made me feel as though her words were gospel.

"It's been a long year, hasn't it?"

I snorted. "Endless."

"Any word on your job?"

I shook my head. "Not yet. The school should let me know soon."

"You're not worried?"

"I am, but I worked there most of the year. I think that'll help me. Serving lunches in the school cafeteria isn't glamorous, but it meant I was around for the kids, had all the same days off they had, and it paid enough for us to live on with the child support and alimony payments from Trevor."

"Then I'd say you're doing well."

I forced a smile for my aunt because the alternative was admitting to her, and myself, that I felt like my entire existence was coming apart at the seams. I took the job because it meant I wasn't sitting around all day waiting for my kids to come home. I felt useless. When Trevor and I got together, he convinced me not to get a job right away. First, it was so I could plan our wedding. Then, it was so I could get pregnant. Then raise the kids. I always planned to start working once Alexis was in school, but at that point, Trevor and I were having problems, and I didn't want to rock the boat.

Now, I was thirty-two with the work history of a teenager. My degree only counted on paper since I'd never used it. And no one would hire someone a decade out of college with zero experience in the field they claimed to be an expert in.

"Do you remember the old garden?" Aunt Gina asked, dragging me from one thought to another.

This one full of hot, steamy nights, falling in love, and learning all about what two people who loved each other could do together.

The first time I met Sebastian was in that old garden. I was reading a book when he walked through, pausing to smell one of the roses. It made me laugh, and that laugh caught his attention. We started talking, and over time, the garden became one of the many places at the Inn where we spent time together.

And the place I finally gave myself to him on one summer night after I turned eighteen. A night that still ranked number one on my top ten list of most romantic moments.

"Yes, of course," I finally choked out, knowing Aunt Gina was waiting for an answer.

"I finally decided to fix it up this summer. It's been such a mess since Uncle Rob died. He was the one who always maintained it. I miss sitting out there and watching the boats."

"It was always so beautiful. I loved being there when I used to visit."

Aunt Gina nodded and folded her hands in her lap. A ghost of a smile lifted her lips. "Uncle Rob and I used to sit there and talk for hours. The garden was always so special. I always hoped you or Gavin would get married there."

"Well, maybe you'll get your wish this summer," I whispered, knowing Gavin's proposal was a secret. Although, if he didn't do it soon, the entire town was going to tell Piper. Secrets didn't last long in MacKellar Cove.

"I hope so," Aunt Gina said. Her bright, happy smile had the opposite effect on me.

The garden was where I promised Sebastian I'd come back. Where we talked about getting married. Standing beside my brother while he got married was something I looked forward to, but doing it in the garden where I once thought I'd be married was going to be a challenge.

"You should go out and see it," Aunt Gina suggested. "Maybe you can help with the design. I'm not getting around as easily as I once was. I think you knew that garden almost better than I did."

I finished my lemonade and nodded slowly. "I'd like that, Aunt Gina. I want to help any way I can while I'm here. I don't want to just be three more mouths to feed. I want to pay my own way."

"You know family doesn't pay here," Aunt Gina scolded me.

"I know, but Piper and Gavin own the Inn now. I don't want Piper to worry that she's going to be saddled with Gavin's freeloading baby sister."

"Piper would never say that, or think it. She's wonderful, and she adores you. She's with Alexis and Cameron right now, planning fun summer activities."

"She is? I figured they'd be with Gavin. I didn't want them bothering Piper."

Aunt Gina dismissed my concern with a wave of her hand. "Piper is not bothered. I assure you. Go out and see the garden, then take a shower and get unpacked before dinner. You'll feel better."

I looked down at the tee I'd thrown on that morning and the cotton shorts that were designed for someone to run in, an activity I never willingly did. I was kind of a mess, probably smelled like urine, and definitely needed a shower. Before I scared off the guests, I decided Aunt Gina was right.

"Will you watch for the kids? In case they need something?"

"Of course. But I'm sure Piper will be fine with them."

"Thank you, Aunt Gina."

I walked the glass back to the kitchen and put it in the dishwasher. I was looking forward to getting to know Piper, but I was nervous about it. She was, hopefully, going to marry my brother, she bought my family's inn, and now she was taking care of my kids. I couldn't imagine her perception of me was all that great.

But I wasn't going to worry about that immediately. I

pushed through the back door and out into the sunshine and early summer heat. If it was already close to eighty at the end of June, it was going to be miserable in August. The breeze off the water helped, but I preferred spring and fall weather so I could wrap up in a blanket and sit by a cozy fire.

I walked down the path toward the family house. I smiled to myself as memories of summers long past came back to me. I was going to do everything I could to make this a great summer for my kids. I resisted everything about MacKellar Cove when I first came, but I fell in love with everything the small town had to offer by the end of that first summer. Almost twenty years later, I knew my life would be different if I had trusted that love just a little more.

But I wasn't strong enough to do that. I let fear dictate what I did. I couldn't say I regretted the choices I made, but if I could go back and make new ones, I also couldn't say with certainty what I would do.

I rounded the house and smiled when the garden came into view. Trellises lined with flowering vines created a wall between the garden and the house, hiding anyone inside from those outside. Every six feet, there was a break in the trellis, with an entrance to the garden and a new path inside.

As I got closer, I heard voices. If Aunt Gina wanted me to help with the design, I figured I should go meet the gardeners. It was a big enough job that I was sure she hired a dedicated crew.

I walked through the closest opening and felt my entire body relax. The water lazily drifted past, gently bumping against the shore with each wave. The garden paths were intact, but the plants were overgrown and dying. A lot of work was needed to make it what it once was.

A laugh drew my attention away from the water toward the people I'd heard. I took a step toward the laughter, a smile lifting my lips when I recognized Piper's friend, Sofia. I opened my mouth to call out to her when I saw the person she was talking to. The man she was laughing with. The one and only person I wanted to avoid for the summer.

The one I just told Aunt Gina I would work with.

Sebastian Parks.

I turned and ran.

2

SEBASTIAN

Sofia tipped her head back and laughed. At my expense, of course. She was helping me in the garden because she knew Zoey and her kids were arriving that day. And Sofia was doing her best to distract me.

The sun blazed down on us, and when I dropped one of the few surviving plants onto the ground and all the dirt splattered like a crime scene, Sofia lost it.

I picked up a chunk of dirt and threw it in her direction. She squealed and ducked out of the way, laughing the entire time.

"You're supposed to be helping, not making this take longer," I snarled at her.

"I'll help clean up, too," she offered. "And maybe even come back and help another day."

She chuckled and focused on the section in front of her. I paused with my dirt-covered hands on my hips and looked around. I told myself I was not looking for Zoey, but I found her anyway.

All the breath in my lungs fled like it did the first time I noticed her, really noticed her. The late afternoon sun hit her golden brown hair and made it glow. She wore a loose tee and shorts that did nothing for her curvy figure. Her hair whipped around her face, blocking her gaze from mine.

And then she ran.

I knew she saw me, but before I could say or do anything, she was gone. She disappeared between the trellises, back to the house or the Inn or wherever I wasn't.

My lungs spurted and stalled before they started working again. I sucked in a painful breath, painful because I'd stopped breathing, not because of Zoey. I'd stopped loving her a long time ago, and I wasn't going to let myself fall back in love with her.

"Are you going to make me do all this by myself?" Sofia asked.

I looked at her kneeling on the ground. Her head was down, and she was focused on the decaying flowers in front of her. She tilted her face toward mine, and I could tell she saw what just happened. The way I froze at the sight of Zoey and the way she ran at the sight of me.

Sofia raised an eyebrow and said nothing about either. She was a good friend. She never pushed me for more than I was willing to share, which was usually not much. Sofia was the kind of woman I should want in my life. One who understood me and always went out of her way to be there for me. But there'd never been that spark between us. We instantly felt like we'd known each other forever, and like we'd been siblings or best friends or something like that forever.

I glanced back at where Zoey disappeared to and admitted to myself that it was for the best. She was there for the summer, and we could simply avoid each other. She was already starting. I would just follow suit. Keep my head down and work, and stay away from the Holbrook family.

"Yeah, I'm coming," I told Sofia. I dropped to my knees a few feet away from her and resumed pulling out dead flowers.

Sofia and I worked side-by-side for another thirty minutes before she announced her back was killing her and stood. "I'm going to a yoga class in the morning with Willow. You should join me."

The teasing note in her voice had me rolling my eyes. "You know how I feel about yoga."

She laughed. "I do. But one day I might change your mind."

"Not likely. I'll take a chance on Zoey again before I'll try yoga."

Sofia snorted. "Maybe you should do both."

The glare I sent her should have been enough to stop her train of thought, but it obviously wasn't strong enough. She kept talking.

"I'm just saying maybe you need closure. She left before, without a word. At least this time you know she's leaving. But with Gavin here, she's going to be back. You're going to run into her again and again. I don't like seeing you so upset."

"You're such a girl," I countered. It was my usual retort when she said something one of my guy friends would never say.

"Why, thank you. I didn't think anyone noticed." She stuck her tongue out at me.

Sofia stretched, then dropped back to her knees once more. Again, I hoped that was the end of it. And again, I was wrong.

"Piper said Zoey almost didn't come this summer because of you."

"Why do you care about this?" I snapped.

She looked at me with one brow lifted, a gentle *fuck you* in her eyes. I was being an ass, but Sofia had an unlimited tolerance for it. She never blinked or pushed back. She always let me get it out of my system, then helped me see where it was coming from. There were times I really didn't like her.

"I care about you, Sebastian. Zoey seems nice enough, but you're my friend."

"Are you… do you…" I didn't know how to ask her what I needed to know.

"I'm not interested in you. I'm not laying in bed every night wishing you looked like you do right now when I ran the other way. I adore you, but like a brother who needs his ass kicked to keep his head on straight. Not something more."

I sighed heavily. I was that needy son-of-a-bitch who always asked. She never questioned our friendship, but I continually worried she was interested in more than a friendship.

"We understand each other," she continued. "I don't have a lot of people I talk to or am close to. Piper was it for a long time. The people in my building are great, but I go into their homes and fix things. We don't hang out together. You're my friend. When you're not being an ass."

I barked a laugh. She was right. "You know that's my usual state."

"Trust me, I know."

I chuckled with her, and we settled back down to keep working. The garden was going to take most of the summer to get back into shape, especially since I could only work on it after my day at the lighthouse. Sofia helped when she had a free afternoon, but we were still on the first major section.

"You know you're going to need to bring in more help when things get further along, right?"

I nodded and stood. The garden was a semi-circle that framed in part of the shoreline. A fountain used to sit in the middle, but it broke years ago and was discarded. Over the last five years or so, the garden had slowly degraded to the state it was currently in.

"The first thing we need to do is finish tearing everything out and make a plan. But yeah, planting all these is going to be nearly impossible."

"Especially to do all this in just a few months."

Sofia was skeptical about the project in the first place, but I couldn't say no. Gina was the only person in the world I considered family, even though we weren't. I would do anything for her, including fix up the garden that made me think of Zoey with every inch of plants.

"What did the garden look like before? When it was maintained?" Sofia asked.

I looked around at it and saw the garden in my memory. The fountain was the centerpiece, but around that were grass pathways that wound around the large space. Kids used to use the garden for games of hide-and-seek because of the benches and bird baths, but also because of the plants that varied in height and created the perfect places to hide.

"It was almost magical before. I worked here when I was young. I would have lunch out here. The trellises created a world inside the garden that felt like nothing bad could happen here. This spot, this garden, was where so many major moments in my life happened."

"Really?"

I nodded slowly before realizing what I was admitting to. Sofia wouldn't judge me, not the way others might, but there was still a lot we never talked about. Our parents and our childhoods were the biggest ones. Neither of us asked, and neither of us offered anything.

"Anyway, I know the garden is important to Gina, and I know Gavin wants everything done for the wedding, if he ever asks her, so we're going to do the best we can."

Sofia tried to catch my gaze, but I evaded hers. I knew she would see the truth in my eyes. The truth that being in the garden was harder than I wanted to admit. That standing there was taking a piece of me. The garden had brought both good and bad to my life. Most of the time, intertwined. Like meeting Zoey and losing her while standing there. Finding a place that felt like home and losing the only home I'd known. The garden was a part of me, and I would do everything in my power to make sure it was what it used to be.

Sofia didn't ask anymore questions. She worked with me until her phone rang with a tenant who needed her help. She promised to be back again the next evening. "I'll bring dinner."

I shook my head. "You know Gina will lose it if we don't have dinner at the Inn. Especially on a Friday night."

Gina had signed over the Inn the Gavin and Piper, but she still worked in the kitchen. She loved to cook, and she took pride in feeding as many people as she could. I'd been eating Friday night dinner with her for so long I couldn't remember a time when I didn't. Sofia had been pulled into the tradition over the last few months, too.

"Ooh, I forgot what day it is. Okay, dinner first. Then we'll finish this section."

"Sounds good. Thanks. I appreciate the help."

"Any time. Make sure you get something to eat tonight, too."

I met Sofia's gaze and nodded. We both knew I was not going up to the Inn for dinner. Not with Zoey and her family around. Normally, I'd have most of my meals there, but everything had changed. Everything.

I dug back in and worked another thirty minutes after Sofia left. The sun was fading, and I knew it was only a matter of time before Gina would come looking for me, so I finished up and headed home for the evening.

The cottage I called home was simple, but the most important part was it was quiet. I liked my quiet, and my alone time. It meant I could have my thoughts and no one would intrude on them.

Too bad people could intrude on my cottage.

I'd just gotten out of the shower and finished getting dressed when there was a knock on the door. I hadn't missed any calls or texts and rarely got visitors. At that time of night, not many people ventured all the way down to my cabin.

I flipped on the exterior light and opened the door, half expecting to find no one there. Instead, Gina and Alexis were on my porch.

"Sebastian!" Alexis shouted before she threw herself at me. Her little arms wrapped around my thighs and her head hit my hip. "I missed you!"

"She insisted on coming to see you tonight. Zoey tried to get her to wait until tomorrow, but I said I wanted to bring you something to eat and offered to come down here with her," Gina explained.

"Did you walk? You shouldn't be out in the dark like this," I asked, ushering them both inside.

Gina shook her head and stepped into my cottage. She went straight to the kitchen and set the covered tray down on the island. "I took the landscape cart. It has nice, bright headlights."

I shook my head at Gina. The woman was fearless. She was also in her late seventies, which worried me constantly. She thought I was being ridiculous by not wanting her walking around at night, but it was for her own safety. Something Zoey needed to learn if she was willing to let her aunt and child go off alone after dark.

"Zoey shouldn't have let you come down here alone."

"Do you think she could have stopped me?" Gina challenged. The gleam in her eyes said she knew exactly why I was upset, and that it had nothing to do with her safety and everything to do with being annoyed by Zoey.

I grumbled a response and turned to Zoey's daughter. Alexis reminded me of her mother. So much that it hurt to be around her at times. When Zoey and I first met, she hung around me the same way. For the first summer or two, I told myself she was an annoying kid, but by the third summer, I admitted to myself that I liked her. She was a teenager, and far too young for me, but I found myself looking forward to the time we spent together. We talked like I'd never talked to anyone else. I shared things with her that I've never admitted since.

And she took all of that and turned her back on me.

"How was your drive?" I asked Alexis. I couldn't think of anything better to ask.

"Not fun. I had an accident and Mommy said a bad word when the police officer gave her a ticket."

I looked at Gina for confirmation. A quick raise of her brows was all the answer I got, with a slight shrug of acceptance. There was definitely more to that story, but it wasn't my business. None of it was.

"Well, did you have a fun afternoon? Is it nice to be here?"

Alexis shrugged. "I guess. Mommy wouldn't let me find you. I wanted to come say hi when we got here, but she said you were busy."

"I was busy. Aunt Gina has me working hard in the garden."

"We used to have a garden. When we lived with my daddy. But he got to keep it when we moved out. Mommy said she misses her garden."

I nodded, unsure what else I could say. The last thing I needed was for someone to invite Zoey to help me in the garden.

"I'm going to have dinner at the house tomorrow night. My friend, Sofia, is coming, too. Are you going to be there?"

Alexis nodded and yawned at the same time. "I am. Will you sit next to me?"

"Sure. I think that'll be fun. Sofia will be happy to see you again, too."

"Is Sofia your girlfriend?"

I considered lying to her because I knew she would tell her mother all about our conversation, but there was no way I would put Sofia in that position.

I shook my head. "No, she's not. She's just a very good friend."

"My mommy says my daddy has a lot of friends now that they aren't married anymore. She doesn't let us stay with him because his friends like to sleepover. Does Sofia sleepover here with you?"

Ouch. As much as I wanted to think Zoey got whatever she deserved by marrying that asshole instead of me, I still felt bad for her.

"No, Sofia doesn't sleepover here very often. She has her own apartment."

"Aren't you lonely here by yourself? I could sleepover sometime and keep you company. Or my mommy could."

"I'm good. Thanks," I told her. The last thing I needed was my home smelling like, or reminding me of, Zoey.

"I think maybe it's time to get you into bed, little miss," Gina said, stepping in and ending the conversation.

"Okay. Good night, Sebastian. I'll save you a seat tomorrow night."

I walked Alexis and Gina to the door. Alexis hugged me tight once more. I patted her on the back and tried not to fall for the adorable little girl that was impossible to not like. Gina kissed my cheek and called for Alexis to slow down so she didn't get too far in the dark. I watched them until Gina started the golf cart and turned back toward the Inn and disappeared up the hill.

I went back inside and heated up the dinner Gina brought me. It wasn't long before my dinner was gone and I was fading, trying not to have dreams about an adorable little girl and her mother who could never again be mine.

3

ZOEY

"I understand. Thank you for calling," I repeated for the third time. I just wanted to end the call. But he kept talking.

"I really wish there was something we could do, Ms. Holbrook. I tried, but there aren't any positions at other schools within the district. I will provide you with a good reference. I was really hoping to keep you." Christian was a nice man, and a good boss, but he was not a miracle worker. Unfortunately for me.

"Thank you for that. I appreciate it."

"Will you let me know where you end up finding a job? I'd really like to know you land on your feet."

"Sure, I'll let you know."

"Thank you, Ms. Holbrook. And I really am sorry."

"Thanks."

I finally managed to hang up the phone and closed my eyes. My chest was tight, and my lungs were too full. There was a tickle in the back of my throat that was suspiciously similar to how it felt when I cried.

It wasn't that I was so disappointed to lose the temporary

job I had for more than half the year working in the school cafeteria. It was a good job, and an important one, but I couldn't say I felt it was what I wanted to do forever. Still, it was a job. A job that paid a decent amount and allowed me to work while my kids were in school and be home any time they were. It was pretty close to perfect.

And now it was gone.

The child support and alimony I received every month covered most of our expenses, but not everything. After a few months, I was getting into debt, which was why I took the job in the cafeteria. That money helped pay for the fun in our lives, like trips to the movies, Cameron's soccer, Alexis's dance, and all the books the kids could want. It also meant we weren't eating ramen noodles or mac and cheese every night.

Without that job, I couldn't provide for my kids the way I wanted to.

The scratchy feeling in my throat sent a tear running down my cheek. I wiped it away, but another one followed right after it. I closed my eyes and gave in to the overwhelming feeling of disappointment in myself. The choices I made a decade ago to avoid this were coming back to bite me in the ass, and pushing me right back into the situation I tried to avoid all along.

Except this time, I had two kids involved. Funny how history seemed to repeat itself. Or, you know, not funny at all.

Gavin's voice reached my ears before his heavy footsteps echoed up the stairs. I stuffed all the emotions down and erased any evidence of my tears. Eventually, I would tell him what was going on, but not yet. I needed to figure out a next step before I started talking to everyone about it.

By the time he knocked on my door, I had my hand on the knob and was getting ready to walk out. I plastered on the best fake smile I could dredge up and opened the door. "Hey. What's going on?"

He tilted his head to the side. He knew me too well and saw something, but he also saw the pretend grin I was hiding behind and didn't push. "I was just coming up to see if you were interested in going outside with me and the kids. They want to have a water balloon fight. I'm outnumbered. I need all the help I can get."

I laughed and nodded. "Yes, you do. They're feisty."

"And sneaky," he added. He winked and led the way to the stairs and outside, where the kids were lying in wait for us.

The first balloon exploded against the porch railing next to me. I screamed and jumped away. "What the heck?"

"They have help!" Gavin ducked away from me as the next one popped on my feet.

I laughed and walked down the last step, scanning the yard for them. The wide open space didn't have many places to hide, but giggles told me where to search.

Behind the Inn's truck.

"It's game on!" Gavin shouted, racing toward the truck with a balloon in each hand.

Piper shouted, "Run! He's armed and dangerous!"

Cameron and Alexis squealed and took off toward the open grass. Both were carrying brightly colored balloons that they'd forgotten about. The smiles on their faces and the pink in their cheeks made my heart feel like it was going to burst like one of the water balloons.

This was why we came.

Gavin popped a balloon on Piper's head, and she laughed loudly. She handed him a balloon, and they both went after the kids. I leaned against the paint-chipped porch railing and watched the four of them run and laugh and play.

I felt the same way they did when I was little and used to visit MacKellar Cove. I laughed and had fun. I knew life could be like that. Uncle Rob would joke around with Gavin and I, just like Gavin was doing with my kids.

It seemed like a lifetime ago that I felt that way. I imagined my life would be like that. Hard work running the Inn, but plenty of happy, playful times to balance it out. I wanted that for myself and my children.

I would have had it, too, but I changed everything before I could. And my children were shortchanged. Instead of all their summers being like this one, we would only have one summer of fun. Once we got back to Pittsburgh, I was going to have to find a job, likely one that meant they would go to an after-school program and camp throughout the school breaks and summer. I let myself get swept up in the fantasy world of what life was like if you had money, and I was finally learning the price for that choice.

"Come play, Mommy!" Alexis called out.

I faked another smile and walked out behind her. She dodged a balloon thrown her way and took off. The four of them weaved around the yard, staying away from the cove and the garden.

I tore my eyes from the garden and tried to forget about Sebastian. I wanted him to be happy. It wasn't fair to wish things were different.

A water balloon hit my side and soaked my clothes. The stream of water trickled down my leg and squished into my shoe. I scoffed and looked around for the culprit, knowing before I spotted my brother that he was the only one who would do it.

If I was only going to have one fun summer with the kids, I might as well try to enjoy it. I grabbed a balloon and went in search of a target.

AFTER THE WATER BALLOON FIGHT, we all showered and got cleaned up for dinner. Aunt Gina was picky about Friday night dinners, so we were all dressed nicely and ready to go to the Inn on time. Even Cameron was wearing a collared shirt and khaki shorts. He was complaining about them, but he wore them.

Alexis skipped ahead of us on the walk over to the Inn. She was definitely in a hurry for dinner. The water balloon fight took more out of her than I realized. I hoped that meant I could put the kids to bed early and start looking for jobs right away.

Alexis disappeared into the Inn, leaving Cameron and me to follow behind her. His slumped shoulders sat not too far below mine and reminded me how fast he was growing.

"Thanks for cleaning up the water balloons earlier. You were a big help."

He shrugged those too-big-for-his-age shoulders and said nothing. Third grade was going to bring a lot of changes. I hoped one of those changes wouldn't be losing my oldest.

"Why didn't Dad come with us?" Cameron asked when we got to the door.

I paused and pulled my hand back from the handle. "You know Daddy and I aren't married anymore."

"I know he doesn't live with us, but I don't really know why. Why can't I live with him?"

The pain that shot through my chest would have been comical if it weren't so damn hurtful. I forced a smile. "Daddy works long hours and isn't home much. Just like when he lived with us. We decided it was better if you and Alexis lived with me."

"I don't think it's better. I wanted to see him this summer. He said we could go to a baseball game."

How many times had Trevor made promises to him and not kept them? Of course, I always had to be the bad guy and either break Cameron's heart or have an excuse ready when Trevor did. I never wanted Cameron to feel like he wasn't important to his dad. It was a horrible feeling, one I wouldn't wish on anyone.

"We're not that far from Pittsburgh. We'll make a baseball game work."

I was done being the one disappointing my son. I had to make the summer fun. I had to.

Cameron shrugged and let himself into the Inn. I took a deep breath and followed him, hoping everything would work out.

The kitchen smelled like heaven. Aunt Gina scooped vegetables from the pan on the stovetop to a large bowl. When she saw me, she nodded for me to carry it into the dining room.

I kissed Aunt Gina's cheek and asked how her day was.

"Good. It's Friday."

I smiled and wished I had half of her excitement for life. I grabbed the bowl and walked into the dining room. I scanned the room for my kids, knowing they had to be there somewhere. Cameron was hanging around Gavin, but Alexis was… Where was Alexis?

I set the bowl down and moved through the crowd of people. There was a small part of me that said nothing had happened to her and that she was safe in the Inn, but the bigger part of me tended to be paranoid and anxious when my kids weren't in sight.

I kept walking through the main dining room that over-flowed with people chatting and laughing. She wasn't in there. I headed out to the overflow dining room, the one that was always open in case there were that many people for dinner. Finally. Toward the back of the room was a small table, and at that table were Alexis, Sebastian, and Sofia.

Great.

My relief was short-lived, but the encounter was inevitable. It had been twenty-four hours since we arrived, and I knew it wouldn't be long before I had to say hello to Sebastian. After seeing him and Sofia in the garden the day before, I was looking forward to speaking to him even less, but obviously, my daughter didn't have the same worries.

"Alexis, I was looking for you," I said, flashing an apologetic smile at Sofia and deftly avoiding Sebastian's gaze. It was easier to apologize to his girlfriend than it was to address the man himself.

"Sebastian said I could have dinner with him and Sofia."

"Ms. Sofia," I corrected her. I'd lost the battle in getting her to address Sebastian as Mr. Sebastian, but she was not going to be overly familiar with his girlfriend.

"She said I could call her Sofia," Alexis argued.

I glanced at Sofia and caught the wince before she smiled at me. "I'm sorry. I didn't realize it was an issue."

"It's fine," I told her, forcing another smile. I wasn't upset with her, or Alexis, but the entire situation was more than a little unnerving.

"Will you join us?" Sofia asked.

I opened my mouth to respond, but nothing came out. I closed it again as my gaze drifted to Sebastian. He was looking past me, as though I wasn't even there. I deserved it, but it still hurt. He hadn't acknowledged me at all. Not that I'd spoken to him, but this was his girlfriend.

"I have Cameron, too. And I'm sure you two want a quiet dinner alone," I said, hoping my smile wasn't as fragile as my heart.

"There's no need for that. Why don't you grab another chair and you can all sit with us? I'd love to get to know you all better," Sofia insisted.

I wasn't sure how to get out of it and found myself agreeing. "I'm going to help Aunt Gina. I'll be back shortly. Alexis, stay here."

"I will, Mommy. Sebastian told me I couldn't get up because he didn't want you to worry. I won't leave him." Alexis smiled up at her favorite person. My gaze followed hers and collided with his. His gaze held me prisoner for a long moment, making it impossible for me to look away or think about it. His eyes darkened, almost imperceptibly, then closed, breaking the hold he had on me. When they opened again, he did not look at me, dismissing me without a word.

I thanked Sofia and Sebastian quietly as I hurried away. An entire dinner with them? It was the least I deserved. I knew that without a doubt as I left them behind. It was going to be a long summer.

AUNT GINA THANKED everyone for coming and introduced Cameron, Alexis, and me to the crowd. Throughout dinner, guests stopped at our table to say hello and welcome us back for the summer. It was nice to have the distraction from the uncomfortable dinner situation we were in.

Cameron sulked through most of dinner, not saying much to either Sofia or Sebastian. I wanted to apologize for him, but my behavior wasn't much better. I didn't know what to say to either of them, and I definitely couldn't ask what I wanted to ask.

How long had they been together?

Were they happy?

Why was I so stupid and gave him up?

For years, I told myself I hoped Sebastian was happy. That I hoped he moved on and had made a life for himself. When I found out he hadn't, I felt bad for him, but I also felt a little bit of hope. It wasn't fair, and it wasn't right, but it was there. My marriage was already over, and for a minute, I wondered if I would get a second chance with Sebastian.

At the end of the day, I got exactly what I deserved. I tried to make a better life for myself and my family by chasing something that wasn't real, and I was paying for it. Instead of accepting love and trusting that it would be enough, I let myself get dazzled by flash and fortune. I should have known it wouldn't last, but I was young and foolish and thought I was doing the right thing.

"It's nice that you have the summer off and can come up here for so long, Zoey," Sofia said, bringing me back into the conversation she and Alexis were having.

I nodded and opened my mouth to agree when Alexis answered for me.

"Mommy works in my school cafeteria. She feeds me lunch every day. It's so cool."

I forced a smile for her and pressed my lips together. Letting her think I still had the job wasn't right, but I wasn't ready to share the news with anyone.

"That is cool. It's nice you get to spend time with the kids during the day. And you're right there if they need anything."

"It is nice. I enjoyed it a lot."

Sofia's smile faltered at my flat tone and closed comment. I left no room for her to continue the conversation. It wasn't entirely conscious, but I felt uncomfortable with her.

"Can I go?" Cameron asked.

"Where are you going?" I asked him.

"I'm done. I want to go play a game."

"I love games," Sofia said. "What game are you playing? Can I play with you?"

"It's online."

"Oh, well, I probably wouldn't be very good at that." Sofia glanced at Sebastian and tried to keep her smile in place. I wondered how she did that. How she could appear so content in the face of such rudeness from myself and my son?

"I'm sorry about his attitude. He had plans with his dad for the summer, and I ruined them by coming up here," I explained, hoping Sofia would forgive our attitudes.

"I understand. Traveling is tough as a kid. You have an idea of what the summer will be like, but it's never quite the same as the picture in your mind. My dad used to make big plans for the summer. Usually, it meant I was more or less on my own. It was tough," Sofia said with a kind smile for Cameron.

"My dad was going to take me to a Pirates game. He promised."

"Nice. I'm more of a Yankees fan," Sofia said with a glimmer in her eye.

"I like the Yankees, too. I played baseball last summer. I wasn't really that good, though."

"Maybe we can find a glove and a ball around here somewhere and play catch sometime. One of my friends used to play for his college team. He might be able to give you some tips." Sofia winked.

Cameron smiled for the first time since we walked over from the house. He nodded, and I wanted to kiss her. No wonder Sebastian chose her. She was kind and thoughtful and willing to go out of her way for a child she barely knew. Hell, I wanted to date her.

"Thank you," I whispered to her when Cameron wasn't paying attention. He'd forgotten about his video game and was finishing his dinner.

"You're welcome. I meant what I said, too. I'd be happy to play catch or kick a soccer ball or whatever to spend time with him. You have two amazing kids."

I gave her a grateful, watery smile. Not many people told me that. Trevor spent more time complaining about all the things I should be doing instead of all the things I had done for the kids. He wanted Cameron to be tougher and Alexis to be less talkative. He wasn't willing to see that his kids were developing personalities right in front of us, and that we should help them be whoever they were meant to be. But Sofia got it. My ex's new girlfriend got it. What could I say? "Thank you."

4

I pushed all thoughts of finding a new job and Sebastian and Sofia out of my head through the weekend and enjoyed the time with my kids. If Cameron was going to be upset because his father was an ass, unfortunately, he was going to have to also learn to let it go because Trevor was unlikely to change. Alexis was her usual bubbly self, but she was asking every five minutes if we could go see Sebastian.

So much for putting him out of my mind.

By Sunday afternoon, I was almost regretting the trip. Cameron was still in a mood, Alexis was making me a little crazy, and I felt like I couldn't just sit down and relax because we weren't at our own home. It was my job to entertain my kids, and I was failing at it.

"What are you doing tonight?" Piper asked, joining me outside where the kids were playing tag.

I gestured to them. "Probably more of this. Why? Did you need something?"

"Yes. I need you to come with me to book club."

I immediately shook my head. "No, I couldn't."

"Why not? You know Blake and Sofia, at least. And you'll be here all summer. You can't possibly sit here every Sunday night and not come. It's fun. And everyone will be happy to see you."

"I don't know. The kids are being difficult right now, and I'm not sure if being here is going to work. And I… I'm not sure I should have come here for the summer." I almost admitted I needed to find a new job, but I couldn't tell Piper before I told Gavin. He'd be hurt.

"Then you definitely have to come. Hopefully, we can change your mind about staying, but if not, you need to come see everyone before you go."

"I don't know." I looked out at my kids. Alexis was smiling, but Cameron was starting to look bored. I wanted them to have a good summer. It had only been a few days, but if we were home, they would have friends to get together with and all their toys and stuff. We could go to the community center pool and go for walks and figure out things to do. Instead, they were already bored.

"Gavin will watch the kids tonight. You come with me. I promise, it'll be fun."

"What'll be fun?" Gavin asked. He wrapped Piper in his arms and kissed her quickly.

"I'm trying to talk Zoey into going to book club with me. She said she might go back to Pittsburgh because the kids aren't having fun."

"Go to book club and enjoy. I'll watch the kids and we'll figure out some fun things to do this summer," Gavin said.

"I can't have you watching my kids all summer," I argued with him.

"Why not? They're two of my favorite people on the planet, and I miss them."

"Yeah, but you have an Inn to run. You have guests. You're busy."

"I'm never too busy for them. Go out and enjoy. I'll manage them for the rest of the day." He walked toward the kids with his arms above his head, his hands crooked into claws, growling and snarling like he was a monster. Alexis squealed and ran, but Cameron just chuckled. Gavin went for Cameron until Cameron started laughing and ran from him.

"See? They're in good hands," Piper said. "Come with me. It'll be good for you to have a night off. It sounds like you don't have many."

I snorted. "I don't have any."

"Well, now you do. Every Sunday night."

I finally let go of my reluctance and agreed. It would be good for me to get out and be around other adults, even if they weren't adults I knew well. And it would give me a chance to get to know Piper before she became my sister-in-law.

"Wait. I haven't read the book. What book is it?"

Piper shook her head. "Don't worry. Half of us never read the book. It's more of a chance to get together, eat cake, and talk about men."

I groaned internally. Maybe it wasn't such a good idea. I was sure to bring the rest of them down. But it was too late to back out.

PIPER MET me in the living room when it was time to go. Gavin had the kids somewhere, and he assured me he would take care of getting them to bed at a reasonable time, with their teeth brushed and pajamas on. He'd always been the fun one, but he still respected bed time. Thankfully.

Piper drove and talked the whole time we were on the way there. It was a short trip, but she managed to tell me about all their plans for the Inn. Including the plans for the garden. I couldn't help but wonder if she knew how special the garden was to me, but I doubted she did. No one besides Sebastian knew, and he was in there tearing it to shreds, so it clearly no longer meant the same to him.

We parked near Book Boyfriends Unlimited, and Piper knocked on the door. We waited for someone to let us in, and Piper smiled widely when it was Finley Jameson. I still had a hard time believing these women were friends of mine. Or at least willing to let me into their circle. Finley and Blake were the girls I saw when I would visit and wished I could be like when I was their age. I still wished I could be more like them, but now I was getting an inside look at what it meant to be them.

Finley hugged Piper, then me, and said, "I'm so happy you came. Piper said you were in town for the summer. We were all hoping you'd join us."

"She talked me into it."

"Well, hopefully it isn't so hard to convince you to come back."

Finley's smile was genuine and true, something I hadn't had enough of in far too long. I couldn't remember the last time someone wanted me around. The feeling stuck in my throat and stopped me from answering with more than a nod.

"Karissa brought a chocolate cake for tonight. Are you up for it?" Finley asked.

"You had me at chocolate. Or cake. Either one and I'm in," I told her.

Finley laughed and looped her arm through mine. I let her lead me to the back where everyone else was sitting in chairs and talking.

I pasted on a smile and accepted the welcome the others gave me. Piper sat next to Melody Holland. Blake pulled me down onto the empty seat next to her. Elise handed me a piece of cake. I felt like I was one of them.

"Any proposal yet?" Blake asked quietly.

I glanced at Piper and shook my head. "No. I don't know what he's waiting for."

"Neither do we. It's killing me. And if he's going to plan the wedding for the end of summer, he needs to get moving," Elise said.

"When are you getting married?" Blake asked her.

Elise snorted. "I'm not sure we ever will. We keep talking about it, but I don't know."

"Do you not want to get married?" I asked her.

"My college boyfriend was abusive," Elise said.

I drew back and stilled. "Wow. I'm sorry."

"Thanks. I've learned over the last year or so to be able to say that without feeling like it was my fault. But anyway, when I was with him, I felt like I wasn't worth anything. I left him and decided I was not going to ever get married, or date, for that matter. But Colin... he's amazing. I never saw someone like him in my future. I know he wants to get married, and I feel bad that I've been putting him off."

"If it isn't right, you shouldn't get married. Trust me," I told her.

Elise shook her head. "It's right. I love him. I want to spend the rest of my life with him. I just need to let go of that last bit of fear. I keep telling him to plan a trip somewhere and we can just elope, but he won't do it. He wants me to agree and for us to actually plan it. Not that we have to have a big wedding, but impulsive is not his nature."

"I'm not very impulsive either," I admitted. "The one time I was didn't end well."

"What happened?" Blake asked.

"I married my ex. Now, he's my ex."

They laughed like it was a joke, but I was serious. Going

on a date with him was a split second decision based on fear and uncertainty. If I'd have taken a minute to think things through, I never would have said yes to him. It was too late for that now.

I took a bite of my cake and let Blake try to talk Elise into marrying Colin. I was about to ask a question when Finley returned from letting someone else in, followed by Sofia.

I choked on my cake and tried to play it cool. Sofia scanned the room until her gaze landed on the empty chair next to me. I wanted to tell her it was saved for someone else, that I spilled something there, anything to keep her from sitting next to me.

But there was nothing I could say. Sofia took the seat, and I was stuck with her. Again.

"Hi, Zoey. I didn't know you were coming tonight."

I smiled and swallowed the bite of cake I choked on. "Piper invited me."

"Good. It's nice to see you again."

I smiled and shoved more cake in my mouth so I didn't have to speak to her. God, I was a child.

"How's the garden coming?" Blake asked.

"It's a big project," Sofia said. "Sebastian is meticulous about every plant in there. If it can be saved, he wants to save it. He said the garden is a special place, and it deserves to be treated that way."

My head snapped her direction, wondering if I heard her correctly. There was no way Sebastian still thought of the garden as special.

"He's been working there for a long time. He probably has a lot of memories of the garden and how it used to be," Blake said. "I would think it's hard to let some of that go."

Sofia nodded. "Yeah, he's definitely having trouble letting it go. He loves the garden. He wants to make sure he does everything he can to make it what it used to be."

"Excuse me," I said, standing. "Is there a bathroom?"

Blake pointed toward the back hallway. "First door on the left."

"Thank you," I said as I rushed toward it.

I pushed into the dark room and flipped on the light before closing the door. I could not sit there and listen to Sofia talk about the garden like she was. Like it was a living, breathing thing that Sebastian loved. Not when I knew he'd rather destroy it and flatten the space and never have to look at it again.

I sucked in a deep breath to calm the emotions rioting through me. I soaked a paper towel and patted my face and neck. Then I drew in another deep breath and let it out slowly. I couldn't leave, but I was going to have a hard time coming back.

I unlocked the door and opened it, only to stop short when I found Sofia right outside.

"Sorry," I said, ducking my head and moving to walk past her.

"Actually, I wanted to speak to you."

"Oh?"

"Yeah. Listen, I know it looks like Sebastian and I are together. A lot of people think we are. But we aren't. We never have been. We're friends. We are very similar and we understand each other, but that's it."

"I'm not sure why you're telling me this."

Sofia raised one all-knowing brow and nodded. "Just in case you were curious. He isn't dating anyone at all. He's throwing himself into making the garden what it used to be. Years ago. Because he still loves it. And wants it to be happy."

"He wants the garden to be happy?" I asked.

Sofia nodded. "He does. Very much so."

I knew what she was trying to say, but I also knew it wasn't true. Sebastian knew I got what I deserved when my marriage imploded. He knew it was justice for what I did to him. And there was no way he wanted me to be happy.

"Okay, well, thanks, I guess."

Sofia nodded, then moved past me into the bathroom. I stood there for a long moment before going back to my seat.

"… exciting! I can't believe how much you've done," a woman I didn't know said to Finley.

"Thanks, Goldie. I never would have been able to do all this without your help," Finley said.

"When is the signing?" Elise asked.

"Three weeks. And we have another one at the end of summer. And I have a book fair right before school starts over Labor Day weekend," Finley told her.

"It's smart to invite authors who have ties to the area to come in for a signing. And to partner with other events going on in town. There will already be more traffic, and it should help you know everything is going to be okay," Blake said.

Finley nodded. "I hope so. These last few months have been stressful. If these events bring in even half of what Goldie is projecting, I'll be set for a while. Long enough to get me through the winter."

"Are we talking about the signings?" Sofia asked, returning to her seat next to me.

"Yep. Goldie has some projections that are really good. So good it makes me anxious. I couldn't have done all this without you," Finley said to Goldie.

"You're the one doing most of the work. I'm just giving you ideas and dates to consider. You're making all of this happen," Goldie replied.

"You two make a good team," Blake said. "We're all so grateful to you for helping out."

Goldie shook her head. "I am the one who's grateful. You've all been so willing to help me with all the town events and promote everything we're doing at the tourism center. You're all making me look good."

"I don't think that's hard to do," Finley said. "You're bringing in a lot of people, and we're all benefiting from it. I'm not going to complain. But I will do everything I can to make you successful."

"That's all I'm trying to do. Make everyone successful. I hope it's working."

"I've had a ton of new sign-ups on my app, so it's definitely helping me out," Karissa said.

"Doesn't that make you mad?" Finley asked in a teasing tone.

Karissa shrugged. "It used to, but I'm accepting it now. A lot of people aren't willing to go through the entire setup just for a hookup, so I don't think it's too bad. At least, I hope not."

"What's your app?" I asked. I didn't think any of them knew it, but I had a degree in computer science. I'd considered developing apps at one point, but it wasn't a knowledge base I had at the time. I still didn't, and my degree was almost a decade old, but computers still interested me.

"Karissa has an online dating app," Blake said. "You should sign up. Even though you're only here for the summer, it's a good way to meet locals."

"Don't listen to her," Goldie said. "The app is cursed. All of these women met their boyfriends or husbands on that app."

"That's not entirely true," Blake said. "I knew Ian before, but the app gave us a new way to communicate."

"And it almost ruined your chances," Elise said.

"Only because I was stupid," Blake countered. "You're one to talk. Book Boyfriends Wanted set you up with Colin and you rejected him."

"Yep. I was not ready for him," Elise admitted.

"It helped give Ramsey and I a second chance. I'm all for it," Melody said.

"If I could say something," Karissa interjected. The room quieted and everyone turned to her. "I designed it to help people find love. It's a dating app, but there are no pictures allowed on the app. Real names aren't used. You can't send a message to someone until both of you accept the match. It's based on romance novels, book boyfriends. We all have our favorites, so the entire thing is designed to pair you with someone who's like your favorite book boyfriend."

"That's… different," I said.

Karissa laughed. "It is. And that was intentional. We would all sit here and talk about how we wished men in real life were like men in the books we read. I decided to figure out a way to find the ones who are. What's your favorite romance novel?"

"Ever?" I asked.

Karissa nodded. "Ever."

"The Time Traveler's Wife," I admitted.

"Whoa. Okay. Great choice, sad, but amazing book. What is it you like about Henry?"

"He's resourceful. He can do pretty much anything. And he adores Clare and would do anything for her."

"So, you want someone you can count on. Someone who will choose you."

The simplicity of her words hit me straight through the heart. I'd never thought of it that way, but she was right. I married Trevor because he made me feel taken care of, but aside from financial support, he was never there for me. Not the way—

"Yes, I guess I would say that's true," I answered her.

"You would be paired with men, or women if you chose that option, who are loyal and looking for commitment.

People who are open to adventure but want to share that adventure with someone else," Karissa said.

"You should fill out a profile," Blake encouraged. "Even if you never meet up with anyone, you should do it. Your divorce is final, right?"

"Yes, for almost a year now."

"Then you should do it. Start slow and low pressure."

"I don't know. I came here because I missed my brother, and because my ex is not involved with the kids. I want them to have a good summer, especially Cameron. Trevor made him promises he was never going to keep, and now Cam is disappointed even more. I just want them to enjoy these few months. If we stay."

"You have to stay. There is so much going on this summer. And it sounds like you all need a break. You should stay," Blake said.

"Amber would love to get together with Alexis," Melody said.

"And Ian can take Cameron out on a boat. Fishing maybe," Blake suggested.

"We'll all help to make this summer amazing for you and your kids. Give us a chance," Elise said with a pleading smile.

I looked around the room at the women I barely knew and admitted to myself that I wanted to get to know them better. I wanted to be there. And I wanted to give my kids the summer they all said we could have in MacKellar Cove.

"Okay, we'll stay."

"Good. Then let's sign you up because you need to have fun this summer, too," Blake said.

I snorted a laugh and shook my head but handed over my phone. I didn't have to accept any of them. But maybe I'd meet someone who made me believe in love again.

5

SEBASTIAN

I yanked another dead plant from the ground and tossed it into the wheelbarrow next to me. I dug through the soil to look for any remaining roots or pieces of it, doing my best to make sure nothing from the old garden was left behind.

Zoey and her kids had been in town for almost a week, and ironically, the garden was the only place I felt like I got a break from them. She still filled my mind when I was there, but I stayed on the far side. Close to the water and far from the benches and grassy section we called ours.

Nothing was ours anymore, and it never would be again. The garden was a gift for Piper and Gavin. It was a reminder for Gina of what it used to be. It was a beautiful spot to sit and watch the water. But it wasn't Zoey's and mine. Not anymore.

The back door to the house slammed shut, setting my teeth on edge. Gina was always so quiet and having other people around was getting to me. I missed the winter season when I could be outside and be completely alone. Instead, there were people everywhere.

I yanked up another plant while listening for whoever rushed out of the house. More than likely, I wouldn't have to talk to them, but I also didn't want someone sneaking up on me.

The rapid pace of running came toward me. Then the tear of vines, or roots. The gentle slap of it hitting the ground had me turning to see who was helping me to rip up the garden.

"There are plenty more over here if you're looking for something to tear apart," I said when I spotted Cameron across the garden.

He looked up at me quickly, surprised at being caught. "I'm sorry. I didn't mean to ruin anything."

I shook my head. "You didn't. I'm tearing pretty much everything out. Why don't you come rip some of these out?"

He hesitated for a long minute, then finally dragged his feet over to where I kneeled on the grass.

"Grab the plant close to the ground and pull slowly so you get the whole thing out. You might have to wiggle it a little if it's a stubborn one."

He grabbed the next plant and did as I instructed. The roots came up with the stems, leaving nothing behind that would ruin the garden later.

"Good. Toss it in the wheelbarrow so we can trash it later."

"You're just throwing them away?"

"They're dead, so yeah. Aunt Gina wants the entire garden replanted this summer." I leaned back on my heels and looked around. There was still a ton of work to do. I'd only pulled out about a third of the plants, maybe a little less. I figured it would take two or three more weeks to remove everything. The larger bushes and trees that stopped blossoming years ago were going to require equipment to be removed. Summer would be half over by the time I could start getting plants back into the ground.

Cameron and I worked side-by-side silently for twenty minutes or so. He tugged the plants from the ground and tossed them into the wheelbarrow, his attitude declining with each one.

"Who made you mad?" I finally asked him.

"No one," he grumbled.

"I slam doors and rip plants when I'm happy, too."

He looked up at me with a curious glare. He knew he was caught, but he didn't want to say what happened. Fair enough.

We kept working until he sighed heavily. For an eight year old, he had that sound down to a science.

"My dad promised to take me to a baseball game this summer."

"And that's changed?"

"Duh. He's not here. And we're not in Pittsburgh. My mom never should have brought us up here."

I wasn't going to argue that point with him. "Can't you go back and visit? It's not that far."

"My mom said we can, but now she's not sure. My dad promised, and my mom won't let me."

I definitely wasn't up on their family dynamic, but from the little Gavin had told me, Zoey was probably protecting Cameron from finding out his dad was a worthless ass.

"Why would your mom keep you away from your dad? Has your dad ever been mean to you?"

"No. Like how?"

"Do you do a lot with your dad?"

"Not really, I guess. I mean, we try, but he works a lot."

"Yeah, that's the tough thing for adults. What did you do with your dad last summer?"

"We were going to go to a baseball game, but he had a work trip. He took my sister and me to dinner once. We stayed at his place sometimes. He's just really busy." His frustrated tone told me to back off.

"I'm sure he is. It sounds like he has a really important job. Does he like his job?"

"I guess. He's always working. Why would you work a lot if you didn't like it?"

I shrugged. "Sometimes adults have no choice. We have bills to pay and people to take care of. Even if your dad doesn't love his job, he might keep doing it because it helps your family. That's not a bad thing."

"Do you love your job?" Cameron asked me.

I nodded, my lips turning up in a smile as I looked out over the water. "I do. Do you see that lighthouse out there?"

"In the water?"

"Yep. I maintain that lighthouse. There's a low spot in the river. From the lighthouse to the shore where we are is too shallow for a lot of ships, so the lighthouse makes sure they stay in the deeper water. If it doesn't work, ships could get stuck. I go out there every day to make sure everything is working properly."

"What about in the winter?"

"In the winter, too."

"Isn't it cold?"

I chuckled. "Extremely. But I don't mind it. I work alone and I get to keep people safe and I get paid well for it. I'm happy."

"My mom isn't happy. She needs to find a new job."

"What was her old job?"

"She worked in the cafeteria at my school. She told me she was going to do it again next year, but I saw her looking online for another one."

"Maybe she's just seeing if there are other options. Like something with computers."

"Why would she do that?"

I narrowed my brows. "Because she knows a lot about computers." Zoey was studying computer science in college when we were together. She was excited about the opportunities it would open up for her.

"She doesn't know anything about computers. She's a mom."

I pressed my lips together to hide my smile. He was very matter-of-fact and clearly did not know about Zoey's skills.

"Well, I'm sure she'll figure out something."

"Yeah. This is boring. I'm going to go do something else now."

I coughed to hide my laugh. "I don't blame you. It is pretty boring. But it's my job for right now so I need to keep going. I hope you get to see a baseball game this summer. If I hear of one, I'll let you know."

He nodded as he ran off, dirty hands and clothes. Gina was probably going to kill me, but a little dirt was good for the kid.

I kept working for another hour until I finished the section I was in. I raked up the dirt and turned it over so it was loose and to make sure we didn't miss any roots. I left all the tools where they were and went back to my cabin for a quick break and some water.

The late afternoon sun was scorching, and I was baking in it. There was a gentle breeze off the water that made the July heat tolerable, but it was still warm.

It was getting close to dinnertime, and my stomach was rumbling. I thought about going up to the Inn for dinner, but I was doing my best to stay away. Alexis would insist I sat with them, and I couldn't tolerate dinner more than once a week with Zoey. Not yet anyway. Maybe not ever.

I left my cottage and went back toward the garden. The sun was drifting lower in the sky, casting an orange glow on everything. It lit up the Inn and reminded me of why the garden was so special.

Instead of taking the path I'd used to go to my cottage, I walked up the twisted one that branched off toward the house. I walked slowly, not in a hurry to get anywhere. The guests would be sitting down to dinner soon, with Zoey's family joining them. I would return to my cottage alone after I stashed the tools and made sure everything was secure for the night.

I turned toward the garden and heard the unmistakable sound of someone crying. A whimper, then a sob, followed by a sniff as someone tried to pull themselves together. I thought about turning around. My phone vibrated in my pocket, and without thinking, I pulled it out.

GINA

Please come to dinner tonight. It's important.

I tried not to groan. I could never say no to her. Not when she said something was important. She didn't ask much of me, not really. I jumped to help her, but she never asked it. If she wanted me at dinner, I'd be there.

I texted back a quick message that I'd be there and kept walking. I forgot about the person crying until I realized I was heading straight for them. As soon as I saw her, I knew I should have picked up the tools earlier and avoided the garden so late in the evening.

I wanted to hate Zoey. More than anything in the world, I wanted to hate her. I wanted to hate her kids, too. I wanted to feel like she got what she deserved when her husband chose his work over her, over their family. But all I felt was pain.

Her pain was my pain. And seeing her sitting on the

bench crying almost tore me in two. Watching her from a distance and knowing she was out there so she could have some privacy to let her emotions out killed me. It was ironic that she had to go outside in the open for privacy, but the bench was out of the main pathways. It was relatively private.

Once upon a time, it was our bench.

That bench was where we sat the first time we had a conversation. It was where we sat the first time I kissed her. It was where we sat when I told her I loved her, and where she told me she'd come back to MacKellar Cove so we could be together.

When I found out she married someone else, I wanted to yank the bench from the ground and throw it in the river. Let it sink to the bottom and die, like I thought I would without her in my life. Instead, I left the bench there as a reminder to myself not to forget what happened.

I stopped walking by the bench. I'd almost forgotten it was still there. I'm not sure what made me walk that way, but as soon as I saw her, I knew I couldn't ignore her. I couldn't go on without stopping to talk to her.

"Are you okay?" I asked.

My voice was rough and less than kind. She jumped at the sound and quickly wiped the tears from her eyes. She nodded and stared past me to the water rushing by, even as her body shook with the emotion still coursing through her.

"You're not okay. What happened?"

"You don't want to hear about my ex-husband. I'll be fine."

"Ah," I said, stepping away. "I didn't realize you were still in love with him."

She snorted. "Not even a little bit. I've been invisible to him for years. He isn't worth my tears."

"Then why are you sitting here crying over him?"

"I'm not crying over him. I'm crying because he's refusing to spend time with Alexis and Cameron. He was a shitty father when we were married, and he's proving to be an even worse one now that we're divorced."

"He lives pretty far away. It can't be easy to make the trip."

She scoffed and glared up at me. I caught a glimpse of the girl I once knew, the woman I once knew. The fire was long gone by the time she came back to MacKellar Cove, extinguished by the man who stole her from me.

No, that wasn't fair. She was an adult. She made her own choices. He didn't steal her. She chose him.

"Are you seriously on his side? The side of my husband who is refusing to take a weekend off of work so he can spend time with our children?"

I shook my head. "I'm not taking sides. I don't have any skin in this one. You made sure of that a long time ago."

I started to walk away, but she was up and in my face before I took two steps. "How dare you! We were over years ago. A lifetime ago. You have no right to pass judgement on my life or to make me feel like I did something wrong."

"Then why are you asking me, Zoey? Why the hell do you care what I think?"

She clamped her mouth shut and took a step back. She took her heat with her, the heat I didn't even realize had seeped into my body until she pulled it away. The heat that ignited me. The heat that I still craved with every inch of myself.

"I'm sorry," she said. Back to meek.

"Why? Why are you sorry? Are you sorry because you destroyed me all those years ago? Are you sorry because you fell in love with someone else? Are you sorry because you weren't really in love with me? Are you just sorry because you stood up to me? Or got in my face? Or defended your choices? What are you sorry for, Zoey?"

She sucked in a ragged breath and closed her eyes. "All of it. For all of it. Except the one thing."

"What? What one thing?"

"I was in love with you. So much it scared me. But we had to hide what we had. You thought people would judge us, and that... you were the first boy I loved. My first kiss. My first everything. Hiding that made me feel like I wasn't as special to you. Or that we were doing something wrong. Things were so different with Trevor. He took me out, showed me off. He made me feel like I was more to him."

"You married him because he had money?" I spat.

She shook her head. "I married him because I thought he loved me, and I thought you didn't."

I raked my gaze down her body and tried to forget the way she felt in my arms. It had been years, but the memories of her were seared into me. If I closed my eyes, I could feel her. But memories... memories only got me so far. Memories were nothing compared to the real thing. And the real thing was standing in front of me. The real thing was looking up at me with those big, sad eyes that made me want to drive to Pittsburgh and ruin her ex for making her feel that way, then thank him for sending her running back to me.

I don't know who moved first, but the surprised squeak she let out said it was probably me. My arms circled her waist and dragged her body to mine. She felt different, but the same. Like déjà vu.

Maybe that's all it was. My mind playing tricks on me. Telling me Zoey, my Zoey, was back.

Then she parted her lips under mine and slid her hands up my back, and I knew it wasn't a dream. It wasn't a fantasy. It was Zoey.

Instead of the young woman I knew years ago, she had

the curves of an adult woman. She was more experienced, more jaded, more everything. She was different, but she was the same.

And I fucking hated her, but I also still loved her.

And that was why I tore myself away and stomped off across the lawn away from her. Because I also hated myself.

6

───────

ZOEY

I watched Sebastian's retreating form and touched my fingertips against my lips. They were still wet from him, swollen and sore. I licked them, desperate to taste him once more.

Sebastian kissed me ran on repeat through my head as he snatched up the small pile of tools and disappeared in the distance. He kissed me. I didn't do anything, but he kissed me.

What the hell did that mean?

Sebastian had done everything to prove to me he thought nothing of me. Sometimes he was angry, but most of the time, he was indifferent. He stayed away and kept to himself, which was fine because it was almost better than the dismissive look I usually got from him.

But he kissed me.

What the actual fuck?

He vanished from my line of sight, and I was finally able to look away from where he'd been. I couldn't remember the last time I'd been kissed, which said nothing for the last time I'd had sex or felt desirable. Trevor was long done with me when we divorced, and a part of me assumed I'd never have another man touch me again.

But Sebastian *kissed* me.

If Sofia hadn't told me they weren't together, I'd be mad at him for cheating on her, but without thinking about her, I was simply confused. There was no reason for him to kiss me. One minute we were arguing and the next he had his lips against mine, his tongue requesting entry, and me hanging on by a thread.

"You okay?" Gavin's voice broke through. I jumped. I hadn't heard him approaching me.

"What? Yeah."

"You sure? Because I called your name five times. You're pretty lost. Did he upset you that badly?"

"You saw?" I asked. I was not really interested in rehashing the whole thing with my brother, but it wasn't like I had other friends I could talk to. Or anyone, really.

"Well, I heard more than I saw."

"Excuse me?"

"You were pretty loud on the phone. I heard you yelling at Trevor, then I saw you rush out the back. I figured you needed a few minutes to cool off. Are you better?"

Trevor. I'd forgotten about the call with him that sent me out of the house and into Sebastian's arms in the first place. "I'm fine. I mean, I'm not and it's not, but I shouldn't be surprised at this point."

"Want to tell me what happened?"

I looked at my brother curiously. "With Trevor?"

He chuckled. "Of course with Trevor. What else would I be talking about?"

"Nothing. Sorry. He just got to me, I guess. He promised to take Cameron to a baseball game this summer, but then said he couldn't. That was the first thing. Now, since we're here, he doesn't plan to see the kids all summer. He's not going to visit, and he doesn't want to have them come see him."

"Are you surprised by that?"

I sighed. "No, but it still makes me mad. He pushed for kids. When we got married, he wanted kids right away. He didn't want me to start working because he wanted us to have kids. And now, he barely pays attention to them."

"Listen, I'm not one to defend Trevor, but do you think he's always known that he wasn't the one you wanted to be with?"

"He doesn't know anything about Sebastian."

"Maybe he doesn't know his name, but he might know there was someone else. You never told him about your past?"

"No. He didn't want to know. He always said whatever happened before we were together wasn't important. What mattered was that we were together and building a life together. Why would he say all that and then do this? Why is he punishing our kids?"

"I don't know, Zo. I wish I had an answer for you."

I sighed, wishing he did, too.

Gavin shuffled his feet and looked out at the water. One of his many tells that he wanted to change the subject but wasn't sure how.

"What is it?"

He looked up at me with a guilty look. "I was kind of hoping I could get your help. But now it feels like I shouldn't."

"Help with what?"

"I was, um, going to propose to Piper tonight."

"What? That's great news. It's about time. I figured you wouldn't get your summer wedding with how long you're taking."

"Well, that's why I want to do it now. I wanted you and

the kids here, and Sofia is going to come for dinner tonight so the people we're closest to are here for it. But I was hoping you could help me with something. You can say no."

I smiled and looped my arm through his. "Of course I'm not going to say no. You and Piper are everything I always wanted with Trevor. You're right for each other. And I'm honored you'd want us here, and that you would want anything from me to pull this off."

He hugged me close, and I felt him shaking. "I just hope she says yes."

I laughed. "She's going to say yes. She loves you."

"I know she does. I love her, too. That's why I want this to be perfect."

"Tell me what I can do."

GAVIN DIDN'T SAY much through dinner. A part of me felt sorry for him, but he was being ridiculous. Piper looked at him like he was her entire world. There was no way she wouldn't say yes. Eagerly.

Sofia seemed to be in on the whole thing, too. She kept looking at Gavin with a dreamy, happy look on her face. It made me like her, even though I really didn't want to. It wasn't fair to her, but she was Sebastian's friend and maybe fuck buddy once in a while, and I was jealous of her.

There, I said it. Only to myself, but I still admitted that I was jealous of Sofia. She was cute and friendly and probably perfect for Sebastian. She didn't mind getting her hands dirty, and she worked maintenance, which told me she was smart and strong and not afraid to do whatever was needed to make something work.

All qualities I did not possess.

She talked and laughed with Sebastian when she wasn't

watching Gavin and Piper. She was completely at ease with Sebastian, who avoided looking even close to my direction. How was him kissing me my fault? It didn't matter. It wasn't going to happen again. It was clearly a mistake, and I didn't need to know why he did it.

I looked at him again and saw the tightness around his mouth and the tension in his shoulders. He was eating and pretending nothing was off, but I could see it. He was uncomfortable.

He slid his gaze to mine, catching me staring at him. Instead of looking away immediately, he glared at me. Ruthless and mean, a glare that made me wish I could crawl under the table and hide until it was time to tuck my tail between my legs and go back to Pittsburgh. A glare that made me regret ever coming back to MacKellar Cove. A glare that said he hated me.

I ripped my gaze from his and resisted the urge to rub the ache in my chest. Tears pricked at my eyes, but I refused to let them fall. I was to blame. For making him hate me in the first place. For inserting myself into his life again. Hell, maybe I was the one who kissed him. With the way he stalked off and glared at me now, maybe that was my fault.

"If I could have your attention," Gavin said, forcing me to put aside my thoughts of Sebastian. It was go time. "This summer is the first summer that I will be here to help run the MacKellar Cove Inn. This place is special to me. My sister and I spent our summers here as kids and being back here means the world to me."

The small audience Gavin had made agreeable noises as he took a second to gather himself.

"I want to offer a toast to Aunt Gina. She's been in charge of this place forever, and she's going to officially retire this fall, become a snowbird, she tells me. This place won't be the same without her."

"To Gina," people said around the room, raising their glasses.

I stood, hating how all eyes in the room turned to me, but it was for Gavin. "Aunt Gina has been the heart and soul of this place for years, but she's leaving it in good hands." Gavin snuck out while Piper was looking at me. "My aunt and uncle always made the Inn feel like home for everyone who came here. Many of you have been coming here for years, and I hope those of you who are new will come back and see the next generation take over. My brother and Piper love this place as much as Aunt Gina and Uncle Rob did. They will fill these walls with all the happiness and joy that have always been here. They will continue to make memories here. Starting right now."

Piper tilted her head to the side and gave me a confused look. I only smiled back, then nodded behind her.

Piper turned and laughed when she saw Gavin in the doorway. "What are you doing over there?"

I pulled out my phone, hit record, and nodded to Gavin.

He took a breath and focused his entire attention on Piper. "I've never known anyone who's had so much faith in me. Who's been willing to argue with me by day and love me by night. Who wants all the same things I want and isn't afraid to tell me when I'm being ridiculous. And I don't ever want to give that up."

Tears streamed down Piper's cheeks. It was clear she knew what was going on, but she stood still and let my brother say his peace while I made sure I was capturing the entire thing.

Gavin lifted the sign he had made so she could see it. "There are a few things we haven't talked about, but I had this made. We can get it changed if you want. I wanted something that makes our partnership more obvious to anyone who walks through the door. Something that says you belong to me and I belong to you."

I pressed my fingers to my lips to keep my sob from escaping. Piper read the sign out loud. "MacKellar Cove Inn. Established 1977. Proprietors Gavin and Piper Holbrook." Her eyes lifted to meet his. "Gavin?"

"I'm not sure how you feel about changing your last name, but I took a chance."

"Why would I change my last name to yours?" Piper asked, defiance and sarcasm thick in her tone even as tears filled her eyes.

"Well, that's the next thing I have." He walked over to her, leaving the sign leaning against the wall. He reached for her hand and dropped to one knee. "I'm hoping you'll make all of this official. That you'll let me lay claim to your every happiness, your every desire and joy and excitement. That you'll give me the honor of being your partner in business and life, as your husband and lover and friend and whatever else comes our way."

Piper sniffed and smiled at him. "I would love nothing more."

He calmly slid the ring on her finger, then stood and lifted her into his arms in one move. She laughed and kissed him, cupping his face in her hands as they whispered something I couldn't hear over the cheers of the small crowd who'd witnessed Gavin's proposal.

Gavin and Piper pulled back from each other with a laugh, and I stopped the recording so I could congratulate them. I hugged them both and said how happy I was for them before they were swept into the rest of the crowd. Gina poured champagne for everyone and glasses were handed around to celebrate Gavin and Piper.

Sofia and Piper gushed over her ring, and Gavin stood

proudly by, the conquering hero who won the woman of his dreams.

I thought back to my own engagement. Trevor took me to dinner at a nice restaurant. Nothing overly fancy, but nice for college students. When they brought out dessert, there was a ring on top of my cake. The waitstaff lingered, watching us.

"So, what do you say?" Trevor asked. His eyes glittered with the knowledge that I'd never say no to him. That I was infatuated with him.

I couldn't say yes. The word stuck in my throat. But I knew marrying Trevor was the best option for me. He spoiled me and he loved me and he would support me. He would take the financial burden of my future on and give my parents some much needed breathing room.

All I had to do was give up on the dream I wanted for almost half my life.

So I nodded and accepted his kiss and his ring and a future with a man I knew would take care of me. A man I loved, in my own way. A man who loved me, or the idea of me, I still wasn't sure which one.

I smiled at the guests and took my seat again. Piper and Gavin deserved their love. They deserved a happy life together, with kids if they wanted them and all the things I didn't get. They deserved the dream because they waited for the kind of love that lasted forever. Unlike me. I had that love, but I chose something else. I chose good enough because I didn't trust in forever.

I sipped my water and looked around the room. The back of my neck tingled, putting me on edge. I forced my smile and looked for whoever was watching me.

I never expected it to be Sebastian. Or for his eyes to be soft. For his gaze to linger on me. He didn't see me watching him, and I pretended not to be as his stare caressed my skin like large, warm hands, heating me up. My entire body felt warm. Between my legs pulsed with desire.

The last thing I needed to do was get involved with Sebastian again. We were a bad idea. He hated me, and I wasn't staying in MacKellar Cove. I just needed to do what I promised myself I would do from the beginning.

Stay away from him.

WEDDING PLANS CAME TOGETHER QUICKLY over the next week. It helped that the location was already set and Aunt Gina insisted on catering it herself. She agreed to hire help for some of it, but Piper and Gavin wanted a small wedding, so it wasn't much more than the Inn could handle.

Piper was still amazed at how Gavin pulled off not only the engagement but the beginning of wedding plans without her having any idea what he was doing. She was blissful and floating every time I saw her, so I figured it was good.

Sofia was spending more time at the Inn to help Piper with the wedding planning. They'd officially set the date for the third Friday in August, which meant we had about six weeks to pull it all together. Piper's biggest task was finding a dress.

"We should just go down to Syracuse and look," Sofia told her at lunch.

They were sitting at a table for four in the dining room, and Piper called me over to join them. I had no excuse not to, so I sat next to Piper and smiled.

"Maybe you'll help me," Sofia said. "I'm trying to talk her into going to Syracuse to find a dress. She keeps saying she'll wear something she already has."

"I'm not going to find anything that can be ready in time,"

Piper whined. "Places don't have off the rack dresses in my size."

"What about New York?" I suggested.

"Ooh, yes, we could totally do that," Sofia said.

"I don't know that New York would be any better. Finding a dress at the last minute is not going to happen." Piper looked more disappointed than I'd ever seen her.

"What about classifieds? Or online? There are always dresses available online," I suggested.

"Isn't that bad luck?" Sofia asked. "I wouldn't want a dress that someone bought and didn't get married in or bought and ended up divorced or something. I thought people saved their wedding dresses."

My cheeks heated at her words. I knew she wasn't trying to be mean, but her tone felt like an attack. Like my dress was the reason I ended up divorced. "Mine was from a consignment shop."

"Really?" Piper asked.

I nodded. "Yeah, but I guess Sofia is right because I'm divorced now. Maybe if I'd gotten something new, things would have worked out. Excuse me."

I forced my lips to turn up into a smile none of us believed and walked away.

Maybe I should feel bad about the way I spoke to her, or maybe I should feel better because Sofia wasn't as perfect as I thought. Maybe I just wanted an excuse to not like her because I knew she was a better match for Sebastian than I was. Maybe I was just a bitch and I needed to blow off some steam.

I walked outside and let the lull of the gentle waves against the shore draw me closer. The soft hum of a motor met my ears and drew my attention from the river and the nondescript boats going past. Because that motor was attached to a boat that held Sebastian.

I watched as he docked the boat and climbed out. He walked down his dock to his cabin nestled between the trees that lined the shore. He disappeared inside.

One encounter was enough. I promised myself I'd stay away from him, and I knew I was upset because of what Sofia said, but even with all that, my feet carried me to his cabin. It was a very bad idea, but I needed answers. I needed to know why he kissed me. And I was going to get them. Then I could move on from Sebastian Parks.

7

SEBASTIAN

I'd just sat down for lunch when someone pounded on my door. I glared at it, hoping whoever was there would give up after a few seconds and go away.

I was wrong.

The pounding continued, telling me whoever was outside my home really wanted to get in for some reason.

I set my sandwich down and sighed heavily. I didn't have long for lunch, but apparently, I was going to have even less time.

I stomped to the door and yanked it open, nearly getting punched in the face when Zoey raised her hand to pound on the door again. She was out of breath and sweating. Anger drew lines across her face, around her mouth and eyes. She stared at me for half a second, her narrowed eyes shrouded. She looked behind me into the cabin I'd called home for the better part of the last decade, then pushed her way inside like she had a right to be there.

My eyes followed her, my brain and mouth stalled for a response. She hadn't said anything, but something was clearly on her mind. So I waited.

65

"Why did you kiss me?" she finally asked. Her tone was sharp, angry, maybe a little confused.

I expected the question at some point, but given it'd been more than a week, I almost thought it wouldn't come. I glanced outside to see if anyone else was around, then slowly closed the door. I leaned back against it, not wanting to have the conversation with her, especially when she looked like she did. Her full breasts rose and fell with every strained breath she took. Her eyes showed fury-banked pain. And every muscle in her body was tense.

Fucking hell, she was gorgeous. The Zoey I used to know was quiet and demure. Sure, she was curious and wanted to know everything, but she never challenged anyone. She went along with whatever everyone else wanted, including me. I tried to push her to tell me what she wanted, for years, but she always insisted she was happy.

This Zoey? This Zoey made me hard in an instant. Same, but different from the younger version. This Zoey had enough baggage to shut down an airport, but she wasn't afraid to push back.

I was in trouble.

"What difference does it make?" I asked her.

"I want to know. I need to know."

"Why?"

"You hate me. You've hated me for years. Why would you kiss me?"

I shrugged and pushed off the door. I stalked toward her. "Maybe it was nostalgia. Maybe it was desire. Maybe you were there and crying and didn't matter enough for me to care what you thought and I just wanted to shut you up."

The last words had the effect I wanted. She flinched, coiling into herself like I'd physically attacked her. I wanted to hurt her. I wanted her to know the pain she caused me.

But seeing her actually hurt did something to me. Knowing I was the cause of it was even worse.

"Is that true?" Her voice was small and scared. Beaten. Abused.

I ran a hand through my hair and over my beard. I wanted to tell her it was. That I hated her as she said. That she meant nothing to me. But even I wasn't that cruel.

"No. It's not true."

"Then why, Sebastian? Why did you kiss me?"

"Because I still can't resist you, okay? Because seeing you upset made me want to make it all better. Because I've missed you all these years. And you standing in my home has me desperate to throw you on my bed and explore the woman you are now. No matter how much I dislike you, I still want you."

"What?" she breathed. That was obviously not the answer she was expecting.

"You destroyed me, Zoey. I've never been able to get over that. Or over you. I never got any answers about what happened and why you didn't come back. And now you're here demanding to know why I kissed you. What right do you have to ask me anything?"

She took a step back and bumped against my table. Her eyes were wild and unfocused, like she was trapped and scared. "I shouldn't have come here. I was so mad. And Sofia said my dress was cursed and Piper was talking about shopping. And I..." She looked up at me. "I'm sorry. I won't bother you again."

She moved toward me, toward the door. My cabin was small. Too small for her to move around me. Too small for me to not feel the air shift as she drew closer. Too small for me to not breathe her in. She stopped in front of me, far enough away that we weren't touching but close enough that it wouldn't take much before we were.

She lifted her gaze to mine. It was all there in her eyes. The pain, the regret, all the words I'd waited years to hear. She didn't say them, but I could feel them. It wasn't enough. But it was more than I'd gotten so far.

And this was Zoey. My Zoey. In my home, a few dozen feet from my bed. We'd only ever had stolen moments and hurried privacy. To be able to stretch her out onto a bed. To strip her clothes off and worship her body. To show her all the things she missed by marrying him instead of coming back to me...

I took one step toward her and bent down to wrap my arms around her waist. She squeaked with surprise when I lifted her into my arms. Our lips came together as I took a step toward my bedroom. I still hated her, but I needed her. I could hate her after. After I let my body love her. After I reclaimed her as mine. After she was gone and I was alone again.

Zoey kissed me back as I walked, her hands diving into my hair and holding on tight. She was no longer the shy young woman I'd loved. She was strong and smart and in control. She knew what she wanted, probably knew what she liked, and she wasn't afraid to tell me.

I moved to release her onto my bed, but she kept her thighs tight around my body and dragged me down with her. I yanked her shirt up so I could feel her bare skin. She moaned and arched into my hand. Our movements were hurried, desperate. Just like it had always been, but not.

Zoey tugged at my shirt and finally released her legs so I could take it off. She pulled off her shirt while I removed mine. I stepped back and unbuttoned my jeans, shoving them to the floor as she wiggled out of her shorts.

I looked down at her and had to bite the inside of my cheek to resist saying something I would regret. She was stunning. Sure, her body had changed, but she was a woman.

She'd had two children. She'd lived a life since the last time we were together. As much as I hated that the life wasn't with me, it made her into a softer, rounder, fuller version of the girl I fell in love with years ago. Her stomach bore the stretch marks of pregnancy and the loose skin it left behind. Her thighs were thicker than I remembered. Her bra and panties were simple and shouldn't have been sexy, but on her, blue cotton was the hottest thing ever.

She watched me as I watched her. Panic slid into her eyes, waiting for me to say or do something harsh. If she had any idea what I was thinking, she wouldn't worry, but I wasn't ready to open myself up to her again. Sex was one thing, emotions were another.

I toed off my boots and kicked my jeans aside, then went to my nightstand and grabbed a condom. I turned back to her and raised an eyebrow, questioning if she was ready for this.

She licked her lips and lifted her hips. She hooked her thumbs in the sides of her panties and eased them down, slowly, like she wasn't sure.

I waited, my breath frozen in my lungs, as she bared herself to me. She let her panties fall to the ground, then shifted her body to move onto the bed properly. Her head rested on my pillow, like she belonged there. Her bra stayed on, but everything else was bare.

It wasn't a romantic scene. It wasn't a seduction. It wasn't anything other than sex between two consenting adults. I pushed my briefs off and rolled the condom on without meeting her gaze. She was there, and she was naked. I didn't need to watch her eyes as they drifted to look at my dick. I just needed her to spread her thighs and let me in.

I was a fucking liar.

I crawled onto my bed and over to her. She spread her legs for me, not shy or timid or anything else like I remembered her being. I positioned myself at her entrance, using every last bit of control I had not to push inside her in one thrust.

I pressed against her, her tight heat challenging me. My head spun and other parts of me tightened, but I had to ignore those other things. This was sex, not love. This was not going to turn into anything. I was using her for an orgasm. Just like she was using me.

Her body opened for me with each slow thrust into her. Zoey didn't say a word, just laid back and moaned every so often. I wanted to know how she felt, if it was like riding a bike and it felt as good for her as it did for me, but I couldn't take it if she said no, so I didn't ask.

Her feet drifted up the back of my legs, widening her entrance so I could sink inside her fully. I groaned when my body met hers, nearly coming instantly at the feel of her around me. She was tight, like it had been a while. I didn't want to know. I didn't ask. It wasn't my business.

She arched her back and met me with each stroke. Her hands stayed at her sides, twisting and turning against my sheets. I wanted them on me. I wanted her to need to touch me the same way I needed to touch her. Desperate. Aching.

I slammed hard into her, making her gasp and moan. "Sebastian," she whispered, her strained voice telling me she was feeling all the same things I was feeling.

"Fuck, Zoey," I replied. It was all I could say. All I would let myself say.

I thrust deep into her again, sending us both closer to where we needed to be. Her head turned to one side, then the other. Her face twisted with need. She was close, but it was out of reach.

I shifted our position so I could get up on my knees. I lifted her with me, hitting her in a different spot at the same time I pressed my thumb against her clit. In an instant, she splintered, screaming out her orgasm as she clenched hard around my cock and demanded I follow her.

Fucking hell. I lost my damn mind. I pounded into her, unable to stop my body from taking everything I needed, everything I'd missed. I grunted with each stroke, my thumb still pressed against her clit and demanding she come again. I was close, my spine tingling and my throat tightening. I needed her to come, to wring me dry, to say my name and tell me I was the one who made her feel so good.

"Sebastian," she whimpered. "Oh, God." Her words garbled and mumbled until she shouted my name again and let go.

She was so fucking beautiful. Her eyes were clenched tight, her entire face tense. Her neck and chest were flushed and beaded with sweat. Her body pulsed around me, forcing me over the edge without warning. I slammed hard into her, my orgasm so powerful I nearly blacked out. I roared my release, her name mixed with praise to God for how good it felt.

And for bringing her back to me, although that part I kept to myself.

I collapsed onto her a moment later, all my energy drained and my body unable to support itself. She wrapped her arms around me and simply held me. Our bodies cooled together, the two of us one in the moment.

I could have stayed there all day, making love to her and reminding myself of the plans we had for our future, but the thought of it sent me to the bathroom. We no longer had a future. We could have, but she threw it away. It was too late for us, and I couldn't let one afternoon of spectacular sex make me forget that.

She was still on my bed when I walked back out. Sprawled across my sheets like it was her bed. It was my turn to be angry now. She didn't belong there.

"I need to go back to work," I said as I reached for my clothes.

"Oh, yeah. Um, sorry. I wasn't thinking."

I didn't answer as she climbed off my bed and started dressing. I yanked my clothes on piece by piece, angry at myself for giving in to her and angry at her for inserting herself into my life again. She wasn't welcome, and she wasn't permanent. The only reason it happened was to get her out of my system. To have one last time together so I could release the hold she had on me.

Except I already wanted her again. I wanted to taste her and touch her and make her come over and over again. I wanted to watch her ride me and take her from behind. I wanted her in the shower and on the kitchen table and in front of the picture window in my living room. I wanted everything with her.

"Are you mad at me?" she asked softly, her quiet tone loud in the silent house.

"This was just sex," I snarled at her. Maybe a little at myself, too.

"Okay," she replied. She dragged the word out, making it into a question.

"No emotions, no declarations. Sex only."

"I understand. I didn't come here for this."

"Maybe not, but you're the one who showed up at my home and pushed your way inside."

"I… guess I shouldn't have done that. I just needed to know what was going on with us."

"We're not going to get back together, Zoey."

"I know." The finality of her tone hurt. She had no interest in getting back together. It was good. That was what I wanted.

"Good."

We finished dressing in silence. Years ago, there was

never silence between us. We were always talking about our lives and our future. We shared everything. But she was a stranger now. She'd had a life I wasn't a part of, and I'd had one without her.

She looked up at me when she was fully clothed and smiled half-heartedly. I didn't know what to say to her. Thanks felt like she was a hooker, but saying nothing felt rude.

We made it to the door, and both stopped. She turned back to me again.

"Just say whatever it is you want to say," I told her.

She sighed and smiled. "I just wanted to say thank you, but that sounds weird."

"You gonna leave a few bills on the table, too?"

She rolled her lips in and nodded sharply. "I shouldn't have said that. I'm sorry."

She reached for the doorknob, but I knew I couldn't let her leave like that.

"That was a dick thing to say. Sorry. This is… I don't know what this is. It's awkward and strange and…"

"Really good," she finished for me.

"Yeah," I admitted. "It was really good. But I can't get pulled back into your orbit, Zoey. You're going back to Pittsburgh. You have kids with another man. You have a life. You already chose someone else. I can't go through all that again."

"I know."

"This can't be more than sex."

"What are you saying?" she asked.

"I'm saying if you want to come back sometime, I'd be open to that. But we're not hanging out or going out or anything that involves more than just sex. We're not dating. We're not getting back together."

"But you want to sleep together over the summer?"

I shrugged. I wanted whatever I could get from her, but

sex was all I could handle. "We were good together. Great. And all I'm saying is this is all I can offer you. If you aren't interested, that's fine."

"I am," she blurted. "I am."

I nodded once. "Good."

"Good."

We stared at each other for a long minute, then opened the door and walked out. I made it back to the lighthouse before I realized I never ate my lunch.

But it was worth it.

8

ZOEY

Four days after my surprise sex with Sebastian, I was still trying to figure out what the hell was going on with him. I'd avoided him, even going so far as to skip Friday night dinner with claims of a headache.

The sex was out of this world amazing, but I wasn't sure what it meant. For him, sex was no big deal. For me, it was huge. He was only one of two men I'd ever slept with, and even though we'd been together before, I wasn't sure I could keep my feelings out of it.

So instead, I just stayed away from him.

"What the hell is wrong with this?" Piper growled as I walked into the foyer. She was scowling at the computer. Never a good sign.

"What's going on?" I asked.

She looked up at me and forced a smile. "Sorry. I'm having computer issues. I didn't realize anyone was here."

"Want me to take a look?"

She scoffed. "At this point, I'll let the kids look. I'm so lost, and there's no way to screw things up more than I have."

I stepped behind the counter as she stepped away. "What's going on with it?"

She tugged her ponytail holder out of her light brown hair and finger-combed it. She shook her head. "I installed new software a few weeks ago for scheduling, and now it's not working. We had a couple show up a little while ago that had emails showing their reservation, but I had no record of them at all. Thankfully, we had the room available, but I have no idea if there are others who are going to show up unexpectedly."

I clicked through and found the software she was talking about. I went into the settings and reviewed how it was installed and what happened. It was a simple fix, but not one most users would have known to look for.

"It's done now. I updated the software itself, and I changed the background settings so that everything gets sent to the Inn's email account and also recorded on the online booking site. That means people won't be able to double book rooms, but also it means you'll have a true record of everyone who's made reservations."

"I thought we already had all that set up. That was why I bought the software."

I nodded and clicked through a few more things to make sure every part of the software was active. "It's how it was designed, but there was a trial period where you could test out the software without additional charges. You were paying for the full system, but it was treating your system like it was in the trial period, which means there was a disconnect."

"How did you know that?"

"I have a degree in computer science."

"Seriously? I didn't know that."

I nodded. "I've never used it, so it's more on paper than anything else, but yeah."

"Paper is what everyone starts with. I've been trying to figure out what was going on for an hour. I thought I was going to have to hire someone to fix this. Thank you."

I smiled. "You're welcome. I'm glad it wasn't too complicated."

"Me, too. Now I can see all the reservations that were made on this system and match them up with our calendar. Sometimes I think the way Gina did it was easier, but I know most people want to book online instead of calling."

"Once you get used to it, you'll be fine. Did you ever figure out what you're going to do about a dress?"

She wrinkled her nose. "Not yet. But I wanted to tell you Sofia feels bad about the things she said. She didn't mean to hurt your feelings."

"It's fine. My marriage wasn't meant to be. But I don't put a lot of stock in all the superstitions around it. People get married every day without following all the supposed rules and their marriages are successful. The dress should be something that makes you feel amazing. That's it." I reeled in my frustration when I realized I was practically shouting at her. "Sorry. I just meant—"

"You meant you love your brother, and you believe in us. Thank you."

I smiled. "I really do. You could walk down the aisle in what you're wearing right now and Gavin would still love you and want to spend the rest of his life with you. The dress is nice, but it's not necessary. All that matters is that whatever you decide to do is right for you guys. Not everyone else."

Piper nodded thoughtfully. "That's true. I was never one of those girls who had big ideas for their wedding. Not that I think there's anything wrong with doing that, it just wasn't me. I wasn't sure I'd actually get married until I was an adult, and even then, it wasn't until I met Gavin that I wanted to. Wedding dresses are big and heavy and not me at all."

"So, don't get a traditional wedding dress. Find a dress that makes you feel good. Or wear shorts and a tee shirt. Or whatever you want to wear. Gavin didn't fall in love with you in a dress. He fell in love with you."

Piper grinned happily. Her entire face glowed, and she couldn't have looked happier. She reached out and hugged me tightly. "Thank you."

I nodded and hugged her back. "You're welcome. I'm really happy you two found each other. And that he managed to fix things after he messed up so badly."

"It all worked out in the end."

"It did."

"Now, we just need to get you and Sebastian together again."

I scoffed. "Not happening. He still hates me."

"I thought I saw you coming out of his cabin last week. What was that all about?"

My cheeks heated. I pressed my lips together and shook my head to buy time I wasn't going to get. "Just getting a few things straight."

"Oh, yeah?" Piper asked, her eyes curious and all-knowing.

I was not about to admit anything to her. She would be even more relentless than she already was. "There is nothing going on, so don't even start."

She shrugged. "That's not what it looked like, but if you say so. Have you had any matches yet?"

The app they signed me up for. I'd forgotten about that. "I'm not sure."

"You should check. Maybe Sebastian will come around if he finds out you're seeing someone else."

"I'm not going to mess with his head. He deserves better than that."

"True, but I think he's still interested in you. I've seen the way he looks at you when you're not paying attention."

"Probably with anger and hatred."

Piper chuckled. "Nope. Not either of those."

"He's been very clear that he is not a fan of mine. I'm going to give him his space this summer."

"I think—"

"Oh, Zoey, Piper, good. Can one of you walk some lunch out to Sebastian for me? I told him I'd bring him lunch today since he's working in the garden. But I don't want to leave the kitchen right now," Aunt Gina said. Her dark gaze flipped between Piper and me.

I opened my mouth to say I couldn't, but Zoey beat me to it.

"I'm going through these reservations. I already see one that's double booked. I need to make some calls and find out what I can do for these guests. Zoey just fixed the computer system for me, but now I have a ton to do." Piper started to back away.

"I could do that for you," I offered.

"Oh, no, I couldn't ask you to do that. Besides, it's my screw up. I can't let you take the blame for it. I have to grovel."

Piper grabbed the computer and moved into the front room before I could say anything else about it. I scowled at her back, then turned to Aunt Gina, knowing I had no excuse.

"Zoey, take Sebastian lunch. It's hot out there and I'm sure he's hungry. He's doing me a favor by fixing up the gardens. We owe him lunch, at least. I have a tray ready. Come grab it."

"Okay," I said. Dammit.

I BALANCED the tray and tried not to scowl at it. It wasn't the tray's fault I was carrying lunch out to Sebastian. Or Sebastian's. It was all Aunt Gina. Or Piper. Maybe they concocted it together to get me and Sebastian to talk. Or maybe I was being paranoid and a little crazy. Probably that one.

Sebastian was on his knees on one of the paths when I spotted him. There was a bench close to him so I headed there to put his tray down. I could set it down and then leave and avoid talking to him. That was for the best.

I made it to the bench without him looking up, but when I set the tray down, he turned to see me.

"Hey," he said, sounding surprised. Maybe a little happy?

"Hi. Um, Aunt Gina asked me to bring you the lunch she made. So, um, yeah. There it is."

"Thanks."

I forced a strained smile and backed up to leave.

"You're not going to join me?"

"Um, no?" Why did that sound like a question?

"It looks like she sent enough food for both of us."

Sebastian nodded toward the tray that I'd just spent the last five minutes trying not to spill. I hadn't even noticed there were two sandwiches, bottles of water, covered cups with lemonade, cookies, and napkins. What the hell?

"You didn't notice?"

I shook my head and felt my cheeks heat. Maybe he would think it was from the sun. Not likely.

"Have you eaten?"

I shook my head again, wondering if my mouth was going to join in the fun and function. Which led me to all the things I wanted to be doing with my mouth instead of talking to him.

My gaze drifted to his lips. They were beautiful lips. Full

and soft. I even liked his beard and the way it tickled my skin when he kissed me. Trevor was always particular about being clean shaven, but Sebastian made me appreciate a man who was a little rougher. More manly. One I didn't have to worry about taking my appointment at the salon to get my hair or nails done.

"Zoey," he said, seeing the word on his lips before it registered in my mind.

"Hmm?"

"You can't look at me like that." His voice was gruff and harsh and did the trick.

I took a step back and dragged my gaze from his mouth. I focused on the water over his right shoulder and nodded. "Sorry. I should just go."

He sighed like I was an inconvenience. "Eat your lunch."

The words were a command, issued with no room for me to argue. It bristled. "Who said you get to decide what I do?"

"Fine, don't eat. I don't really care right now. I'm hot and tired and sore and hungry. So I'm going to drink the water and lemonade and eat my lunch. If you don't want yours, then feel free to run back inside and hide from me some more."

"Who said I was hiding from you?"

He snorted and shook his head, then dropped onto the bench next to the tray. He grabbed one of the sandwiches and took a large bite, a quarter of the sandwich disappearing into his far too tempting mouth.

He set his sandwich down and opened one bottle of water. He tipped it up to his lips and drained half of it before he took a breath and screwed the cap back on. Then he picked up his sandwich again and took another massive bite.

He looked up at me as he chewed, not saying anything, just watching me with one raised brow and an amused quirk to his lips.

I groaned and sighed and finally sank onto the bench on the other side of the tray. I lifted my sandwich and took a bite. I chewed slowly, watching the water instead of the man next to me.

Sebastian finished his sandwich and water before I'd eaten half of mine. The silence between us felt uncomfortable. We'd never been at a loss for words with each other. Even when we didn't speak, we would sit close and hold each other and let our bodies speak for us. Sitting in silence when there was so much we should say was awkward.

"Are you ready to tell me why you're avoiding me?"

"I'm not—" I started, but we both knew it was a lie. "Fine. After… the other day, I figured you would want some space."

He nodded slowly and stared past me to the water. "So, you regret it."

He wasn't asking. He honestly believed his words. But they weren't true. "No," I hurried to say. "I don't. I feel guilty because… well, for a lot of reasons, but I don't regret it."

"It wasn't any good?"

I actually laughed at that. "Um, no. I can't say that either."

"Then why are you giving me space?"

"Because you don't like me. Because I pushed my way into your home and we had sex and you still hate me."

"Did you think that was all going to change just because we got naked? Because I haven't liked every woman I've slept with. Hell, some of them I didn't even know. Having sex is not going to make me fall in love with someone."

No matter how many times I prayed Sebastian would find someone else, and how many times I hoped he was happy and had a good life, and how many times I wished for him to move on, hearing about all the other women he slept with felt like a slap. A hard one. One I deserved.

"You're right," I said stiffly. It took all my strength to keep the tears in my eyes instead of letting them fall in front of him. "You're right. You said that the other day. No emotions, no feelings, no connection. If it happens again, it's just sex. Just like the other day. There's nothing between us anymore and won't be again."

"Exactly. It's what we both want. The sex is good, so we should enjoy it, but it was everything else between us that got messy and complicated. Neither of us needs that right now."

"True." I set the rest of my sandwich down and stood. "I should go. I can come back later and get the tray if you aren't done."

"Nah, I'm good," he said. He shoved the last bite of his cookie into his mouth and wiped his lips on his napkin. He tossed the napkin back on the tray and stood. "Thanks for bringing me lunch. Tell Gina thanks, too."

I lifted the tray. "I will. Bye."

"See ya," he said. He pulled his work gloves back on and went back to working on the garden.

I hurried away, doing my best not to drop the tray or let anything spill.

I made it to the Inn without incident and handed the tray over to Aunt Gina at the sink. She asked if Sebastian liked his lunch, and I assured her he did.

"Did you eat, too?" she asked, more than a little suspiciously.

"I did. Although I'm not sure why you sent food for me on the tray. I could have eaten here."

Aunt Gina waved her hand, sending bubbles flying into the air. "There was no reason for that. You and Sebastian needed to talk."

"There is no me and Sebastian, Aunt Gina."

She snorted. "Not a one of us believes that, Zoey. You two are still in love with each other, and now that you're divorced, you two can have a second chance."

I shook my head sadly. "That's not going to happen, Aunt Gina. Sebastian hates me, with good reason, and there's no way he'd ever give me another chance."

"I'm not so sure about either of those things, dear. But I'll let it go for now."

"Uh huh."

Aunt Gina smiled and ignored me. If only I had anywhere near her level of confidence. Then again, if I had her confidence, a lot of things would be different in my life.

9

SEBASTIAN

I couldn't get the image of Zoey holding back tears out of my mind. I hated when women cried. Usually, they were happy to let the tears go and use them to get what they wanted, but it was worse when they held back. When they tried to stop them. I hurt her.

Fucking hell. I didn't want to hurt her. No matter how many times I thought about how good it would feel to have her show up one day and see me happy with my new woman, it hurt to see her cry and to know it was because of me.

Maybe her staying away was for the best. Maybe I should find someone else. Avoid her like she was avoiding me. Move on with my life for real instead of wishing I could for a decade and not really giving another woman a chance.

Before I lost my nerve, I opened that stupid dating app and accepted a handful of potential matches. I was sure nothing would come of any of them, but I had to be willing. Even if Zoey and I slept together again, her life wasn't in MacKellar Cove. She would go back to Pittsburgh and move on again. She'd find someone else. Someone who wasn't me.

I shoved my phone back into my pocket and got back to

85

work. The garden was finally coming along. I'd taken a little more time on it over the weekend to get the last of the weeds pulled out, and it paid off. I had a better idea of what the space looked like, and by the end of the following week, I hoped to be able to put in orders for all the plants.

"Hey," I heard to my right.

I leaned back on my heels and looked at Cameron. He kicked the dirt and scowled at it. He was wearing a pair of jeans and a t-shirt with a video game character on it. His gaze flickered to the weeds in front of me, then back to me.

"Hey," I replied. "Want to help?"

He shrugged like that wasn't why he was there. "I guess."

I smothered my smile and nodded like I didn't know that was why he'd joined me. I handed over an extra pair of gloves I bought for him after he helped the week before and nodded to the weeds I'd been pulling. "These are a little tougher. I can definitely use the help."

Cameron nodded, his unruly blond hair falling over his eyes, and kneeled next to me. "Okay."

I watched him for a long minute. He grabbed the weed at the base like I showed him the week before. He pulled slowly, wiggling it when it resisted. The dirt loosened as he tugged until the weed came flying out in his hands. Dirt went flying everywhere, showering both of us.

Cameron looked up at me with wide eyes full of fear. "I'm sorry. I didn't mean—"

"There's no reason to be sorry. It happens."

"But I got you dirty," he said softly. He ducked his chin and tugged his lip between his teeth.

In less than two hours, I'd made two of them cry. All I had to do was find Alexis and steal her favorite toy, and my day would be complete. Jesus, I was an asshole.

Or Zoey's ex was an asshole. It was hard to imagine the kid was so upset about getting me dirty when I was kneeling in the dirt, but as his shoulders shook, I knew there was more to it.

I picked up a handful of dirt, grabbing it from under his nose so I knew he would see. His watery gaze lifted with my handful of dirt. He watched as I lifted it over my head and let go of the dirt all over myself.

His eyes went wide, staring at me like I was completely nuts. I shrugged like it was no big deal, then rubbed my dirty gloves on my face and over my clothes, making sure the dirt stuck and didn't just brush away.

"Why did you do that?"

"Because dirt washes off."

"But my dad always gets mad when I get him dirty."

I clenched my jaw so tight it hurt. I forced it to relax and put my dirty hand on his shoulder. "I don't know your dad, but when I work in the dirt, I expect to get dirty. Even when I'm not working in the dirt, I expect to get dirty. It's a part of life, and if I got upset every time I got dirty, I'd spend all my time avoiding the fun things in life. Do you think it's fun to play in the dirt?"

He paused, then nodded hesitantly.

"Me, too. I also think it's fun to get other people dirty." I reached out quickly and touched his cheek with my dirt caked glove, leaving a brown line on his face.

His eyes went wide again, then curled up into a grin. He stuck his hands into the dirt and lunged at me, smearing his hand over my shirt.

I laughed with him and nodded. "Good one. I might need to wash this shirt twice."

Cameron giggled, sounding like an eight year old for the first time. He was too young to be so serious. One more thing I wanted to hunt down Trevor for and teach him how to treat the people he was supposed to love.

Cameron and I worked together for almost two hours

before he started to slow down. We chatted about his favorite video game and school and a little about his family. He told me he didn't see his father much and missed him, but it also sounded like maybe he didn't. It was tough to hear because a kid should love their parents and miss them all the time.

My own parents had retired and moved to Hawaii years ago. I wasn't very close to them and never had been. I knew how Cameron felt about his dad because I was pretty much the same. My parents made sure I had what I needed growing up, but they didn't go above and beyond. I learned to accept it and never felt like I belonged anywhere until I met Gina.

I didn't want the same for Cameron. He wasn't supposed to miss his father yet. He was supposed to have a relationship with him and believe his father would always be there for him.

"I'm getting kind of thirsty," I said as the sun blazed down on us and Cameron sat back for the third time in a row.

"Yeah, me, too," he hurried to agree. I admired the kid for not wanting to appear weak or like he couldn't keep up.

"What do you say we go find some water and take a break? I could use one. How about you?"

"Yeah, I think I could use a break."

I smiled and stood, waiting for Cameron to do the same. He looked up at me as I shook the dirt from my hair. Most of it didn't come out and had turned to mud, but Gina would have a fit if I didn't at least try to be a little more presentable.

"Can I help you again?" Cameron asked before we got to the Inn.

"Yeah, of course. Any time."

"I know I'm slow," he said, sounding regretful.

"So am I. It's hot out here. It's smart to go slow so we don't overheat."

"But if I was faster we'd be done sooner."

I shrugged and tried not to let him know how much his words bothered me. "Sure, but only if we didn't pass out or something. Not everything in life has to be done fast. Some things are going to take time. Gardening is one of those things. I've been working on it since before you got here. You aren't slowing me down. You're a big help, and I'd be happy to have you join me whenever you want."

"Yeah?" he asked, suspicion and hope vying for dominance.

I nodded. "Absolutely. Sometimes Sofia helps me, but she works a lot."

"Is she your girlfriend?"

"Nope, just a friend."

"My dad has a friend who's a girl."

"Oh, yeah?"

Cameron nodded. "Yeah. But my mom doesn't have a lot of friends. She works and is home with us. She says we're her friends."

"That's nice," I said, unsure how to take what he was saying.

"I guess. But my mom likes girly stuff like my sister. Neither of them like to do things I like to do."

"Like what?"

He shrugged. "Like play with cars or go outside."

"Well, come find me. I like those things."

"Yeah?"

I nodded. "Absolutely. I have to work, but my work is outside. You can come with me to the lighthouse sometime. If your mom says it's okay. And you can help me in the garden whenever you want."

"What about cars?"

"Love 'em."

Cameron smiled, and I felt like I finally did something

right. Something to make someone in his family happy. My chest ballooned up, and I felt ten feet tall.

"Thanks!"

I grinned and opened the door for him to walk into the kitchen ahead of me. At least someone liked me.

NINE DAYS LATER, I was staring at the empty garden and wondering what the hell I'd gotten myself into. It took me weeks to clear all the dead debris. David from the garden center recommended I test the soil. He told me it was healthy, but he recommended waiting a week or two before trying to put new plants in.

Of course, I couldn't just let it rest. I needed to work the soil so it would be better suited to accepting the new plants. Which meant tilling the entire garden at least every other day and adding new soil in low spots and lime to balance the pH.

It was not what I signed up for.

"Are we all set?" David asked me. I'd seen him around town but didn't know him before I had to order a ton of plants. He was older than me, probably at least a decade, with gray hair and weathered, tan skin from years in the sun at the garden center.

I sighed and nodded slowly. "I guess I don't really have a choice. The owners are getting married out here in a month. I wanted everything done in a few weeks, so I'll do what needs to be done to make it happen."

"Ooh, really?"

"Yeah, why? Is there a reason we can't get it done by then?"

"No, we can, but we need to get the plants on order and

the delivery and planting scheduled if you need our help. You're not doing this alone, are you?"

I had planned to. Gina didn't want to spend a ton of money on labor when she was already spending thousands on plants. I didn't mind providing free labor, but I couldn't ask the garden center to do the same.

"I was going to. I hoped I could stagger the delivery of everything so I had time to get one section done at a time."

David looked around and blew out a breath. He was a big man, not as tall as me but close. He had short hair and wide shoulders. He looked as though he could carry a tree from the truck down to the garden without breaking a sweat.

"It's a big garden. Things can sit out for a while before they need to be planted, but if you're doing this for a wedding, you probably don't want to risk that anything goes wrong."

I shook my head. "No, definitely not. Can you look at when everything can be delivered and if you can get a crew out here to help?"

David nodded. "Yeah, of course. I'll get you prices on everything. If you want it all done in a day, I'd suggest five guys. I'll send you a quote this afternoon, and we can be in touch about getting it set up."

I nodded, knowing I didn't really have a choice. The wedding was a month away, but I wanted the plants in at least a few weeks before the wedding so they weren't as fragile when people were walking all over them.

I walked David to his truck and thanked him for coming by to check out the garden. Between the plants he suggested adding to what I'd already picked out and the help of his crew, I had a feeling the garden was going to end up costing more than Gina had planned or hoped.

Wanting to give Gina as much of a head's up as I could, I headed into the Inn to find her. As soon as I opened the door, my phone buzzed. I stepped inside and pulled it out to see an alert from Book Boyfriends Wanted.

MomOf2 had messaged me. We'd traded occasional messages over the last two weeks, and she was replying to my last question about the worst date she'd ever been on.

MOMOF2

My ex thought a company dinner counted as a date. It was our anniversary, and he asked me to get a babysitter for the kids. Told me to get dressed up. I bought a new dress and went to the salon. It had been a while since we'd had a real date, so I was excited. He was sweet and affectionate until we walked into the restaurant and his boss and boss's wife were there. We were led to a table for six with a client and his wife already there. It was horrible.

I chuckled and moved into the sitting room so I could reply to her.

BETHELIGHT

Did you make him make it up to you?

MOMOF2

No. I should have, but he never saw anything wrong with it. He even said I should have been happy because it was a restaurant I'd been wanting to go to for a long time. He was clueless.

BETHELIGHT

Sounds like there's a reason he's an ex.

MOMOF2

More than one.

BETHELIGHT

Well, better to be past it than still having to deal with fake date nights and men who don't know when they're being first class assholes.

MOMOF2

So true.

So, opposite side. What was your best date?

Zoey's face as a teenager popped into my mind. I loved her for years before I got my hands on her, but when she turned eighteen and we could be together, we went out on our first date. She was sweet and innocent and had no idea how crazy she made me.

We met outside the Inn because we weren't sure how Gina would take us going out. She climbed up into my truck and slid across the seat so she could hold my hand. She was wearing a blue sundress that had a short, flirty skirt that lifted in the breeze when we walked by the river later that night.

The night should have been innocent, but it was charged with sexual tension and the crazy kind of chemistry that only existed when there was a deep connection between two people. In the fourteen years since, I hadn't ever felt the same.

That was also the night Zoey and I slept together for the first time. The night I told her I loved her. The night we started planning our future.

A future that never happened.

BETHELIGHT

I have to think about that one. Need to get to work now. Talk later.

I tucked my phone away without waiting for an answer

from her. Of the matches I'd had in the last two weeks, she was the only one I was still talking to. One of them was only interested in hooking up, which should have been fine, but felt wrong after I'd slept with Zoey. The others didn't click with me. But this one, the woman who was unapologetically herself, made me laugh and kept me interested.

Maybe moving on was possible.

Gina was in the kitchen like I figured she'd be. She was humming a tune to herself and mumbling something when I walked in. She turned when she heard the door swing.

"Oh, Sebastian, you're here. How was the meeting with David?"

"That's why I wanted to find you."

Gina put down what she was holding and gave me her full attention. "That doesn't sound good."

"I don't know how bad yet, but it's going to be more money."

"How much more?"

I shook my head. "I don't know. He had some suggestions for more plants. He said what I ordered wouldn't be enough to fill all the spaces. He wanted to add height and color and texture to it all and said he'd work with what you and I had already planned out, but he wanted to make it what it used to be."

"I understand that. I figured he'd want to add some plants. He also knows the budget and won't go too far over it."

"On plants, yes."

"What else is there?" Gina asked. Her sharp gaze narrowed as she studied me. "Sebastian?"

"Labor."

"Ah," Gina said, the word carrying too much weight. "I should have included that in my budget. I ask you to do far too much."

"It's not that, Gina. I should have worked faster at getting everything out, but now, David said I need to let the soil rest and treat it so it'll accept the new plants. We can't get started for at least a week, and that'll be almost three weeks before the wedding. If we don't get everything planted next week, I'm afraid the plants won't be well established in time for Piper and Gavin's wedding."

Gina scowled and drew a breath. She turned back to whatever she was cooking and worked silently. She was trying to come up with another idea, which made me feel like shit. She'd always been able to turn to me when she needed something, and for years, I did everything for her without complaint or thought. I never accepted her money, and I wouldn't now, but I knew if I worked around the clock for a week I wouldn't get all the plants in. And I couldn't work around the clock. I had my own job to do.

"I'll have to make it work," Gina said simply after a few minutes.

"Let me see what the price is from David. I should have gotten everything done earlier."

"No, Sebastian. This is not on you. I put too much on you and it isn't fair. I've been leaning on you for years."

"Gina, I agreed to do this. I'll figure it out. I promise."

"Sebastian—"

"Gina, no. I will figure it out."

She drew a deep breath and let it out slowly. "Okay. But tell me if you can't. Please."

I nodded and promised her I would, even though I knew it was a lie. I'd do anything for Gina. She was the closest thing I had to family, and I wasn't going to let her down.

10

David sent me the quote for having his crew help me plant everything in the garden, and I nearly choked on the number. Not because the guys weren't worth it, but because it was almost as big of a number as we were spending for the plants themselves. There was no way Gina could afford to pay that. And no way I could cover it and not tell her.

I spent the evening trying to come up with options and feeling like a failure for taking on the project without a better idea of what it would take. I was constantly jumping to help Gina. I'd done it forever. I was sure a shrink would say it was my misguided attempt to win Zoey back, using her aunt as a proxy for the woman I loved and hoping it would get back to Zoey that I was around and reliable and took care of anything that needed to be done.

Hell, maybe that was part of it. I chose to believe it was just because I loved Gina like family and wanted to help her.

It didn't really matter what the reason was because I'd finally agreed to something I couldn't do.

I was looking at the plans again when there was a knock

on my door. I wasn't expecting anyone, so I ignored it, but the person knocked again, quietly. Almost like they were trying not to let me know they were there.

I walked over to the door and opened it quickly, hoping whoever it was hadn't already left. Zoey was a few feet away with her back to me.

"Zoey?"

She turned and looked at me over her shoulder. "Hi. Um, sorry. I guess I should have called you first or something. But I, uh, don't have your number, so…"

I tilted my head to the side and took her in. She was wearing a pair of cotton shorts with a drawstring that hung down to her bare thigh. Her tank top clung to her curves and teased me with the way it cupped her breasts. Her hair was pulled back into a ponytail and her lip was between her teeth.

She looked like the girl I fell in love with decades ago.

"What are you doing here?"

"I…" She looked around as if someone was going to jump out at her and scare her.

It made me even more curious, and maybe a little uneasy. What was going on? I crossed my arms and leaned back against the doorframe, waiting her out. Eventually, she would talk.

"I wanted sex, okay? You said this," she gestured between us, "was sex only. No emotions, no connection, just sex, and I… should never have come here."

She turned and stomped off toward the house. At the word sex, my cock hardened. Hell, at the sight of the woman who used to be my girl, my cock hardened. It was Zoey. I couldn't say no to her. I didn't want to.

"Zoey," I called out, hoping it would stop her.

It didn't.

"Dammit, Zoey, stop."

That stopped her. I hurried over to where she was. Her arms were crossed, and her toe was tapping impatiently on the ground. She looked like a pissed off teenager instead of a grown-ass woman who'd just asked me for sex.

"Why are you leaving?"

"Because this was a bad idea. Because we are a bad idea."

"Yeah, we are," I agreed, shocking her. She sucked in a breath and drew back, but I pushed on. "We know we're a bad idea. That's why I said sex only. Because when we talk, we piss each other off. When we get involved, we fight. But when you're naked and under me, or naked and on top of me, or naked and standing in front of me, we're good."

Her breath was shaky and needy. She licked her lips and looked up at me with eyes that begged me to lay it out for her.

"If you want to walk back up to the house right now and slide your fingers over your clit and pretend they're mine, I'm not going to stop you. But if you want me to touch you until you scream my name, then fuck you until you can't scream anything, turn your ass around and get naked."

Her eyes widened. The pulse at the base of her neck fluttered rapidly. Her breasts heaved with each breath she took. Her nipples fought against her bra for freedom.

I prayed silently that she would choose my house. That she would do as I suggested and get naked and spread herself out on my bed. I prayed that she would steal my attention for a little while so I could stop obsessing over how I was going to help Gina.

And I nearly fell to my knees when she brushed past me and shook her ass as she walked into my house.

I followed her like the puppy I was. As soon as the door closed behind me, she whipped her shirt off and tossed it on the floor. She kicked her shoes off next. Then her shorts and panties were pushed down her thighs and pooled at her feet before she stalked to my room, crawled onto my bed, and positioned herself on my pillows.

I couldn't remember the last time I saw something so sexy. Until she reached down between her thighs and stroked herself.

"Fucking hell," I murmured, hurrying to strip my clothes off while keeping my eyes on Zoey the entire time.

"It's been a while since I've been with anyone. Before a few weeks ago, it was almost two years," she said calmly as she spread her folds and dipped a finger inside herself. "I have gotten really good at making myself come quickly. But being with you was… I want you, Sebastian." She met my gaze as she said those final words.

There was a part of me that hated her for saying them. That was angry she would use those words, words that she knew would make me do anything. She said those same words to me the first night we made love, and every time after that. I told her nothing would ever happen unless she was okay with it. That she had to be the one who initiated it. Those four words were her signal for me to take charge.

I wasn't a puppy. I was Pavlov's dog, and Zoey was my treat. And I could not say no.

I kept my gaze on her fingers, manipulating her body as I moved toward the bed. When I reached the edge, I crawled onto the mattress, positioning myself between her thighs. She didn't stop touching herself with me right there, letting me watch from less than a foot away how she liked to come. A stroke, a flick, a rub. A moan came as she lifted her hips. I blew a breath on her, my cock pulsing when her sensitive skin puckered from the cool air.

"Sebastian," she whimpered.

That was my cue. I pressed her thighs wide and opened her up. I licked her from her entrance up to where her fingers lazily teased her clit, then nudged her fingers out of the way with my tongue. I repeated the same thing she'd been doing to herself, slowly, drawing out her pleasure until she was writhing beneath me and begging me to let her come.

Maybe it was punishment for leaving me all those years ago or maybe it was not being able to stop, but when she crested that first wave and moaned loud enough to alert the neighbors, if I had any, I didn't let up. I lashed at her wet skin, pressing a finger deep into her as she started to come down.

Her entire body jerked and tightened around my finger. Her legs tensed and closed around my ears. Her words became nonsensical and louder as she laid there and took everything I gave her.

I added a second finger and sucked hard on her clit, sending her tumbling without warning. My name flew from her lips, and I hated myself for what I was doing to her. To myself.

But I still couldn't stop.

I withdrew from her body and kept my gaze away while I grabbed a condom from my nightstand. I needed her so badly that I couldn't take a deep breath, but I didn't want to. For not the first time, I wished I could have fallen for someone like Sofia. Someone who saw things the same way I did and wanted the same things I did. Or the woman I was messaging. Or any of the others I'd dated or slept with over the years. If I'd been able to fall for any of them, I wouldn't be rolling a condom on and positioning myself at the entrance of the one and only woman I'd ever loved, the one and only woman who'd ever broken me.

But I hadn't fallen for any of the others, so I thrust hard into Zoey, groaning when she pulsed around me and moaned loudly. She reached for my hands, but I ignored hers and went up on my knees, using my hands to lift her hips to mine in offering.

I watched as her body stretched to take me in. As her pink flesh slid around me. I kept my gaze locked at where we met so I didn't memorize every inch of her womanly body. Every scar and freckle and stretch mark she gained bringing her children into the world, children another man gave her.

Just like the last time, neither of us spoke a word. The only sound in my cabin was our bodies slapping together in an erotic rhythm. She tensed around me and tipped her head back, drawing my attention up her body to her twisted face. Her mouth opened soundlessly, but her eyes were squeezed tight as if she was in pain.

I released one of her hips and pressed my thumb to her clit. Instantly, her face changed to one of pure pleasure. The silent O turned to a long moan that became frantic and incoherent as she came hard.

The pulsing of her body demanded I follow her over the edge. I pounded into her, trying to let my mind go blank and let Zoey be some faceless woman. I tried, but I failed.

My eyes devoured her as I raced toward the edge. I only had seconds, but it felt like hours as her eyes locked on mine and time stretched between us. All the times we'd made love came back to me like a flood, crashing over me and blending past and present into some twisted sense of belonging.

Her eyes widened as if she was feeling the same thing, and at that moment, my body tensed and released with a shout of her name and a mind-numbing force that had the edges of my vision fading to darkness.

I caught myself just before I collapsed on top of her and rolled to the side. My pulsing cock slid from her body and continued to send aftershocks through me. My eyes stayed closed for a long moment as I tried to center my mind and remind myself that it didn't matter how amazing the sex was, it was just sex.

When I had the strength to move, I rolled off the bed away from Zoey and went to the bathroom. I closed the door with a loud click, hoping she got the hint and got off my bed and got dressed. The only way I could function around her was to be the angry ogre I'd become since she left. Gavin and the other guys had started to bring out a more human side of me, but I couldn't be that guy with Zoey. Not when I knew she would only destroy him.

I gathered my clothes as I walked out of the bathroom and put them on, ignoring the mixed emotions I felt when I saw Zoey had done the same. She was waiting for me in the kitchen, nibbling on a nail and staring at the door like she couldn't wait to run through it.

"You leaving?" I asked.

She nodded. "Yeah. Should we exchange numbers?"

"Why?"

She nibbled her lip for a second. "In case you want to get a hold of me or something."

"Nope. No need. You know where to find me."

Her eyebrows narrowed, and she studied me for a long minute. I resisted the urge to shuffle my feet and let her know I didn't like being assessed since she always found me wanting.

"I feel like I'm taking advantage of you."

"Why?"

She shrugged and didn't answer. I lifted an eyebrow because I knew there was something she didn't want to admit to.

"Because I'm coming down here for sex. Or I did today. Last time wasn't intentional. And it feels like a shitty thing to do."

"Sort of like promising to come back and then marrying someone else?"

She opened her mouth to argue, fire sparking in her eyes, then she closed her mouth, and that fire dimmed again. "Maybe this is a bad idea."

I shrugged and headed to the fridge, pretending not to care either way. "Up to you. If you don't want to do this again, have a nice life. Otherwise, you know where to find me."

I grabbed a beer and went to the couch. I pulled the plans onto my lap and waited, unable to breathe or think or function, until she was gone. I didn't want her to leave, but I knew she would. She always left. And the sooner she did, the sooner she reminded me of who she was and what she was like, the better it was going to be for me.

A few seconds later, the door closed quietly. I turned and found my cabin empty. And tried to convince myself it was for the best.

THE LAST THING I wanted to do the night after sleeping with Zoey was hang out with her brother. But I told Gavin earlier in the week that I'd be going, so he was waiting for me.

Piper usually worked at O'Kelley's on Thursday nights, but she was working fewer hours there and more at the Inn, so Gavin was looking to ride together since he wasn't going to hang around and bring Piper home after her shift ended. I wasn't sure how long she was going to keep working at O'Kelley's, but Hudson said she had a job as long as she wanted one.

We walked in, and I was reminded once again why Hudson was hoping to hold on to Piper as a server when I saw him cleaning up glass with a worried-looking server watching him.

Yeah, she was going to be fired.

Gavin and I shook our heads and went to the bar. Knox Randall was behind the bar pouring drinks. "What are you doing here?" I asked him.

Knox looked up at me with a grin and a head-nod. "Sebastian Parks. I didn't know you knew your way to a bar. How the hell are ya?"

I chuckled and shook my head. Knox owned Al's Hardware, the one and only hardware store for hours. He took over for his dad a few years ago and made the place an even bigger success than it'd been under his dad. I liked both men but hadn't ever seen either outside the hardware store.

"You're one to talk," I told him. "And you're pouring drinks? A man of many talents."

Knox pushed a beer in front of me and nodded. "Yeah, well, I had to pay my way through college somehow. Bartending was always good money, and I never went home alone."

He winked and jerked his head toward Gavin. "Want a drink?"

"Beer's good."

Knox nodded and started pouring. "How do you know this one?" he asked Gavin.

"Known him forever. My sister should have married him. Now, I'd like to think he's a friend," Gavin said without a glance in my direction.

Good thing because his comment about Zoey had me almost choking on my beer. I took an extra second to swallow it and met Knox's gaze.

"No shit. I haven't known Sebastian to settle down. I figured he'd be a bachelor forever and always had been."

"My sister did a number on him, but she's paid for it.

Married an asshole who treated her like she didn't matter. They're divorced now, and we're hoping she and Sebastian will get back together."

"She's leaving in a few weeks," I growled.

"And I'm hoping she'll remember why she loved this place, and you, and will stay," Gavin said succinctly.

I shook my head. It wouldn't do any good to argue with Gavin about Zoey. Or anyone else. Zoey was her own woman, as she'd proven many times.

"Well, this is interesting. When I saw Hudson earlier, he said I should stop by, but I wasn't expecting to get all the local gossip from a bunch of dudes hanging out."

"Oh, please, I think you start half the local gossip," Ian said with a smile. He took the seat next to Gavin and clasped hands with Knox across the bar.

Knox tipped his head back and laughed. "Probably true."

"How are ya?"

"I'm good, man. How are you? How's the wife?"

"Blake's good. Things are going well. I was going to head down to see you next week. See if I can put in an order for the winter. There are a few projects I need to get done around the shop."

Knox nodded. "Sounds good. I'll see what I can do for you."

"Thanks. Are you joining us?"

"Yeah, that was the plan. Until Hudson heard glass breaking and walked off grumbling under his breath about having to fire another server." Knox shrugged like it was no big deal.

"He's had it rough. Good of you to pitch in," Ian said.

"That's what we do around here, right? Pitch in and make it work," Knox said with a smile.

The wheels started turning in my head at his words. It had been months since Gina asked me to fix up the gardens, and the other guys had offered to help, but I kept insisting I'd take care of it all myself. I thought I could, and I knew they were all busy with their own jobs and lives and didn't need to help.

But things had changed, and I actually did need the help.

"Hey, can I ask you guys a favor?" I interrupted.

They all turned to look at me.

"I got a quote for planting everything at the Inn, and it's more than Gina or I can afford. I was going to try to find a way to make it work, but would any of you be willing to help me put some plants in the ground?"

"Yeah," Ian said without hesitation. "Do you know when?"

I shook my head. "Not yet. Next week sometime. Maybe the week after if it takes that long to get everything in."

"I can move things around in my schedule and help out. Blake might, too. Just let me know when."

"Thanks."

"You know Piper and I will help. It's for our wedding, after all. And our Inn," Gavin said.

"I don't mind helping," Knox said. "I'll take the trees." He flexed his large muscles and nodded.

I rolled my eyes at him, but I appreciated the help. As the rest of the guys arrived, they all agreed to come over whenever the plants got there to help.

Looked like I had my crew.

11

ZOEY

"Please, just give it a chance," I said. I was not going to resort to begging my kids, but I was getting close.

We'd been in MacKellar Cove for almost a month, and they were arguing daily about going home. They didn't have friends in MacKellar Cove and didn't know how to make friends. A few people who stayed at the Inn had kids, but mostly, it was adults. Which left my kids extremely bored.

Melody offered to get her daughter and Alexis together, but I felt like it was a pity playdate. I hesitated to take her up on it since we didn't really know each other, but I was waffling on that, too.

All I did lately was second guess everything.

"Fine," my kids grumbled from the backseat.

I breathed a sigh of relief and promised myself a very large glass of wine that evening for my trouble. Because dealing with two crabby children was hard enough, but pretending in front of the entire town that I was whole was even worse.

"Is Sebastian going to be there?" Cameron asked.

"Sebastian? I don't know. Why would you ask?" I blurted, wondering where the question came from. Did he have a tone? God, I was paranoid.

"I was just wondering."

I looked in the rearview mirror at him, but he was staring out the window. He didn't talk to Sebastian much at dinners, so I couldn't figure out why he cared. Unless he thought something was going on between Sebastian and me.

"I like Sebastian," Alexis said. "He's nice."

I looked at her, and she stared out the window with a smile on her face. I had no idea what was going on with my kids, but I was going to do my best to play it off.

"Sebastian has a lot of work, so we'll see. I'm hoping there'll be some kids you guys can play with. Then you can make friends."

They both grumbled in agreement, less excited than I expected. For two kids who constantly complained about not having friends, they didn't seem all that interested in making new ones.

I rolled my eyes and focused on the road. The streets were busier the closer we got to the center of town where the summer fair was being held. I found a spot on a side street not too far away and hoped the kids would enjoy the afternoon.

Gavin and Piper said the fair was something new the town was doing. One of Piper's friends, Goldie, was the tourism director for the area, and she suggested it to bring visitors to the town, but also to bring residents out to celebrate what made MacKellar Cove special.

Rides and food trucks were set up around Catherine Park. People wandered down the sidewalks and across the streets in the area. The roads weren't technically blocked off, but with so many people, cars couldn't get through.

The excitement of the fair made the kids' eyes light up. I

asked what they wanted to do first and was surprised when they both said riding a few rides and even agreed on which ride to start with.

"The spinny thing," Alexis said, pointing to a ride that made me dizzy just looking at it.

"Yeah, that looks awesome," Cameron agreed.

"Let's go," I told them, praying they would not ask me to go on with them.

We got into line, and the kids were big enough to ride without me, so I happily waited while they sat next to each other in one of the carts and the attendant secured their belts.

The ride started with a jerk, then they spun. I held my breath as I watched them disappear, then reappear in seconds. The smiles on their faces let me relax a little.

"Zoey!" I heard from behind me.

Knowing I didn't know very many people, I hesitated before I turned around. I was sure whoever it was wasn't talking to me. When I looked, Melody Holland was waving at me with her husband and daughter by her side. She pointed to me, and they all walked over.

"Hi," Melody said with a quick hug. "How are you?"

"Good," I lied. I hadn't seen Melody since book club the weekend we arrived. I made excuses not to go back every weekend since. Piper and the others were nice, but I felt weird being there. They were Piper's friends, not mine, and they weren't going to become my friends. Not when I wasn't staying in town.

"We've missed you at book club. Piper said you've been busy with the kids."

I nodded, knowing none of them believed my lie, but I wasn't going to change it now. "You know how it is."

Melody smiled. "I do. This is Amber. She was hoping to meet Alexis today. I'm glad we ran into you. Is Alexis here?"

I nodded and turned back to the ride as it slowed. "She's on that ride with her brother."

"I want to ride, Mommy!" Amber said excitedly.

"We will. Let's meet Alexis first. Maybe you two can ride some things together. And we can eat lunch or something. If you're okay with that."

"Yeah, of course," I told her. Being nice wasn't hard for me, but I still felt uncomfortable around Melody and her perfect family. Mine had fallen apart, but hers was still together and happy and everything I wanted.

Ramsey lifted a hand to wave to someone, then told Melody he was going to say hi to a client and nodded to me before walking away.

"Sorry," Melody said. "It's tough to be at these things because he knows everyone. Oh, is that Alexis?"

I looked to where she pointed and saw my kids running toward us. They collided with my legs and began talking rapidly.

"That was awesome. We need to ride more. Can we do something else, Mommy? This is so much fun!"

"Good, and of course. First, this is Amber. Amber is six like you, Alexis. She lives here and wanted to go on rides with you guys."

"Hi," Alexis said simply.

"Hi," Amber answered.

"Did you see that one?" Alexis asked, pointing to another ride.

"Yeah, let's go," Amber said.

Alexis looked back at Cameron, who also nodded, and the three of them took off toward the next ride.

Melody laughed. "I guess that went well."

I chuckled with her. "I wish it was that easy to make friends as an adult."

"Oh, my God, right? When I first started hanging out with

Blake and the others, it was because my marriage was falling apart and Blake kind of took pity on me."

"What?" I blurted before I could stop the word.

Melody smiled wryly. "Yep. I lost our second child, but I was determined to have another kid. He fought hard because losing Steven almost killed me, physically and emotionally. Willow… It was a whole big thing, and Ramsey and I separated for a while. Blake and Ian had just started dating, and Blake and I started talking some, and she invited me to book club. Finley and I were never friends, and I really didn't know everyone else so I did not want to go, but Blake wore me down. It was awkward at first, but after a few weeks, I enjoyed it and let my guard down a little. And they helped me to put things back together with Ramsey."

"Wow," I breathed, more shocked than I could say. She said something at the one book club I attended, but I brushed it off as conversation and not reality. I saw Melody and Ramsey as picture perfect, a happy little family without a care in the world, but they weren't. Not by a long shot.

"I know. Most people see us and have no idea, but I almost lost all of it. I'll be forever grateful to Blake and the others, along with Ian and Hudson and the guys for helping us."

"Mommy, that was awesome!" the kids said as they ran back to us. "Can we go on another ride?"

Melody and I looked at each other for permission, then both laughed when we realized what we were doing.

"Of course. Just let us know where you're going so we can follow you," I told them.

Melody nodded. "And stay together."

The kids decided on their next ride, then took off together. We stood and watched them run off with smiles on our faces. It was good to see them happy.

"You should come to book club tomorrow night," Melody

said. "And we should plan a playdate for the girls. All three of them, if you're up to it. Our neighbor has a boy a little older than Amber, probably Cameron's age. I can invite them over, too. He's a single dad, so it'll be later in the day, if that's okay."

"You don't have to do that," I protested.

Melody shook her head. "Honestly, it'll be fun. Ramsey can grill something, and Derek will probably be up for it. Oh, ha. That's him now."

I looked to where Melody was pointing and saw a tall, Black man with a white tee stretched across his chest. He was smiling at his son, a mini-me version of the man with a matching smile and short, dark hair. They were talking to Ramsey and walking toward us.

"Hey," Ramsey said when they reached Melody and me. "I saw Derek and Jude when they walked up to the fair. I mentioned Cameron and thought Jude might want to have a buddy to ride rides with."

"Hey," Derek said, reaching out to me. "I'm Derek, and this is Jude. Ramsey tells me you're here for the summer, and Gina Holbrook is your aunt."

I nodded and shook his hand. "Yep. My kids are less than thrilled to be here without their friends. My brother and I came here when we were younger, and I loved it, so I wanted to bring my kids here."

"It's a great place to raise them. How old is your son?"

"Cameron is eight."

"So's Jude. He'll be in third grade next year."

"Cameron, too."

"Great. It's easy for kids to make friends."

Melody and I laughed. "We were just saying the same thing about our girls."

"You have a daughter, too?"

I nodded as the kids ran over. "This is Alexis and

Cameron. Cameron, Jude is going into third grade like you are. He was hoping to ride some rides with you guys."

"Cool. We were going to do that one next. Wanna come?" Cameron said.

Jude looked up at his dad and nodded.

"Go," Derek said. "Have fun."

The four kids took off together again, smiles and laughter following them.

"He doesn't get enough time to be a kid. Since my divorce, he's a mini-adult," Derek said.

"I know what you mean. Mine are the same," I agreed.

"Kids are resilient, though. Seeing the excited smiles on their faces makes it all worthwhile. Thanks for dragging us over here," Derek said to Ramsey.

"Happy you were willing," Ramsey said.

"I hope you're also willing to come over one night this week," Melody added. "Zoey and I were talking about getting all the kids together for a playdate. Ramsey can grill, and we can let the kids all play, and we adults can chat. If you have a free night."

Derek nodded. "That sounds great. We're free every night this week. He just finished baseball, so things are quiet."

"Great. How about Tuesday? Ramsey, what's your schedule?" Melody asked.

"Tuesday's good. That works."

"Good," Melody said, looking happy with herself. "This will be fun. I think all the kids need this."

"So do the adults," Derek said with a wry grin.

"Definitely," I agreed. "Let me know what I can bring, too."

"What do you guys eat? Let's make a plan," Melody said as we turned to follow the kids.

The guys held back and talked while Melody and I

planned out food for dinner. She was easy to talk to, and when she asked me again to come to book club, I agreed.

"Good," she said. "Now, I'm going to be nosy and ask what's going on with you and Sebastian."

"Nothing. Why? What do you mean?" I stammered.

She smirked. "Okay, well, that doesn't seem like nothing, but you don't have to tell me. We all teased Sofia for a long time about them because they hit it off so quickly, but she's always assured us nothing happened and they're just friends."

I nodded. "She told me the same thing."

"I believe her. I'm not sure if you do, but I don't think she would lie about that. Piper says the same thing."

"I know. But regardless, I'm going back to Pittsburgh next month. The kids have school, and we have lives there. I couldn't move here. Sebastian still hates me. It's obvious."

"Is he mean? I can't imagine him being that way."

I shook my head. "Not like that. It's just the general feel I get from him. He's made comments about things. The other night I said I felt like I was using him and felt shitty for it, and he threw me leaving in my face."

Melody was quiet for a long moment as we walked through the crowd. I was waiting for her to tell me I was a horrible person, but instead, she asked, "How are you using him? For sex?"

I fumbled to come up with an answer as my cheeks heated with the truth.

"Oh, my God, you are. Good for you!"

I shook my head. "Not really. I mean, I… it's complicated with him."

"It's complicated with everyone. I've been with Ramsey for half my life and it's complicated. But if you're enjoying yourself and you both know the score, then there's nothing wrong with it."

"Yeah, but he wants it to just be sex. No emotions. And I'm not sure I can do that."

"You're still in love with him, aren't you?"

I stared straight ahead and hesitated. After a minute, I nodded.

"You should tell him that."

I laughed. "No. That would not go over at all."

"Can I ask you a question?"

I nodded and waited.

"Why didn't you come back?"

The truth pressed hard on me, but the whole truth was something I'd never admitted to anyone. I'd always given a version of the truth, a version that made me look like a bitch instead of a gold-digging bitch. Neither was preferable, but I learned to live with my choices.

"When I met Trevor, things were different. With Sebastian, we always hid. Because he's so much older than me, he thought people wouldn't accept us, so we never went out. But Trevor took me out all the time and made me feel special. He told me he loved me and wanted to give me everything I ever dreamed of in life. It had been months since I'd seen Sebastian, and all my friends had boyfriends on campus. They were going on dates and planning futures, and all I had were a few old letters and my memories. It felt like it wasn't real, but Trevor was. He was right there in front of me, and he wanted me, and I gave in."

"You never wanted to come back and see Sebastian?"

"I did. I thought about him all the time. I cried more times than I can count because I knew I hurt him. But I also thought we were better off apart."

"Why?"

"A lot of reasons," I told her honestly. "I convinced myself that love didn't happen like ours did. That we weren't really in love. Even that he might be with other women when I was at school. I never imagined he'd still be single now."

"If you'd known, would you have come back?"

I shook my head. "No. My marriage wasn't perfect, and it wasn't meant to last forever, but at that point in my life, I needed Trevor. So, I married him."

Melody let the topic go after that, but I could tell she wanted to ask more. I wasn't ready to admit to anyone, especially a woman I'd only spoken to a handful of times, that marrying Trevor was the only way to keep my parents' heads above water. That if I'd married Sebastian, or moved to MacKellar Cove and started dating him, my parents would have had to declare bankruptcy and would have lost everything.

My parents didn't know I knew, and I wasn't going to start telling everyone around. But the full truth was, I didn't think I had a choice. I needed someone who could afford to support me until I found a job. Someone who would take on my student loan debt and pay for my living expenses.

Maybe I made the wrong choice. But it was my choice, and I'd learned to accept it, and the consequences.

12

$\mathcal{B}$y the time we got home from the fair, the kids were worn out and crashed hard. I grabbed my phone and opened up a new book and poured myself a large glass of wine.

I curled up in a chair near the dark fireplace and covered my legs with a light blanket. It was quiet in the house with Gina already asleep and Gavin and Piper not home. I took a deep breath and enjoyed the quiet for a minute.

My phone buzzed with a notification, and I clicked over to the dating app. I was still undecided about online dating, but I couldn't deny that talking to a stranger and having him tell me he enjoyed talking to me made me feel good.

BETHELIGHT

How's your weekend going?

MOMOF2

Good. We went to a town fair today. It was fun.

117

BETHELIGHT

There was a fair in MacKellar Cove today.
That's where I live. Is that where you were?

MOMOF2

It was. I didn't know we were in the same
town. That makes me wonder who you are
and if we've met.

BETHELIGHT

Me too. I guess we probably have, but I don't
think I'm ready to know who you are yet.

MOMOF2

Neither am I. I'm enjoying talking to you.
Without the added pressure of dating.

BETHELIGHT

I agree. So, what else are you doing this
weekend?

MOMOF2

Well, right now I'm drinking a glass of wine
and talking to you. Not a bad end to my day.

BETHELIGHT

Sounds pretty perfect to me. Although I'd be
drinking a beer.

MOMOF2

Never developed a taste for beer. My ex
thought it was too low-class to drink anyway.

BETHELIGHT

He sounds delightful.

MOMOF2

I know. Another one of the many reasons
he's the ex.

BETHELIGHT

Was he always like that?

MOMOF2

Pompous? Yeah, but I was willing to not notice it when we got together. He was good to me and made me feel like I deserved the world.

BETHELIGHT

I'm sure you do. Sorry he didn't end up giving it to you.

MOMOF2

In a way he did. My kids are amazing, and they are my world.

BETHELIGHT

Sounds like they're lucky to have you.

MOMOF2

There are days I'm not sure they'd agree, but I'm doing the best I can.

BETHELIGHT

I think that's all a parent can do.

MOMOF2

I'm trying.

We chatted a little longer, then said goodnight. I tried to read some of my book, but with my wine gone, I was tired. I tiptoed upstairs and checked on the kids, then crashed.

The next day passed fairly quickly. I asked Piper if I could go to book club with her and had a good time. I was still quiet and didn't open up to them, but Melody sat next to me and we talked more. I was starting to feel like I had a friend. Someone I would have been friends with if I lived there full time.

On Monday, I jumped back into my job search. It had been a month since I found out I lost my job, but I was discouraged by the limited opportunities. I hadn't been doing enough lately to find something. I was reluctant to take on anything that would keep me away from the kids, so I was burying my head in the sand and ignoring the problem. I had to force myself to face it, at least a little, so my savings account wasn't completely dry by Christmas. I knew being in MacKellar Cove for the summer was going to put a strain on my finances, but I was handling it okay. I wouldn't if I had no income when I went back to Pittsburgh.

There were jobs available that I was qualified for, but everything wanted someone to start right away. Cashier, bank teller, administrative assistant. All of them were for immediate hires, not someone who needed to wait another month.

Even worse, most of the jobs I was qualified for had either irregular hours or long hours. I couldn't work at a bank and be there until five-thirty or six o'clock every night. If I was a cashier, I would be expected to work on weekends.

The job I had in the cafeteria was perfect. It was close to the kids if they needed something, the hours were great, and it paid well enough that we were comfortable. But it was no longer mine.

I gave myself a minute for a pity party. If I'd started working out of college like I'd planned, I would have years of computer science experience to fall back on. I would have contacts and a resume and all those things that would help me get a good job. But I listened to Trevor and let him work full time while I stayed home and tried to get pregnant. He assured me I'd never have to work. Too bad he never assured me we'd never get divorced.

I refused to be reliant on him for the rest of my life. It wasn't fair to him, not that I was all that worried about him, but it wasn't what felt right to me. I wanted to show my kids that I was capable of taking care of them, and myself, and that it was okay for both parents to work.

But first, I needed to find a job that would give me what I needed.

I was at the Inn in the sitting room going through job boards when Piper walked in and sat down across from me. I looked up at her and smiled, waiting for her to say something. I wasn't expecting what came out of her mouth.

"I want to hire you."

"Excuse me?"

She scooted forward on the couch and clasped her hands together. "You saved me a ton of headaches when you fixed that computer thing a few weeks ago. And you made it easier for me to see what's going on. It took you five minutes to do what I'd spent hours trying to figure out."

"It wasn't hard," I protested. "You weren't looking in the right place."

"No, I wasn't, but that's because I didn't know where the right place was. Zoey, I need you. I've been talking to Gavin about hiring someone to do a complete overhaul of our entire computer system. Everything from the hardware itself to all the software we use. Optimize it all and make everything not only user friendly, but integrate the systems. I'd also love an update of the website."

I bristled more and more as she spoke. If it was just Piper coming to me, I'd feel like a charity case. Not only were they putting us up for the summer, but she was trying to pay me for it, too? But she mentioned Gavin, so I knew it was not just charity but pity. He talked her into it because I have no marketable skills and he wants to help me out.

"I can't," I told her, making a move to get up.

Piper's face fell. "Really? I mean, I'm sorry, but can we talk about this?"

"Why?" I asked, not bothering to hide my exasperation. "Piper, look, we don't know each other well, and I'm sorry for that. I think you're amazing and I know you love my brother, and I know Gavin loves me, but I'm not going to let you guys treat me like I'm incapable of getting a job on my own."

"What?"

"I don't know how you found out that I lost my job, but I guess since it's out there now, I can admit it. Yes, it sucks, but I'm looking for something else. That's what I was doing when you walked in. I'll find something, but you don't need to make up a job in order to try to help me."

"Zoey, I honestly have no idea what you're talking about. With any of it. At all."

I studied her carefully for a long moment. Her face was open and curious, not carefully blank. Her hands were loosely linked on her lap, not clenched. Even her posture was inviting and relaxed.

Shit.

"You lost your job?" Piper asked cautiously.

I drew a deep breath and let it out. I wasn't ready to admit I'd failed, but apparently, I'd already admitted it. "Yeah. It wasn't exactly my dream job, but it was perfect for now. I worked in the school cafeteria and could bring the kids to school with me in the mornings and was off work before they were. I had all my summers and breaks from school off so I never had to worry about childcare. And it paid enough that, combined with the child support and alimony I get, we were comfortable. But it's gone. It was temporary, and the person who had it before me was able to come back so it was filled. Not by me."

"I'm so sorry, Zoey. I honestly didn't know. Gavin didn't tell me anything."

I shook my head and met her gaze. "He doesn't know. I haven't told him, or anyone else. I haven't been able to say it out loud."

"Shit, and here I am, bringing it all up and making you feel bad about it. I'm so sorry."

"It's not your fault. I was looking for a new job when you walked in, but I'm struggling to find something that won't require evenings or weekends or both."

"Do a lot of computer jobs require weekend work?"

I shook my head. "I'm not applying for computer jobs. I don't have the experience."

Piper tilted her head and gave me a disbelieving look. "Um, yes, you do. Maybe not tons of experience, but you know more than the average person, assuming I can consider myself average."

I chuckled. "Thanks, but the computer world moves fast. My knowledge is old. I haven't kept up with it."

"Well, you still know a lot more than any of us do, and I really would like to hire you to upgrade our systems. You don't have to, but I have been planning to look for someone to do it soon. Before the end of the year. I know you'd do a better job than anyone else because you love this place even more than I do."

I breathed a smile and looked around. I loved the Inn. It was home to me. It always had been, and if I'd made different choices, it probably would be now. But my choices were my own, and I refused to regret them.

"Can I think about it for a few days?"

Piper nodded. "Of course. Like I said, I was going to look for someone by the end of the year, so no rush. Take all the time you need."

I wanted to say yes, but there was something about it that was holding me back. I wanted to talk to my brother, and maybe talk to someone else.

Not that I thought he'd be open to an actual conversation.

I WAS STILL THINKING about Piper's offer the next night on the way to Melody and Ramsey's. I hadn't talked to Gavin about it yet, so I hadn't given Piper an answer. I loved the Inn, and I always enjoyed working with computers, but I needed to talk to my brother.

I was determined to put all of that out of my mind and enjoy the evening, though. The kids bounced in their seats with excitement, and I had to admit I felt the same way. It had been a long time since I'd had a friend.

"Are we there yet?" Alexis asked.

I laughed. "Not yet. But it won't be long."

"This place is pretty. Ooh, I want a swing in my tree."

"We don't have trees at the apartment," Cameron said sullenly.

"I know, but one day we might live in a house with a tree."

Cameron snorted but didn't argue with her. I hated that I couldn't give my kids everything they wanted and more. Being able to give them what they needed felt like a chore most of the time.

I pulled into the driveway and smiled. Their house was adorable and charming and perfect. It was idyllic with its purple front door, white trim, and soft gray siding. It was big, too, but not so big I felt uncomfortable. I knew Ramsey was a lawyer, but most people in MacKellar Cove were not flashy about any wealth they had. Living in an established neighborhood like they did said Ramsey and Melody were practical people. I could relate to that.

The kids scrambled to get out of the car and up to the door. They waited for me to grab the salad I brought and follow them before we rang the bell. It wasn't long before Melody opened the door, with Amber right behind her.

Alexis and Amber smiled brightly at each other and started talking a mile a minute.

"Do you want to see my room?"

"Yes! It's so cool here."

"And you're here! Can I show you my stuffed animals? And my books? Ooh, and my dance?"

Alexis's excited chattered followed Amber down the hallway.

"Well, now that they're entertained. Thanks for coming!" Melody stepped forward and hugged me close. I hadn't had a friend hug me in longer than I could remember. It felt good.

"Thanks for having us. We've all been looking forward to this."

"So have we. Come on in. Cameron, Jude isn't here yet, but you can come into the backyard. We have a swing set and a soccer ball and all kinds of stuff."

"Okay," Cameron said. He wasn't nearly as excited since his friend wasn't there yet, but he would be soon.

Melody winked at me over his head, and I tried to apologize without words. She waved it off and led the way to the backyard.

Ramsey was cleaning the grill when we walked out. He looked up and waved, looking like no lawyer I'd ever met. When he was out in town, he wore nice pants and button-down shirts, sometimes with the sleeves rolled up. But in his own backyard, he was in a tee and shorts. Comfortable and relaxed.

"Can I get you a drink?" Melody asked.

"Sure, that would be great."

"We have beer, wine, water, sparkling or still. And pop."

"Water would be great. Still. Thank you."

"Of course. We don't entertain a ton so it's a nice treat."

"You have a great house. It's perfect for entertaining. And it's cozy and homey. I love it."

"Thanks. We bought it when we were young, before we had Amber. We always talked about having more kids, but it wasn't meant to be. I told you I lost our second when he was twenty weeks. After that, my doctor said I shouldn't risk another pregnancy."

"I'm so sorry," I said. I couldn't imagine that kind of pain.

"Thanks. It was hard, and it almost ruined us, but we finally got through it. How are you doing with being here?"

"Good. I've always loved it here."

"It's a pretty special place." The doorbell rang, drawing Melody's attention. "I'll be right back. Can Cameron come with me?"

"Of course. Cameron! Do you want to go with Ms. Melody to answer the door?"

"Is Jude here?" he asked excitedly, jumping off the swing.

"I think so. Let's go see," Melody said. They walked inside together, Cameron practically jumping with joy.

"Melody was so happy you guys agreed to come over. She's been looking forward to this," Ramsey said when they were inside.

"Me, too. I really like Melody, and Alexis is crazy about Amber. Alexis doesn't have a ton of close friends in Pittsburgh. She talks to everyone, but it's not easy with so many kids in her class."

"How many kids?" Ramsey asked. He turned the grill on.

"Thirty-three last year."

"Wow. That's a big class. Amber has eighteen."

"Really?"

"Yep. The schools here are small, but they limit the classes to no more than twenty. I can't imagine having more than that."

"That would be so nice. My kids have never had less than thirty."

"Small town living," Ramsey said with a smile.

The reasons for moving to MacKellar Cove seemed to be adding up. Not that I could actually consider it, but it was hard not to think about the option.

Cameron and Jude raced back into the backyard together, running right past Ramsey and me. I smiled as I watched them go straight to the swings and climb on next to each other. Their laughter reached me easily.

Both of my kids were enjoying themselves here. I was enjoying it. I was making friends and having fun.

And then there was Sebastian. He was the biggest positive, but also the biggest question mark.

Melody and Derek walked outside, and I pushed all thoughts of Sebastian and moving out of my head. I was there to enjoy time with new friends. And I was going to do just that.

13

When dinner was ready, we helped the kids get their plates. I was balancing one for Alexis and one for Cameron when Ramsey walked up and offered to help Cameron.

"You don't have to. You did all the cooking," I argued.

He shook his head. "That was the easy part. Plus, I'm just standing here. I'm happy to help him out."

"Are you sure?" I asked.

He nodded and took the plate from me. "Come on, Cameron, let's see what we can find for you."

Cameron smiled up at him like Ramsey was his new hero. It had been a long time since he'd had a man he could count on in his life. It was the sad truth of having Trevor as a father.

"I want that, Mommy," Alexis said, bringing my attention back to her.

I held her plate as we walked through the buffet of food Melody set up. Ramsey grilled chicken, burgers, and hot dogs, enough to feed twice as many people as were there. Melody had fries, green beans, and a mixed vegetable medley out next to the salad I brought. At the end of the table were two desserts, compliments of Derek and Jude. One chocolate and one vanilla, Jude explained to Cameron when they reached that end of the table.

"I want both," Cameron insisted.

Ramsey and Derek laughed. "Let's get some dinner in you first, then we'll talk dessert," Ramsey said.

Cameron nodded without any argument. Well, damn. I never got that kind of agreement. Ramsey and Derek settled the boys at the table, then got back in line behind Melody and I with the girls. The men talked sports while the girls focused on the food they wanted on their plates. When they were nearly overflowing, Melody and I set the girls up at the table next to the boys.

"What do you think of the school football team this year?" Derek asked Ramsey.

"I think they're going to be pretty good. But I also heard it might be Coach Mack's last year."

"He's been saying that forever. Until he actually retires, I'm not going to believe it."

"He was a tough coach."

"You played for him?" Derek asked.

Ramsey nodded. "I did. He was good. I was not. Baseball was definitely more my sport. Back then, he coached both. But since the school is so small, I made both teams."

Derek laughed. "I can't picture you on a football field."

"Did you play?"

"I did. I grew up in Tennessee. My ex wife was from the area and wanted to raise our family here."

"And she left, but you stayed?" I asked. I was eavesdropping on their conversation, but it wasn't like I could avoid overhearing them when they were only a few feet away.

"I did," Derek said. He shrugged. "It felt like a great place to raise a kid. Where I grew up was sort of rural like it is here. Smaller town with a good blend of good people. I liked it there, but my parents are gone and my younger sister moved to Texas for college and stayed, so there was no big draw for me to go back to Tennessee."

"I feel the same way about Pittsburgh, but my ex still lives there. My brother moved up here last winter, but my parents aren't in Pittsburgh anymore."

"Why do you stay?"

"Because of my ex. He's not a great dad, but he's still their dad," I said quietly, not wanting the kids to overhear.

"Is he involved?"

I shook my head.

"Maybe it's time for you to make a move. When I got divorced, my ex decided she wanted to live in a city. She moved to New York and gave me primary custody. She would take Jude every other holiday and over the summer, but she got sucked into a different lifestyle. One that didn't blend well with kids. She started canceling on him and one summer said she didn't want him to visit at all. It's been tough on him. I debated moving to be closer to her, but there are too many advantages to living here. He loves it, and honestly, I do, too."

The four of us moved to the table with full plates and sat down. The kids were all eating and talking and not paying any attention to our conversation.

"I've thought about moving," I continued, "but I'm not sure where I would go. I don't really love where my parents are, and moving here isn't an option for me."

"Because of Sebastian?" Melody asked.

I nodded. "It wouldn't be fair to him."

"Who?" Derek asked.

"My ex-boyfriend. I wasn't good to him when it ended. I promised to come back here, but I ended up marrying someone else and not speaking to him for a decade. He's close to my aunt and lives on the property right next to the Inn, so we're kind of in his face. Even being here for the summer feels like I'm hurting him."

"Sebastian will be okay," Ramsey said confidently. "You don't know Sebastian Parks?"

Derek shook his head. "If he doesn't have a third grader, I probably don't know him. I might recognize him if he's ever been in the shop, though."

We laughed. I understood the sentiment well. "What shop?" I asked him.

"I'm a mechanic. I own Stone Auto Repair. I started working there when we moved here, and a year ago, Mr. Stone retired and sold me the business."

"That must keep you busy."

"It does, but I can make my own hours, so it's easier with Jude in school. I can take time off and know the business will still run. There's a great crew there, and the business manager was there before me. The place runs without much help from me."

"He's being modest," Ramsey said. "They all adore him and work hard because he's such a good boss. No one left when Mr. Stone retired because they believed in him and knew Derek would keep everything the same."

"If it isn't broke, I'm not going to fix it," Derek said.

"Probably a good plan with vehicles," Melody said.

"Very true," Derek replied with a laugh.

We continued talking about life and work and the kids while we ate. When the kids were done, they bolted from the table and went back to playing. They chased each other around the yard in a game of tag where the older boys slowed down so the younger girls had a chance to get away.

"Jude is a great kid," I told Derek.

"Thanks. So is Cameron. And the girls. I'm almost

amazed at how well the four of them are getting along," Derek said.

"Me, too," Melody agreed. "I've been around enough kids at enough parties and school functions to know it isn't always this easy."

"No, it's definitely not," I said.

"It's also not always this easy with the parents," Ramsey added.

"That's very true," Derek agreed. "I haven't gotten out much in the last few years. It always feels like meeting new people is a chore. And being a single parent makes it harder."

"It does. I've only been doing it for a year, but it's tough to have a life when you're responsible for someone else," I agreed.

"That's the good thing about having other parents as friends. You're both welcome to leave the kids here any time you need to. Amber and Jude aren't the same age, but they're having fun together," Melody said.

Derek nodded. "They are. And thanks."

"But he's not going to do it," I said for him.

Derek laughed in surprise. "She's right. I can't lie."

"Why not?" Ramsey asked.

"I don't even know what I would do. I'm not ready to start dating yet, and I don't have buddies I get together with or anything," Derek said with a shrug.

"Well, you should. Every Thursday, some of us get together at O'Kelley's. You should come," Ramsey said.

"Thanks, but I don't know," Derek said.

"My brother goes, too," I told him. "I'm always home that night. Maybe Melody and I can get together and watch all four kids. I feel like it's easier when they have buddies to play with. No one feels left out."

"I don't want to put you guys out," Derek said.

"It's not. I promise. I'm only here until the end of

summer, but how can I not want more of this for my kids?" I looked out at them all running around in the yard. They were laughing and their cheeks were flushed from running around. It was a parent's dream. It was why I went there for the summer. To give them a summer to remember.

"I'll think about it," Derek said. "But thanks."

I nodded, letting the subject drop. I knew it wasn't easy to let go. To trust someone else. That was why I offered to partner with Melody. I figured Derek knew her better and might take Ramsey up on the offer if we were both there so Jude had a friend to play with.

We talked and laughed the rest of the night. The kids devoured the desserts Derek brought. I enjoyed a little piece of both and nearly groaned in pleasure at the taste. Derek admitted he didn't bake either of them and got them from Cove Bakery.

"I love that place," Melody gushed.

"I haven't been there. It's good."

"So good. We should go sometime before you guys leave. They have ice cream in the summer, but cakes and cupcakes and pies and so many good things. It's delicious."

"If these are anything to go by, I'm sold. I like to bake, but I've never made anything this good," I admitted.

"I don't like to bake, so I knew this was a better bet. Valentina is amazing," Derek said.

"She really is," Melody agreed. "So talented."

"It's always a good idea to cater to your strengths," Ramsey said. "She's done that. I just hope she doesn't take her talents elsewhere."

"Where would she go?" Derek asked.

"She's not leaving. Her dad is here, and she's really close to him. And I think Harriett knows what a treasure she has in Valentina. She won't leave," Melody said.

"I hope not. It'd be a real loss if she did," Derek said.

The others nodded. I couldn't help but wonder if she did wedding cakes. One less thing for Aunt Gina to have on her plate. She insisted she didn't mind, but Piper was worried she would stretch herself too thin.

Maybe if I could offer an alternative, Aunt Gina would take it.

THE REST of our evening was fun, and we all agreed to do it again before the kids and I went back to Pittsburgh. I had to admit having people to talk to that weren't Piper and Gavin was nice, no matter how much I loved my brother.

The next morning, I finally tracked down Gavin. We'd seen each other over the last few days, but only in passing and always with other people around. I wanted to corner him and get everything out in the open about the job Piper offered me.

"Hey," he said when I walked into the dining room after breakfast. "Where have you been hiding?"

I sat down with him. "I was going to ask you the same thing."

"Things are so busy right now," he said with a sigh. "I had no idea getting married in less than two months was so difficult."

"Well, I think any female could have told you that. If you'd bothered to ask."

He laughed. "Probably true. But I wanted it to be a surprise for Piper, and I think it's all coming together."

"I think so, too."

He smiled in that dreamy way he'd developed after falling for Piper. It was good to see him so happy. It had been a long time since Gavin seemed like himself. Relaxed and enjoying life instead of trying to outrun his past failures.

"I wanted to talk to you about the job Piper offered me."

"Yeah, she mentioned she asked you about it the other day. Did you accept yet?"

"No, but that's what I wanted to talk to you about."

His brows tugged together, and he tilted his head to the side in question.

"Did you talk her in to offering it to me?"

His face relaxed, and he shook his head. "I promise you, it was her idea."

"Really?"

He chuckled. "Yep, really. She couldn't stop gushing about you helping with the booking software a few weeks ago, and she said you were exactly the kind of person she wanted to hire to help us with everything else. Someone she could trust and knew would not only do a great job but would be patient enough to walk us through everything if we didn't understand it."

"She said all that?"

"Yes, because you're amazing, Zo. She knows it. Piper trusts you and loves you, and she knows you would do anything to help make this place successful. I'm sorry you thought I was manipulating you, or her, or the situation, but I promise you, this is all Zoey's idea."

I nibbled on my lip and considered the whole thing. It was a great opportunity, and I loved working with computers. I didn't know what software and hardware was available right now, but it wouldn't be difficult to come up with some options. Or to get it all done in the next few weeks.

"Do you think I should do it?" I asked my brother. Even though he was biased, he was still the person I trusted most in the world.

"Absolutely. When Zoey said it, I felt dumb for not having thought about it before, but everything she said was right, and I know you will go above and beyond. The wheels are already turning in your head. I can see it."

I laughed with him and admitted he was right. "I always loved computers. I like the idea of working with them again, even if it's temporary."

"Why does it have to be temporary? Why can't you get a job working with computers full time?"

"I just don't have the knowledge for a full-time job."

"And I don't have the knowledge to run an Inn, but I'm doing it. You can do anything, Zo. You just have to decide you're going to do it. You've been unhappy for too long. You need to do something for yourself."

"I am," I admitted, not willing to tell him about Sebastian. Maybe it was something stupid, but it was still for me. Being with Sebastian was giving me a little bit of confidence back, and it was fun.

"Good," Gavin said. "I'm happy to hear that. Now do something else for yourself, and for my future wife, and take the job."

I laughed and nodded. "I will. Do you know where Piper is?"

"Probably in the sitting room."

I squeezed Gavin's hand and thanked him, then went to find Piper.

"Do you have a minute?" I asked when I saw her on the couch.

She closed her laptop with a smile and looked up at me. "Of course."

"I've decided to take the job."

"Oh, thank God," Piper breathed. "I was so worried you were going to tell me no."

I laughed and sat with her. "I do have one condition, though."

Piper narrowed her gaze and looked up at me. "What's that?"

"I can't let you pay me."

"What? Why would I not pay you?"

"Because this place is a part of me, too. I'm not one of the owners, but I love it. It's home, and I'd do anything to help you and Gavin make it successful. So, I can't take money for the help. Besides that, three of us are living here for two full months and not paying a dime. Eating and drinking and sleeping in the house. We're taking up space that you and Gavin could be using and eating food that the Inn has to pay for. Doing this will make me feel like I'm paying you back, at least partly."

"Zoey—"

"Piper, I can't. I can't accept charity. Maybe that's ridiculous, but I can't. Not from you guys."

Piper smiled and reached for my hand. "All I was going to say is thank you."

I smiled back and squeezed her hand. We talked for a few more minutes and set up a time when Piper could walk me through everything they had and what she wanted to change. She had things to check on, so I headed back to the house to take a breath and have a mini-celebration with my book and a few minutes alone.

I spent the rest of the day with the kids, playing outside and enjoying the sunshine since it was supposed to rain for the next few days. We had fun, and the kids were worn out and ready for bed a little early. Since I had some free time, I decided to share the good news about the job with Sebastian. I hadn't been back to his place in almost a week, and I was feeling good.

I snuck out of the house at dusk. I had a bottle of wine that I hoped he'd be willing to share with me so we could celebrate. I felt like a teenager again, sneaking around so I could see Sebastian.

I made it down the slope to where I could see his cabin. The outside light was on, illuminating his front yard and porch. Including Sebastian on the porch.

Without a shirt. And not alone.

He was smiling at Sofia, laughing at something she said. Then she put her hand on his chest and pushed him inside the cabin.

And closed the door.

SEBASTIAN

The knock on my door had me jumping up and rushing to answer it. I was hoping it was Zoey. She hadn't been down to see me in almost a week, and I missed her. I didn't want to, but I did.

I'd been lying on the couch and didn't think twice about answering the door without a shirt on. Zoey would have taken it off soon enough anyway, so there was no need for the pretense.

Except it wasn't Zoey at my door.

"Why aren't you wearing a shirt?" Sofia asked when I opened the door.

"I was just watching TV."

"You watch TV shirtless?"

I shrugged. "You don't?"

She laughed and shook her head. "Um, no. Can I come in?"

I hesitated just long enough that she picked up on it.

"Shit, you're not alone, are you?"

I snorted. "Of course I'm alone. I'm always alone. Who else would be here?"

She raised an eyebrow at me in that way Sofia had. I wasn't sure how she did it, but she could read me. I knew without a doubt that she knew about Zoey and me.

"You know, don't you?"

She shrugged. "I was fairly sure, but I was waiting for you to tell me."

"It's not—"

She shook her head and put her hand on my chest. "Inside. I need you to put on a shirt. Otherwise I'm going to be waiting for you to tell me which way the beach is."

I laughed and let her push me inside. She closed the door behind us as I headed for my room. I grabbed a clean shirt and pulled it on while Sofia made herself at home on my couch.

She'd been a good friend. The kind of friend I didn't know I needed until we started spending time together. She understood me and gave me space to be quiet when I needed that or to talk when something was on my mind.

Her figuring out about Zoey but not telling me she knew was typical of Sofia. Hell, even the way she told me was typical of her. Like she didn't mean to say anything and wasn't going to force me to talk about it.

"How's the garden project?" she asked when I finally joined her on the couch. Again, not pushing me to talk.

"I think it'll be okay. I was hoping to get everything in this week, but David needs one more week to get the rest of the plants delivered. We're going to be cutting it close. With everyone who said they'd help, we'll be able to get everything in the ground in one day. It's going to be a big job, but much easier with help."

"Good. I can help, too. I hope you know that."

I nodded and waited. I knew what she wanted to ask, but I also knew she wouldn't. It had to be up to me. "What do you want to know?"

She shook her head. "Nothing. I came here tonight to hang out. I wanted to get out of my place. It's too quiet a lot of the time now that Piper's staying here almost every night."

"Are you going to find a new roommate?"

"I don't think so. I lived alone before Piper moved here. I guess it's time to do it again."

"I don't think I could live with someone. I'm too set in my ways."

"How long have you lived here?" she asked as she got up. Sofia grabbed a glass and poured herself water before joining me again. She acted like she lived here, which I liked. She was the only person who'd ever spent so much time in my cabin.

"Eight years. I used to rent an apartment above a garage in town, but when I got the job at the lighthouse, it came with the cabin. I like my quiet."

She chuckled. "Me, too. It's different from how I grew up, but so much better."

"Your childhood was loud?" I asked. Sofia didn't talk about her parents or growing up. I also didn't ask.

She nodded and wiped the condensation off the side of the glass. "When I was young, it wasn't bad. It was just my mom and me for a long time. She worked a lot, but she liked quiet, too. She died in a car accident when I was a teenager, and I had to go live with my dad. That… That was loud. All the time."

"I don't think I could have handled that. My parents were quiet, but they also were indifferent to me. They made sure I had what I needed, but they were perfectly content to leave me alone for weeks on end when they went on vacation or business trips or whatever. I was always an afterthought."

"Sounds like my dad," Sofia said. "But it made me stronger, I think. I learned to rely on myself. I knew I could do anything because by the time I graduated high school, I'd done pretty much everything."

"Me, too. It sucked in a way, but it was good training for being on my own. I never felt like anyone cared about me until I started working here."

"And met Zoey," Sofia said, not asked.

I shook my head. "No, Gina. Gina and Rob were like the parents I never had. They hired me to do maintenance around the property. Some landscaping, some general maintenance, but odd jobs. They made me feel like I mattered. Like I was important, even though I wasn't." I paused before drawing a breath and continuing. "It was because of them that I resisted Zoey for so long."

"She is a lot younger than you."

"Yeah. And nothing happened between us until she was eighteen."

"I would never judge you. I know you're still in love with her. If you still feel that way after all these years, I can only imagine how it was when you first met."

"It was insane. It was like being struck by lightning. I could tell she was young, so I kept my distance, but over time, we started talking. Sometimes it was just hello, but eventually, we had conversations. We talked about everything and nothing. I'd never had anyone who cared what I had to say like she did."

"You fell for her because she saw you." Sofia's face was a cross between sympathy and confusion.

"It wasn't just that. She wanted to know me. Like when you and I became friends. You talked to me like you understood me. Like we were kindred."

She smiled brightly, pure joy reflected at me. "We are kindred. I can't tell you how many times I wish that meant we were more than friends, but it never has for either of us. I love Piper like she's the sister I never had, and I love you like the brother I never had. I keep thinking life would be easier if we could fall in love, but—"

"It's not meant to be," I finished for her.

She nodded. "Yep. The thought of kissing you is just weird. No offense."

I chuckled. "Ditto."

We settled back on the couch in comfortable silence. It was normal for us to be that way, to just spend time together without speaking. We were similar enough that we understood what the other needed.

After a minute, she asked, "Do you want to talk about Zoey?"

I sighed heavily. A part of me did, but another part of me wanted to pretend there was nothing to talk about.

"You don't have to, but I wanted you to know that if you do, I'm willing to listen. I'm guessing you haven't told anyone else."

"No. I haven't. Most of the time I won't even let myself think about it."

"Why?"

"Because if I think about it, I start to imagine not having to let her go again. But I'm going to have to let her go. I know I am."

"Shit, Seb, I'm sorry."

"It's okay. It's my fault. I saw her crying one day and stopped to see if she was okay."

"Seriously? That's like page one of the manual."

"What do you mean?"

"I mean, I want to be supportive, but at the end of the day, you're the one I care about. Crying in public is a sure way to get a man to notice you."

"She wasn't somewhere most people would have seen her. She was on one of the benches in the garden where you had to be going that way in order to notice her."

"I hear that you want to believe it was unintentional, and

maybe it was. I hope it was because I don't want her manipulating you, but be careful."

I nodded slowly, wondering if Sofia could be right. I didn't think so, but maybe.

"Obviously she wasn't okay?" Sofia prompted me.

I shook my head. "No. Something with her ex. Cameron talked to me the same day and was upset about his dad, too. I think something was going on for real."

"I'm sorry to hear that for them."

Sofia was sincere. Even if she was protective of me, like I would be of her, she wanted people to be happy, even people she didn't like or know.

"I told her we aren't together, you know. I made it very clear to her that nothing has ever happened between us."

"What?"

She sipped her water and didn't look apologetic at all. "I didn't want her to think we were together."

"Why would you do that?"

"Because you love her, and if there's even the slightest chance that you two can be together, I don't want anything to keep you apart. Especially me."

"We're not going to be together."

"Why are you so sure?"

"Because she's going back to Pittsburgh after the wedding."

"And Gavin was supposed to go back after Christmas. Plans change."

"Her ex is in Pittsburgh. There's no way he'd let her move up here with the kids."

"If he's as involved as it seems, I don't think he'll care," she said sarcastically.

"Still, I can't hope for it. If I let myself think about it, I'll end up broken when she leaves again."

"Unless she stays."

"She's not staying, Sof. She didn't come back before, and she's not staying now."

"But—"

"No. I'm sorry. I'm not trying to be harsh, but I can't even consider it. That's why I told her whatever happens between us is just sex. No emotions, no feelings, no anything. Just sex."

Sofia sighed like she was disappointed in me. "You're making a mistake."

"No, I'm not. I'm protecting myself. The only way I can."

"Sebastian—"

"I'm tired. I think I'm going to get some sleep. Finish the movie and crash here. I don't want you driving home so late."

She nodded, and I knew she'd do what I said. Sofia didn't like being out late either, and after hearing about her mom, I understood.

I squeezed her shoulder on my way by and softly closed my bedroom door. I was being an ass, but I couldn't do what she said and get my hopes up. Having them crushed by Zoey again would destroy me. Permanently this time.

ZOEY WAS in the dining room the next day when I walked up for lunch. Gina had an open invitation for me to eat there whenever I wanted, and since I had a slow day, I decided to go eat and hoped to find Zoey while I was there.

Her eyes lit up for a second when she saw me, but they immediately dimmed, and she turned away. I walked over next to her in the buffet line and grabbed a plate.

"Hey," I said. Not the best opening line, but oh well.

"Hi."

"How are you?"

"Great." Her smile was forced and looked like her face would break if she held it for much longer.

"Um, okay. I haven't seen you in a week or so."

"Sorry."

What the hell? She was acting like we were strangers. Again. "What's going on?"

"Nothing," she said quickly. Too quickly. Far too quickly.

"Zoey."

"Yeah?"

"What the hell?"

"Nothing, okay? I saw you and Sofia last night, and I'm backing off."

"Saw me and Sofia what?"

"It's fine, I get it. She's beautiful and smart and funny. You two clearly have a close connection. And I don't want to get in the way."

"In the way of what?" I asked. She didn't answer me, leaving me to try to figure out what she thought was going on as Gina moved between us to set down a bowl of fruit.

"You two doing okay?" Gina asked, clearly picking up on the tension between us.

"Of course. All good, Aunt Gina," Zoey said quickly. She added a small bag of chips to her plate and moved away from the food.

Gina gave me a look that said she wasn't buying it.

"It'll be fine," I assured her, hoping I was right.

I followed Zoey to a table and sat down without asking if she minded. I knew I was pushing my luck. I was the one who said no emotions, and at the first sign of her backing off, I let my emotions get in the way. I wasn't ready to give her up.

"What the hell is going on?" I demanded softly. I didn't want the guests to overhear our conversation.

"Nothing." Zoey pushed her plate away and made a move to stand.

"Sit down," I growled.

She looked at me with a cross between shock and fear in her eyes. She dropped to the chair without looking away from me.

"I'm not going to hurt you, Zoey."

She didn't relax.

"Fuck, I just want to know what's going on. Tell me. Please."

"It's just what I said. I saw you and Sofia last night. At your cabin. And I saw her leaving this morning. I know some people are okay with having sex with more than one person at the same time, but I'm just not. So, I'm backing off."

Realization dawned, and she misinterpreted my understanding as acceptance and made another move to leave. "Sit the hell down," I said. My words and tone were harsh, but I needed her to listen to me.

"Sebastian—"

"Please, Zoey."

She hesitated, but at my please, she sank onto her seat again.

"Sofia came over last night. We get together a lot. We watch movies and talk. I didn't know she was coming over, but when she knocked, I thought it was going to be you and didn't bother with a shirt. When she pushed me inside, she told me to put a shirt on. And I did. We aren't sleeping together. We aren't doing anything together except being friends. She sleeps on the couch, and refuses to let me give up my bed, because she doesn't like to drive late at night. But nothing is going on between us."

"You're allowed to live your life, Sebastian."

"And I am. You're not holding me back from anything."

She held my gaze for a long minute, only releasing it

when she reached for her plate again. She started eating without another word, finishing her lunch before she pushed her plate away again.

"Are we okay?" I asked her as we set our plates in the bin for the dishwasher.

"Yeah," she said.

"I was really hoping it was you who showed up at my door last night."

"You were?" she asked, obviously surprised by my words.

I was surprised by them, too. They were the truth, but I was the one who said we were keeping it to just sex. I was the one who refused conversation and anything personal. She just went along with it.

"Piper wants me to help with the computer systems while I'm here. I was going to tell you about it when I came down last night. I had wine."

"Will you come by tonight? Tell me about it then?"

She hesitated for a second but nodded.

"Good. How about we have dinner? I can cook something for us. If you're okay with that. Shit, your kids. Sorry, never mind."

"No, dinner… Dinner would be nice. I'll ask Gavin if he'd mind bringing them up here for me. And putting them to bed."

"I don't think he'll be happy if you tell him why."

"Gavin doesn't get a vote in my private life."

I nodded once, hoping it was true. Gavin would not be happy if he thought I was taking advantage of her. Or if he thought I would hurt her.

If he only knew the truth… But I wasn't sure I was ready to admit the truth to anyone. Because I wasn't ready to say out loud that I was still in love with Zoey.

15

ZOEY

Gavin raised his eyebrow at me when I asked if he could take the kids to dinner, but he didn't ask any questions. I knew it was only a matter of time before he pressed me, but for now, he let it go.

Once they left the house, I hurried up to my room and tried to figure out what to wear. I didn't want to dress up and look like I was trying too hard, but I also didn't want to look like I wasn't trying at all. It was my first date since my divorce, and even though Sebastian and I had already slept together, I wanted to look nice.

I settled on a pair of jean shorts that made my butt look good and a grape colored tunic that was light and comfortable but hugged my abundant curves in the right places. I slid my feet into black sandals and fluffed up my hair and took a deep breath that did nothing to calm my nerves.

I carried the same bottle of wine on the same path I'd taken the night before. This time, I decided I'd go up to his house no matter what. He invited me, and I had every right to be there.

It was total bullshit, but I didn't see anyone on his porch

to scare me off so I kept up the lie as I walked to his door and knocked.

Sebastian opened the door and immediately turned back inside. "Come on in. I'm finishing up dinner."

I took a tentative step inside and nearly groaned at the scent of whatever he was cooking. It was heavenly. His absent reaction to me was less than, but I wasn't going to dwell on that.

I closed the door and set the wine on the table before I went to the kitchen to see if he needed any help. "What can I do?"

"Nothing, I got it. This is almost done."

"Okay." I stood a few feet away, feeling awkward and uncomfortable. I wasn't sure what to do with myself. He didn't kiss me when I walked in, and he barely looked at me.

I waited off to the side and tried to stay out of his way while he finished dinner. He turned the heat off and left the pan he was cooking in on the stovetop when he finally turned to me.

"I guess I should have asked if you like sausage. I didn't even think. Is this okay?"

"Yeah, it smells amazing."

"I don't cook for other people very often."

"I'm sure if Aunt Gina had her way you wouldn't cook at all very often."

He chuckled. "True. She'd keep me at the Inn as much as possible. But Gina won't be in charge much longer."

"I think she'll always be in charge. But Gavin and Piper will always feed you."

He shrugged. "It isn't the same."

I nodded, understanding what he wasn't saying. It was how I felt about being paid to do the computer work Piper asked me to do. MacKellar Cove Inn was always home, and everything was changing, but there was a part of it that would always be home.

"Are you ready to eat?" Sebastian asked.

I nodded, wondering if he felt as uncomfortable as I did.

He let me serve myself first, then nodded toward the couch. "I thought we could watch a movie."

We settled onto the couch with our food and drinks and about three feet between us. He started the movie, and I gasped.

"Do you not like it?" he asked, pausing with the title on the screen. *The Time Traveler's Wife.*

I shook my head. "I love it. It's one of my favorites."

He looked at me strangely but pressed play and settled back in his seat again.

We watched the movie and ate, the love story on the screen threatening to make me cry. I couldn't help but think about what Piper's friends said when I told them this was one of my favorite stories. Of all the movies to watch, how could Sebastian know I loved this one?

Maybe Sofia told him. The thought made me pause. Why would she do that?

I wasn't sure why Sofia would be on my side, but I couldn't figure out another answer. It was possible Sebastian came up with the movie idea on his own, but if not, Sofia had to be trying to help me. To help us.

I didn't know what to do with that either. I was going back to Pittsburgh in a month. I wasn't going to get a new chance with Sebastian. Not a real one. So what good would it do for us to try?

The movie ended, and the credits rolled, and I was still considering everything. We hadn't talked. Barely said a few words to each other. We watched my favorite movie. He cooked me dinner. But I was leaving soon.

Dating sucked.

Especially dating the ex you thought you could move on from after a lifetime without him, only to find out you were an idiot for leaving him in the first place.

"That was good. I wasn't really sure what to expect."

"You've never seen it?"

"Nope. Sofia recommended it a while ago, but I never looked for it. I was flipping through movies earlier and saw it. Thought maybe you'd like it, too."

I forced a smile. Sofia wasn't trying to help us. It was just a coincidence.

"When do you start your new job?"

"New job?"

"Yeah? I thought you said Piper wanted you to upgrade the computer systems. Did you decide not to do it?"

"Oh, that. Yeah, I am going to do it. I guess I don't think of it as a job. It's for the Inn."

"She's not paying you?"

I pulled my feet under me and repositioned on the couch. "She offered, but I couldn't accept. My skills aren't what they could be if I'd kept up with the market. It wouldn't be fair to have her pay me. Plus, I don't own the Inn, but it still feels like it's a part of me. I couldn't take payment for doing something to help out."

"You should."

"Do you?"

He shrugged. "Sure I do. Gina feeds me all the time."

"And I'm staying here with my two kids, and we're eating almost all our meals at the Inn. That's why I can't accept more money from them."

"Sure, but that was agreed on before. Don't you need the money?"

I drew back at his words. We hadn't talked about my financial situation. We hadn't talked about much of anything. "I'm fine."

"Are you? Because you're looking for a job."

"How do you know that?"

"I don't understand why you wouldn't accept payment for a job that uses your skills. Why you are getting all defensive and not willing to do it?"

"Because I have to stand on my own," I blurted. "I've always been someone else's problem. My parents paid for everything growing up and it almost bankrupted them, then I married Trevor and he supported me from the day I graduated college. I can't ask my brother and his soon-to-be wife to do the same thing. I can't be a drain on the people around me any longer."

Sebastian was silent through my tirade and simply looked at me for a long moment afterward. I was close to telling him everything, but I bit my tongue and waited for him to reply.

"People always want to help those around them. They want to see their loved ones succeed. Being the one who needs help isn't being a problem. We all need help sometimes."

"You never do. You've always been strong and independent."

He shook his head. "Not really. My parents were never there for me. I had no choice but to figure out how to be independent, but it wasn't easy. I messed up a lot as a kid. And as an adult. But when I was at my worst, someone gave me a chance and completely turned my life around."

"Who?"

"Rob. And Gina. They saved me in so many ways. I'd been working for years, but when they hired me at the Inn, and then treated me like I was a part of the family, I stopped being so angry. Growing up, I was mad about everything. I almost got arrested for it. Rob never held it against me."

"Why would he hold it against you?"

"Because I almost ruined the garden."

"You what?"

"The weekend I graduated from high school, my parents went on vacation. They weren't even here to watch the ceremony. I saw all my classmates with their extended families and friends and parties, and it just pissed me off. I hated it. I hated them. I hated this town and everyone in it. I got drunk and ended up wandering around and found my way here. I thought it was a house, one of the rich kids who had everything. I didn't know it was the Inn. But it wouldn't have mattered. I was too wasted to know the difference."

"What did you do?" I asked, my voice barely louder than a breath.

He scrubbed a hand over his face and rubbed his beard. "I don't remember most of it. I was in the garden, and I know I pissed all over the plants. I poured beer on them. I yanked some of them out. Then I set fire to one of the trellises."

"What?"

His face twisted in pain. "That was when Rob found me. He was scared at first, but when he saw me, his fear turned to anger. He had a fire extinguisher and put out the flames, then led me by the ear into the house. He ripped me up one side and down the other. He called the cops, and when they showed up and saw me, they told him my parents weren't around. Everything changed when he heard that. He told the cops he didn't want to press charges and asked if I could stay the night with them. The cops agreed and said they'd be back in the morning to check on me."

"What happened?"

"I passed out, but when I woke up, Rob was on the couch across from me. He stayed up all night to make sure I was okay. I'd almost destroyed… everything, and he was worried about me."

Sebastian paused and swallowed roughly. I waited for him to continue, wanting to hear the rest.

"He offered me a job working for the Inn. It wasn't glamorous, but it was more than I had. When my parents were out of town, he let me stay at the house with them. I more or less lived with them for three years."

"How did I never know this?"

Sebastian shrugged. "I never wanted you to. By the time you and Gavin were coming here for the summer, I had my own apartment and was working my way through school. I didn't want you to know who I used to be."

"I wish I'd known."

He smiled sadly. "I probably would have told you, eventually. But…"

He trailed off, leaving the obvious unsaid. I never came back. I drew a breath and knew he needed more from me. I owed him more. "A few months before I graduated from college, I overheard my parents talking. They were having money problems. College for two kids was expensive, and my mom had a surgery that insurance didn't cover much of. My dad lost his job for a while, and with mom being sick, they were in a lot of debt. Enough that they were talking about filing for bankruptcy. The housing market was low, and they didn't think they'd get enough for the house to cover what they owed for all their debts. It was… It was bad. I thought about not finishing school and starting to work right away so I could help them, but they'd already paid my tuition and couldn't get that money back. I decided to finish school and do whatever it took to help them out."

Sebastian was still, almost to the point of frozen. I couldn't stop talking, though. I had to tell him all of it.

"When I met Trevor, he made me forget about everything going on. He was funny and kind, and he liked me. I hadn't ever dated, and it was exciting. I knew it was wrong when I'd made promises to you, but I couldn't stop myself from falling for him."

"For his money?" Sebastian asked, his voice coming out like a growl.

"The money was part of it, yes. I wouldn't have admitted it then, but now, I know that played into my mind. He was the opposite of you in every way. He took me out and showed me off. He made me feel like he wanted me in a way I wasn't sure you did. And it was clear he had money. He was working his last semester as a teaching assistant, but he had a nice car, and we went to nice restaurants and money never seemed to be an issue. I'm not proud of what I did, but I imagined my life with you and my life with him. After hearing my parents, I knew I didn't have a choice if I wanted to help them. I had to choose Trevor so I could take one burden away from my parents."

"You married him for his money," Sebastian said.

"Partly, yes. I did love him, but I also loved you. I chose him for his money."

"God, Zoey."

"I know. If I'd known what my life would look like, I can't say I'd choose differently, though. We were happy for a while. He was good to me. When Cameron was born, I was out of my mind blissful. I didn't know love could feel like that. Same with Alexis. Even though my marriage didn't last, I'll always love Trevor because he gave me my kids."

"Why didn't you ever tell me?"

I scoffed. "Really? Would you have thanked me for the call if I'd picked up the phone and said, *hey, I met someone else, and I still love you, but he throws money around like it grows on trees, so I'm going to marry him, okay?*"

Sebastian exhaled heavily and closed his eyes. Without opening them, he said, "I would have been thankful there was a reason. Instead, I waited for you. For the entire summer, I waited for you to pull up. I watched the driveway constantly. I turned down dates with other women because I was waiting for you. And then Gina told me you were getting married. I… I wished I was dead."

"Sebastian…"

He shook his head and finally looked at me. "I get why you married him. Even though it ended, it was the right choice for you at the time. I can see that and accept it, even though I disagree, but back then? I had never known what it was like to love another person. I was closing in on thirty when I told you I loved you. I'd never said it to anyone else in my life. I meant those words, more than anything I'd ever said. I wanted to build a life with you. And then I found out you were with someone else? I couldn't figure out why I was still alive. I had nothing and no one. My parents barely acknowledged my existence, and the one person who I thought actually loved me chose someone else."

Tears rolled down my cheeks. I knew I hurt Sebastian when I chose Trevor, but I never imagined it was that bad. I didn't know about his parents, and I never knew he was so hurt. "I'm sorry."

He drew a breath and let it out slowly. "I need you to promise me something, Zoey."

I nodded.

"I need you to say it. I need you to tell me you promise."

"I promise, Sebastian. Anything."

"Don't make me fall in love with you again. Don't lean on me or confide in me anymore. Don't act like we're more than we are. I don't think I'll survive if I let you in and you leave again, and you are leaving. So, just, don't make me love you."

The tears wouldn't stop. The pain in his voice tore me apart. I nodded, understanding exactly what he was asking. If I'd have been brave enough, I'd have asked Trevor the same thing years ago. But I was weak. I fell for his lies and promises over and over again. I let him tell me he would do better, and smiled and trusted when he was, until he wasn't.

Trevor never put me first. He never put the kids first. He was only ever worried about putting himself first. And it ruined our marriage.

I was not willing to do the same thing to Sebastian. To break him the way Trevor broke me. I loved him too much to put him through that kind of pain.

"I promise, Sebastian. I won't make you love me."

"Good. Now, get naked so we can celebrate your new unpaid job."

Whatever he needed. That was my new mantra. Whatever Sebastian needed. My heart would forever be shattered, but it didn't matter as long as he was whole.

J was still feeling the aggressive way Sebastian claimed me three days later when I went to book club. Claimed was the only word I could use for it. He was demanding and possessive. He was also relentless, and I orgasmed so many times I thought I was going to pass out. It was amazing and powerful and disconnected.

He was a man on a mission. I didn't know what the mission was, but with my sore thighs and raw vagina, I had a guess. Not that I was complaining, exactly. More that I was confused.

If he'd told me he loved me before that, I would have thought he was doing it to show me how much I mattered to him. How special I was and how he wanted me to think of him before, during, and after I slept with any other man for the rest of my life. But he didn't tell me he loved me. He told me not to make him fall in love with me, so I was confused and a little empty inside when I left his cabin.

I was chewing on my nail and ignoring the group when Melody said, "Earth to Zoey. Are you in there?"

"What? Yeah." I sat up straighter and attempted a smile. "Sorry."

"What were you thinking about?" Finley asked.

"Oh, um, nothing, really. Sorry. What were you guys talking about?"

"You," Melody said with a kind smile. "We were trying to figure out what was going on because you have the look of a woman who has man trouble."

I looked around the room and tried to resist the urge to bolt when I saw their curious and encouraging faces. Fuck. I did not want to tell them what was going on. I needed to keep it to myself.

"Just tell us," Trinity said. "This group can help. I know you don't know us well, but we like you and we care."

I smiled at her kind words. They meant more than she'd ever realize. I knew she had only known the other women for a year, but that was still a lot longer than I had known them all. But hearing her encourage me made me feel like they wouldn't judge me.

"I guess I do have man trouble," I admitted.

"I knew it," Piper said. She shook her head and smiled. "I told Gavin you were seeing someone. That's why you asked us to take the kids to dinner last week. You had a date."

"Well, not entirely." I risked a glance at Sofia and found her smiling encouragingly at me. If I had to guess, she knew everything. She nodded and confirmed it for me. "I've been sleeping with Sebastian."

The room went silent. No one moved or spoke or even breathed. They all just stared at me.

"What did he do?" Sofia asked when the others couldn't seem to form words.

"It's not that he did anything, really. It's just... I don't know how to explain it."

"He's afraid of falling in love with you again," Sofia said knowingly.

I nodded. "I know. He told me not to make him fall in love with me."

"So, what happened?" Sofia asked.

I sighed heavily and knew I needed to tell them everything if they were going to understand. Hell, I didn't understand, but maybe they would. I started with seeing Sofia and Sebastian in the garden, then Sebastian kissing me when he found me crying. I told them about confronting him and the first time we slept together and what he said after that and about going back to see him. I apologized to Sofia when I mentioned finding her at his cabin, but she understood. Then I finished with what happened when we talked. No one said a word the entire time. They just watched me and listened. And when I was done, they were all frozen.

"Um, what, um…" I stammered.

Sofia groaned and shook her head. "They're all in shock, which is why they're not saying anything. For me, I am going to have a hard time because I haven't had a relationship like yours, ever. He's told me about how you met and his side of things from when you were younger, and we've talked recently, so I'm struggling with what to say to you that won't violate my friendship with him."

"I don't want you to do that. And I don't want you to encourage me to keep sleeping with him. I don't know what I want."

"Why don't you want her to encourage you?" Melody asked.

"It's not fair to Sebastian. I'm leaving. My kids have school and friends and my ex is in Pittsburgh. I have to go back. I was going to avoid him this summer. I didn't want to see him or get involved or anything. I wanted to give him space. He hates me, and I know he hates me, and I don't blame him. And I'm not saying all of this is his fault. It's mine, too. But I still—"

"You still what?" Melody asked.

I chewed on my lip and shook my head. I was not going to finish that sentence.

"She still loves him," Finley provided for me. "Don't you? You're still in love with him. After all these years and two kids and a marriage, you're still in love with Sebastian."

I drew a shaky breath and nodded.

"Fuck," Sofia mumbled.

"Is that a problem?" Trinity asked her.

Sofia looked at me and sighed. "He still loves her, too. I'm guessing that's why he told her not to make him fall for her. He's barely hanging on right now. He's been talking to someone on Book Boyfriends Wanted and was hoping it might go somewhere, but he hasn't reached out in a while because of Zoey. He's trying to protect himself already because he knows he's going to fall apart when she leaves."

"He was talking to someone?" I asked, picking up on that.

Sofia nodded. "Yeah, sorry. A single mom. He liked talking to her, but he felt bad because of what's been going on with you."

I didn't reply to her comment. If I did, I would have admitted the truth. I was fairly sure I was the one Sebastian was talking to online. I could be wrong, but what were the chances there was another single mom on the app who hadn't heard from the match she was chatting with in over a week?

I couldn't decide if that was good or bad, though.

The rest of the conversation happened around me. They all agreed they wanted us to be happy, but they couldn't agree on if that meant we should keep sleeping together or not. Me, too.

The one and only thing that stuck with me at the end was

Melody saying it was too bad I didn't live there. That would solve all of it.

That always seemed to be the issue Sebastian and I had. Since we met, it was our biggest challenge. If only I lived there. If only I moved there. If only I was brave enough.

I WAS WORKING on the computer systems on Tuesday afternoon when Piper came and sat next to me at the dining room table. I'd made it into my office during the times it wasn't being used to serve food. That way, I could keep an eye on the kids as they ran around outside, and I was there in case Aunt Gina or anyone else needed me for anything.

When Piper sat down, I immediately knew something was going on. I turned to her and tried to smile calmly while she worked to find the words she wanted to say.

"Why can't you move here?" she finally asked. "I mean, I know it wouldn't be easy, but why isn't it an option? Really? Because the kids and the ex and all that is a good excuse, but I don't think it's the real reason you don't want to move here."

I leaned back in my chair and thought about the best way to answer her question. "I love it here. When we used to visit, I wished we lived here. Even coming back at Christmas, I wanted to move here, and a part of me still does now. But I can't do that to Sebastian. He deserves a chance to move on with his life, and if I'm here, I worry he won't."

"Because he still loves you."

"Because I hurt him. I was horrible to him, and we talked about it last week, but I was still horrible to him. I always told myself he was better off without me because of what I did, and I still believe that, but I really do still love him. I know it's twisted, and it doesn't seem like real love, but this is the only thing I can give him right now."

Piper nodded slowly and stared out the back window to where the kids were running around outside with Gavin and some kids who were staying at the Inn. "Gavin talks about moving back to Pittsburgh sometimes."

"What? Why?"

"Because of you. He'd probably be mad at me for telling you this, and I'm not telling you to try to convince you to move. But I want you to know Sebastian isn't the only one here. Your brother is, and he loves you and those kids so much. He misses you guys every day. It bothers him a lot that he can't be there for you like he used to be, but he knows running this place isn't the kind of job he can do from anywhere else."

"I didn't know he felt that way," I breathed.

"I know. But I thought you should understand it. He loves you so much, and he wishes you'd move up here. I keep telling him it's your choice and not to push, but after the other night, I wonder if maybe all the reasons you're not moving here are in your head. Maybe being here would be the best thing for you."

I sucked in a sharp breath, her words sinking in deep as Piper got up and patted my hand before she left me alone to replay her words over and over and over.

Maybe being here would be the best thing for you.

There were so many times I wondered and hoped the same thing, but it was hard to imagine I didn't miss my chance.

I kept working, but Piper's words kept playing in my mind. When I was finished with what I was doing, I pulled out my phone. I still hadn't figured out for sure if BeThe-Light was Sebastian or not, but what I did know was he was someone who didn't know me and wouldn't have a suggestion based on anything other than his instinct.

MOMOF2

How do you make a hard decision?

I wasn't sure if he would answer at all, but I definitely didn't expect him to answer so quickly.

BETHELIGHT

It depends on what it's about.

MOMOF2

Let's say you get offered a new job, but it means moving. How do you decide what to do?

BETHELIGHT

Honestly, I trust my gut. I think about what my life would be like if I accepted. Then I think about what is missing from my life as it is. Will the change help me get any of those things?

MOMOF2

What if you aren't sure?

BETHELIGHT

Nothing is ever sure. We could drown this afternoon. We could end up paralyzed from a car accident. We could meet our soulmates the day before we move. Anything can happen.

MOMOF2

Why does the unexpected have to be bad? LOL

BETHELIGHT

Good point. Maybe you take the job and find the person you're meant to be with. Maybe you stay and get a promotion and a huge raise. Maybe you get a third job offer that's even better, and that's the one you take.

MOMOF2

Much better.

BETHELIGHT

LOL. Do you want to tell me where you're moving to?

MOMOF2

It's hypothetical. I'm trying to decide what's right for me and my kids right now.

BETHELIGHT

Having kids makes everything more complicated.

MOMOF2

Do you have kids?

BETHELIGHT

No, but I've sort of been seeing someone IRL. She has kids. I wasn't sure I should tell you.

MOMOF2

I understand. I have been, too. This is the first time I've tried online dating, so I wasn't sure the about protocols or whatever.

BETHELIGHT

Exactly. The rules are confusing. And I'm too old for games.

MOMOF2

How old are you?

My heart raced while I waited for him to answer. If he

said forty-one, I was going to be sure it was him.

I looked out the window at the kids while I waited for the reply to come through. Sebastian walked over to Gavin and the kids. He rubbed Alexis's head when she latched on to his leg. He fist-bumped Cameron like they were old friends. And he typed something into his phone and tucked it away as my phone buzzed.

BETHELIGHT

41

Shit. It had to be him. And I had to tell him it was me.

MOMOF2

I have a confession to make. I think I know who you are.

I watched as he smiled at something Gavin said, then dug his phone back out. His eyebrows drew together, and his smile faded as he read the message. His thumbs flew over the screen before my phone buzzed again.

BETHELIGHT

How do you know who I am? Do we know each other?

I took a deep breath and typed in the message that would end things.

MOMOF2

Look up.

He read the message and drew back. I thought maybe I was wrong, but then he looked up. He looked around until his eyes landed on me standing in the window.

I held up my phone so he knew it wasn't a coincidence. His shoulders slumped. He shoved his phone back into his pocket and focused on Gavin. His mouth was drawn tight across his face. I just stood there and waited.

He finished speaking to Gavin, then stalked toward the Inn. I waited in the dining room for him. He stomped into the room and stared at me.

After a painfully long moment, he said, "You're MomOf2?"

I nodded. "I didn't know you were BeTheLight for sure until today."

"But you thought I was?" he growled.

"Sofia mentioned—"

"Sofia told you?" His tone was a mix of disbelief and anger.

"No, she didn't tell me anything. Do not get upset with her. She mentioned you were talking to someone on Book Boyfriends Wanted. A single mom. It seemed unlikely it wasn't you, especially when I thought about your screen name."

"So, all that was to trap me into admitting it?"

"All what?"

"Your questions about how to make a tough choice. What was that all about? Where did you get a job? Are you leaving Pittsburgh?"

"No, that was all hypothetical."

He scrubbed a hand over his beard and glared at the wall behind me. Again, I hurt him. It was the opposite of what I wanted to do, but it seemed to be the only thing I was good at when it came to Sebastian.

"You're still looking for a job?"

"Yes."

"In Pittsburgh?"

"Yes."

He nodded, then turned and walked out of the Inn. I

watched him walk across the yard and disappear around the corner of the house.

That didn't go as planned.

"Zoey, can you help me with the seating chart?" Piper asked, walking into the room from behind me.

She was staring at the book in her hands, oblivious to what just happened.

I wanted to go back to the house and hide. To bury my face in a pillow and cry. Or bury myself in a bottle of wine and pretend I didn't just hurt Sebastian again. But I couldn't do either. I no longer had that luxury. I was an adult, and being an adult meant making choices that we didn't always want to make.

And helping with my brother's wedding, because at the end of the day, family was all I had, and all that mattered.

17

SEBASTIAN

I stared at the beer in front of me and resisted the urge to throw the bottle against the wall. I was pretty sure Hudson would kick me out if I did, and I didn't want to leave yet.

A year ago, I never thought I'd be sitting in O'Kelley's on a Thursday night with a group of friends. I never thought about a lot of things. Like falling in love with Zoey all over again. I knew I still loved her, but what I was feeling lately was new, not old. I had fallen for her again, and the pain was new, again.

It fucking sucked.

"What's up with you?" Nico asked, not too quietly.

"Nothing."

"Bullshit. What's going on?"

"I just can't right now."

"Can't what?" Hudson asked.

I shrugged. "Function. Breathe. Talk. I was so fucking stupid."

"What did you do?" Nico asked.

"I fell in love with her."

"Sofia?" Nico asked. They all thought Sofia and I would get together eventually, so I guess that was a reasonable assumption.

I shook my head.

"He's talking about Zoey," Hudson said.

"My Zoey?" Gavin clarified.

I growled at him. I actually growled. Because he said she was his. I knew what he meant, but any man staking a claim over her pissed me off. Even her brother.

"Well, shit," James said. "You're going to fight her brother over her? You're fucked."

"Tell me about it," I said miserably.

"What happened?" Hudson asked.

I shot a glare at Gavin, waiting for him to say something. He stared right back at me.

"I don't know anything about this. And between us, she is more mine than yours. She's my best friend in the world. You can get pissed off, but I'm going to protect her."

"Like you protected her from her ex-husband?" I snarled.

"You have no idea what you're talking about."

"I think you're the one with no idea." I shook my head. I couldn't tell him why Zoey married Trevor. The stuff about her parents wasn't public knowledge, and blurting it out in front of everyone would not do me any favors.

"What's going on?" Ian asked, the calm in the middle of the storm. "You fell for her, but didn't you always love her?"

"Yeah, I did," I admitted. "When she came up here, I... I don't know what I thought. I wanted to hate her or punish her or hurt her. I didn't want to fall into bed with her, but I couldn't resist her."

It was Gavin's turn to growl.

"I didn't do it on purpose. It just happened. I told her it was just sex, that we weren't going to get emotionally involved. She agreed. But we ended up paired on that stupid app you all made me sign up for. She figured it out and asked me how I'd make a tough decision, like choosing to move for a new job."

"She's moving? She got a job? Why don't I know any of this?" Gavin blurted.

"She said it was hypothetical, but it doesn't feel like it is. It feels like there's something going on. I just don't know what."

"Did you tell her not to move here?" Gavin snapped.

"Easy," Hudson said firmly.

Gavin's tone and behavior were getting more and more aggressive as I spoke. I got it. He was caught in the middle. We all knew he wanted Zoey to move to MacKellar Cove, and I was fairly sure I was the reason she wouldn't consider it.

"I didn't tell her anything. She asked me her hypothetical question before she told me who she was. I told her when I'm making a choice like that, I trust my gut and think about what life is like and would be like depending on the options. After she admitted who she was, she said it was hypothetical, and she didn't have a job offer anywhere."

"If she wanted to move here, what would you tell her?" Gavin demanded.

I took a breath and tried to push through the pain. Gavin and the others had no idea how those words made me feel. Zoey *did* want to move to MacKellar Cove. For years, we talked about it. We planned for it. We were going to work and save our money, get a small house. We knew it wouldn't be easy, but we would have had each other. She was young, but I had a little money set aside at that point. I was going to surprise her with a house when she moved to town. All things she never knew.

The thought of making plans like that again, of getting my hopes up and having them destroyed all over again, it warred inside me. It was why I told her not to make me fall in love with her again. Loving her and planning a life with her a second time was something I never let myself dream could happen. I still couldn't let myself imagine it.

"I would never stand in the way of her happiness," I finally ground out. "I never have."

Gavin stared at me, his eyes watching me carefully.

I turned away from him and focused on my beer again. I gripped the bottle tightly, once again battling the urge to throw it against the wall and watch it shatter into a million pieces.

The others changed the subject and started talking about sports and the local events coming up. There was a book signing at Finley's store over the weekend. Some of the guys were planning to go with their wives and girlfriends, but I had no interest and tuned them out.

Hudson set another beer in front of me but didn't let go until I looked up at him. "For what it's worth, I know this isn't easy."

I shook my head. It wasn't.

"If I had a second chance with Hillary, I'd take it in a heartbeat, but she didn't put me through what you went through."

"Yeah."

"I know you'd never stand between Zoey and happiness, but you need to think about what would make you happy, too."

"She would," I answered instantly. Zoey was the only thing I wanted for as long as I could remember. As much as I didn't want to hope we could have another chance, I still wanted it.

"Maybe you should tell her that."

I snorted. "No. Because just like I wouldn't tell her not to move here, I also can't tell her she should move here. If she wants me, it has to be her decision."

"It's complicated when she's not by herself."

"Yeah, it is. I love her kids, but they're not my kids. I'm their friend, not their dad."

Hudson nodded. "I don't know if I could handle the step-dad thing. Of course, that also means dating, and I'm not open to that either, so I'm no help."

I smiled at him, grateful he wasn't judging me or throwing me out.

"Anyway, just wanted you to know Gavin isn't the only one with an opinion."

"Thanks, Hud," I said, lifting my beer in silent toast to him. It was good to know he was in my corner.

"WHAT DO you mean you can't deliver everything as planned?" I barked into the phone the next morning. Gavin and Piper's wedding was in two weeks, and the flowers needed to be planted if they were going to get married in the garden.

"I'm sorry, Sebastian. If I could do anything about it, I would. Our delivery truck just crapped out on us. We are getting it fixed, but it's going to be Monday, at the earliest, that it'll be done," David said.

"Can I pick things up?" I asked, desperate for another option.

"I thought about that, too, but this order was going to fill our entire truck. If you came and got it, it would be about twenty trips in a pickup truck."

"Which would take me all day. Shit."

"Trust me, I feel the same. I know this isn't ideal. Even if you had a bunch of trucks, it's still going to take forever."

I paced the area near the water and tried to come up with a solution, but there really wasn't one. Everyone volunteered to help on Sunday, but without plants, there wasn't much we could do. If we picked them up, it would take more than half the day to get everything to the Inn, and there was no way we'd get them all planted. At that point, it just made sense to wait until Monday when the truck was fixed and everything could be delivered.

"I'm not sure I can get the help I need out here during the week," I said, mostly to myself. "I guess I don't really have a choice in all this. When you get the truck fixed, will you let me know?"

"Of course. You're my first priority. As soon as we can, we'll deliver to you."

"Thanks, David."

"Talk soon."

I hung up and dropped my head to my chest. Fucking hell. I had no idea how I was going to make this work. The only reason I had a chance at pulling it off was because of all the help I was going to get, but now…

I sent a text to everyone letting them know the delivery was off and had to be rescheduled during the week. A few of them said they'd try to make it work, but most of them had to work, which I already knew. It was going to be painful, but it was for Gina and Gavin and Piper, and if I was being honest, I was also doing it for Zoey. I wanted to see the look on her face when the garden was back to what it used to be.

I'd just tucked my phone into my pocket when Gavin called out to me. He was on the group text, so I knew he was aware of what was going on. I waited for him to reach me and sighed at his pinched expression.

"Nothing?" he asked.

I shook my head. "Their truck broke down. Monday is the soonest it'll be fixed, and he couldn't even guarantee that."

"Shit. Piper's going to have a fit."

"I know. I'm sorry. I'll get it done next week. But it'll take a while without help."

"I'll do whatever you need. What if we go pick everything up?"

"I asked about that, too. It would be twenty trips."

"Which would take all day and we might as well wait until Monday."

"Yep."

"What about tomorrow?" Gavin asked. "Could we go tomorrow?"

I hadn't thought about that as an option. If we picked everything up on Saturday, it would all be at the Inn for Sunday. "Let me call David back and see."

I tapped my phone and waited while the other end rang. "Cove Gardens."

"This is Sebastian Parks. Is David available?"

"Hold on."

I waited and hoped that it would work out. I didn't know how we would get the bigger items to the Inn, or how I would move everything from my truck to the garden area, but I had to try something.

"Hey, Sebastian. What's up?"

"David, I was talking to Gavin, and he asked if we can pick up tomorrow. We have a crew coming on Sunday to plant everything, and if I can make my trips tomorrow, we can still get it all done on Sunday."

David sucked in a breath. "Yeah, I don't see why not. We have almost all of it pulled. I was going to get the rest out tomorrow, but I can start working on that now. The trees will be the biggest concern. Do you have any straps? We can tie them to something so they don't tip while you're driving."

"I can find some. I'm going to try to get another vehicle or two, if I can. What time tomorrow can we come?"

"We open at eight. I'll be here. Everything is in the back.

There's a loading zone. Give me a call on your way, and I'll meet you back there myself to help load."

"Thanks, David. I really appreciate this."

"We appreciate your business. I'm disappointed I won't be able to see it all finished, but I'll get out there, eventually."

Gavin tapped my shoulder and motioned for the phone. "Hey, hold on."

I raised my brows at Gavin and handed my phone over. "Hey, David, this is Gavin Holbrook. Piper and I would love it if you came to the wedding. It's in two weeks, very casual, but we're getting married in the garden so you'll have a great view."

"You don't have to do that," David protested loud enough that I could hear him.

"We want to. We were going to talk to you Sunday when you delivered everything, but I thought I'd mention it now."

"Thanks, Gavin."

"And bring Mrs. Maxwell, too. We'll have great food, music, dancing, and of course, amazing flowers."

"Thanks. We'll do that."

Gavin talked a few more minutes and promised we would call when we were leaving. He hung up and handed the phone back to me.

"Were you really going to invite him?" I asked.

Gavin nodded. "Piper wants to invite the whole damn town. I get it, but we don't actually know everyone. Or, I don't. She does. But David is helping us to make this happen. We wanted to ask him in person."

I nodded slowly. MacKellar Cove was a special place. Everyone pitched in to help everyone else, and seeing it time and again reminded me how much I loved it there.

"Hey, so, about last night. I wasn't really fair to you about Zoey."

"She's your sister. It's your job to protect her."

"Yeah, but I also know you'd never hurt her. Not on purpose, and if you could help it, not on accident either. The divorce was hard on her and the kids, but her marriage was over a while ago. That was just the last step."

"She told me."

"I always wanted her to end up with you. When she chose Trevor, I really didn't get it. I'm still not sure why she did, not really. She got drunk and told me about you guys once, but she refused to talk about choosing Trevor, and now I guess it doesn't really matter. But I wish she'd moved here and married you instead."

"Everything happens for a reason. I wish she had, too, but that wasn't meant to be. I've made my peace with it."

"Have you?"

I shrugged. "I have to. She's not staying here, and I can't imagine leaving. Maybe that's selfish of me, but this place is home."

"I get it. I really do. I keep trying to talk her into moving up here, but she doesn't want to hurt you."

I nodded. I didn't want her to either, but moving would do the opposite. Or maybe not. We were different people than we were a decade ago. We'd both been through a lot. And maybe we weren't supposed to end up together.

Life always worked out the way it was supposed to.

Gavin talked a few more minutes. He said he'd help with the pick up the next day, but he obviously didn't have a truck, so we still needed help.

After Gavin walked back up to the house, I sent out another text saying we were back on for Sunday, if people could still come out, and asking if anyone was available to help with the pick up.

Hudson and Colin immediately agreed to make trips with me. Colin added that he had straps and tarps and bungee cords to secure everything. Ian jumped in and said he'd drive, too. A few others offered to meet us at the Inn to help unload everything.

It was all coming together. Just in time.

Because of the people in town. How could I leave it? I didn't want to, but was that my only option if I wanted a life with Zoey?

And did I want a life with Zoey?

I was walking up to the Inn when I heard giggles and turned just in time to catch Alexis before she plowed right into me. She laughed and held on tight, and I realized I wasn't sure how I was going to have a life without all of them. It wasn't just Zoey who'd made me fall in love again. It was Alexis with her sweetness and her laughter, and Cameron with his strength and his kindness, and Zoey... with her everything.

All three of them snuck inside my heart and demanded I pay attention. All three of them wrapped around me and made me fall for them. All three of them were leaving in a few weeks... and I knew I'd never be the same.

ZOEY

The grounds around the Inn were a fury of activity all Saturday morning. I helped where I could, but I didn't feel like I was doing much. By lunch, I'd already ditched them so I could eat and get ready to go to the book signing at Finley's store. She asked all of us to come so she had at least some people there to meet the guest author.

I'd never read one of Athena McKenzie's books, but Finley gushed over them. She said they were modern day classics with lots of steamy scenes and book boyfriends you wanted to pluck from the pages. With a recommendation like that, I was looking forward to getting one from the signing.

Alexis asked if she could come with me, but Athena was doing a reading and it was not going to be kid friendly. I promised Alexis another playdate with Amber soon and sent her in search of Aunt Gina. Piper was going to the signing with me, and Gavin was still picking up plants, so Aunt Gina was on babysitting duties.

"Holy shit," Piper breathed when we turned onto Riverview Road. There was a line in front of Book

Boyfriends Unlimited that ran halfway down the block. Parking was nonexistent.

I grinned at the sight. "Good for Finley."

"Absolutely. Help me find a spot so we can get in there and help her out."

Piper turned down one side street after another until we lucked out and found someone leaving. She parked a little over a block away from Finley's store, and we hurried to get inside.

The line had dissipated, but that was only because the inside was wall-to-wall people. The turnout was amazing, and Finley was smiling broadly. She waved when she saw us, but she was talking to a customer and didn't have a chance to say hello.

Piper spotted Sofia and some of the others and headed their way. They were sitting to the side, giving plenty of space for Finley's new customers to have front row seats for the reading.

Athena McKenzie was talking to two women in the front row, smiling and laughing with them. She looked exactly like her picture online with dark hair and light brown skin. Her eyes were kind and welcoming, making it easy to see why she was so popular. I always wondered if people like her, famous people, were the same in real life as they were on the page, but sitting there watching her made me think there was no way she wasn't.

"How's the plant delivery going?" Sofia asked Piper once we said hi to everyone.

"Good, I think. Gavin said they have a ton more to get, but I think they'll get through it all today."

"That's good to hear. Sebastian has been anxious about it. He was sure something was going to ruin the whole thing. I don't think he'll breathe again until after your wedding."

"I still can't believe I'm getting married in two weeks."

"Less than," Sofia said. They hugged tightly, sharing a moment I felt like I was intruding on just by being there. Sofia was Piper's maid of honor, her best friend. I was Gavin's best woman, but I felt like he only asked me because he felt like he should. But I loved my brother, and I was happy to stand up for him.

Finley walked up to the front of the room and got Athena's attention. She finished what she was saying to the woman she was talking to, then joined Finley at the table. They spoke quietly for a minute while the energy and excitement in the room peaked.

I'd never been to a book signing before, and I was just as excited as the others. Murmured words and easy laughter flowed around me as everyone waited for Finley to introduce the woman of the day.

Athena took a step to the side, behind her table, and Finley stepped forward. As soon as they moved, the crowd grew quiet in anticipation.

"Wow," Finley said. "Thank you. I know you're not all here to see me today, but if we haven't met, I'm Finley Jameson. I'm the owner of Book Boyfriends Unlimited. I am so happy to have you all here today, but I'm especially happy to welcome Athena McKenzie." She paused while everyone cheered. Finley continued with a smile. "Athena McKenzie is a *USA TODAY* and *NEW YORK TIMES* Bestselling Author of more than forty romance novels. She spends her time dreaming up the next great love story and chasing her menagerie of pets around her four acre property in Upstate New York. Athena's husband supports her efforts to write by bringing her coffee, chocolate, and wine, not always in that order. He keeps her writing through countless hours of inspiration and plenty of foot rubs. When she's not writing, Athena enjoys quiet walks alone, going to the farmer's market, and sinking into a deep bubble bath. Please welcome Athena McKenzie!"

Finley started clapping as she stepped away, and everyone followed suit. Finley stopped in front of us and smiled at me. Her cheeks were glowing with excitement. This was a huge turnout for her, and I hoped it would help dig her out of the hole she said she was sinking into.

"Thank you so much, Finley. I am so thrilled to be here. I don't do a lot of book signings, but when Finley called, I couldn't pass up coming here today. Finley and I have known each other for years. My husband and I visited this area five or six years ago, and I fell in love with the town, and this store. Isn't it adorable?"

Everyone clapped for Finley, and she blushed deeply.

"If you haven't been here before, I hope it isn't your last visit. Finley is amazing, and I know you'll find a ton of stuff to take home with you. And I hope one of those things is my new book, *Home Tonight*."

More cheers erupted from the crowd. I couldn't help but smile and cheer with them.

"If it's all right with you guys, I'm going to do a short reading, and then I'll answer questions and we can chat. I'm here until Finley closes at five, but she said she'll stay open until I've had a chance to speak to all of you. She's the best."

I glanced at Finley and saw tears sparkling in her eyes. "Are you okay?" I whispered.

She nodded. "I never thought I'd get this kind of turnout. This is more business than I usually do in a month, and that's just sales so far. If half of these people buy a book, I'll do more business than I usually do in two or three months."

"That's great."

"It is. But it's showing me I need to play bigger. The potential is there. And I've been hiding from it because I've been scared of being judged. But I'm not alone. All these women love Athena, and love romance novels, and I've been so stupid to worry that I'd be laughed out of town because I don't sell literary fiction or some high brow crap that doesn't interest me. Romance is a billion dollar industry. I need to embrace it."

"You are. And you will continue to. This is just the first step toward seeing what's possible."

Finley nodded. "It is. It really is. I can't wait for the next one."

I smiled at her, wishing I could feel some of her excitement. I was happy for her, of course, but I didn't have what she had. My opportunities were limited, and my money was even more. I also didn't want to run a bookstore, or any other kind of store. I wasn't sure what I wanted to do, but I needed to figure it out soon so I had a job and could provide for my kids.

I leaned back and listened as Athena read a sensual passage from her book. None of it was graphic, but you could feel the energy of the book. Her voice was sultry and stunning, lulling me into the story and making me excited to read the rest.

When she finished the passage, she explained where the inspiration for the scene came from and the inspiration for the book.

"My husband was my first boyfriend. My first serious boyfriend. We dated in high school, but when we went to college, we lost touch. Years later, we ran into each other at a coffee shop. We exchanged contact information and set up a time to get together. He'd just gotten out of a relationship, so we agreed we'd just be friends, but that didn't last long. We were married within six months, and we haven't looked back since. This book… it's a fictionalized version of our story. It's one I've waited to tell for years because it's so important to me. The reviews have been amazing, and the fan response has been better than I could have asked for. This is truly a book from my heart, and to have so many people love it is just the best feeling in the world."

Athena opened the floor for questions and Finley moderated it for her, helping to get everyone's questions answered. After that, a line snaked around the store as people waited to speak to Athena and get one of her books signed.

Finley scrambled behind the checkout desk to keep up, so I walked over and offered to help. I bagged the purchases while she rang them up. Blake joined us after a few minutes and created a second line for anyone paying in cash.

The three of us worked together to get everyone's purchases ready and smiled as one after another happy customer left with a new book or six.

When the line finally dwindled, Athena walked over to us. "You ladies need a break."

"No rest for the wicked," Finley said with a smile.

"Very true. But your friends over there saved a few books for you, if you're interested," Athena said.

"Really?" I blurted excitedly. I hesitated to help Finley because I didn't want to miss out on a book, but I knew she needed the help.

"They did. No pressure, though." Athena smiled sweetly.

"I want one," Finley said. "I meant to ask you in advance, but I never thought there would be so many people here. You brought in a massive crowd."

"You have an amazing store here. I was so happy to help you." Athena reached across the desk and squeezed Finley's hands.

"Thank you. So much. This was amazing."

"Of course. I hope you'll let me come back sometime."

"Any time you want. Zoey here is at the Inn where you're staying. Her family has owned it forever," Finley explained.

"Really? I love that place. Is Gina your mom?"

"Aunt," I told her. "My brother and I used to come up here for the summer. He moved back last winter, and I brought my kids up here to stay this summer."

"That's so exciting. Family is so important. We live in our hometown. We couldn't imagine settling anywhere else. Our extended families are still there, and it's home. Where is home for you?"

Sebastian popped into my mind. I opened my mouth to say Pittsburgh, but I knew that wasn't the truth. The truth was, home was wherever Sebastian was.

When I didn't answer, Athena quickly interpreted it. "Home is no longer home for you, is it?"

I slowly shook my head.

"Maybe it's time to figure out where home really is, and take that leap." She signed the book in front of her and passed it over to me.

I smiled at her and hugged the signed book to my chest. Maybe it was time.

I WAS UP EARLY the next morning to help with the planting. It was a huge job, but Sebastian had gathered a ton of people to work together. Everyone was given a job and a group to work with so everything could be done at the same time without taking forever.

I had Alexis, Hudson, Ramsey, and Amber with me.

"I'm not sure how much help the munchkins are going to be," Ramsey said as the girls giggled and ran in circles around us.

"Yeah, probably not much. But maybe they can bring us waters or something," Hudson said.

"Are you going to ask my daughter to wait on you?" Ramsey asked, a teasing glint in his eyes.

"Yes. Yes, I am." Hudson showed no remorse, which made Ramsey and I both laugh.

"Probably a good plan. Are we ready to get started?" Ramsey asked.

Hudson and I nodded and started placing the plants in our section. Gavin and Sebastian had everything positioned where they wanted the plants to go. Each section had at least a dozen plants, sometimes many more. The outer areas had the larger plants, and as we moved toward the water, the plants were lower to the ground so the cove and river were visible from anywhere in the garden.

Ramsey, Hudson, and I worked well together. One of us would dig a hole, another one would set the plant in place, and the third one would fill the hole back in and make sure there was enough dirt to keep it secure. It wasn't long before we were almost finished with our small section and in need of water from our helpers.

"Why don't you girls see who else you can give water bottles to?" Ramsey suggested as we stepped back and sipped our water and admired the work we'd finished.

Some of the other sections were also done. The garden was taking shape, and it was stunning. Sebastian kept the same general layout that had always been there, leaving the grass pathways throughout so people could walk around and not step on the flowers. There were benches placed in different areas and the trellises were being threaded with vines. The bigger trees and bushes were still waiting to be set, and Hudson and Ramsey went to help with that task.

"This is stunning," Athena McKenzie said to me. "I am so happy I'm here for this."

"You're a guest. You shouldn't be out here doing this," I protested.

Athena waved her hand. "Oh, please. I love this kind of

thing. Piper told me the whole story last night. So, Gavin is your brother?"

I nodded. "He is. My daughter is running around him. The little girl with dark curls. My son is the blond one talking to Gavin."

"They're adorable. It looks like they're having fun."

"They've enjoyed this summer. It wasn't easy at first, but once they met a few friends, they started to have fun."

"Kids are a challenge we haven't tackled yet. We've talked about it, but there are so many things I love about my life as it is."

"I understand. I got pregnant shortly after we got married. It was the right decision for us at the time."

"Is your husband the one your son is working with?"

I looked at where Cameron was and saw him kneeling next to Sebastian and looking up at him like he hung the moon. The admiration on my son's face took my breath away. I knew they'd been working in the garden some, but I didn't know Cameron adored Sebastian the same way Alexis did.

"Um, no. My husband isn't here. He's actually my ex-husband."

"Oh, I'm so sorry. I guess I should have known since you aren't wearing a ring."

"It's fine." I was still staring at them, unable to tear my gaze away.

"So, he's home, huh?"

"Excuse me?" I asked, finally coming out of my trance when I couldn't figure out her question.

"The guy with your son. He's your home?"

"Sebastian? No, I... It's complicated."

"Of course it is," Athena said with a smile. "But that doesn't mean it isn't worth the effort. If you love him, tell him."

"I hurt him once. Badly. I'm not sure we can come back from that."

"It looks like he can. If he hated you, he wouldn't be so good to your son. And he wouldn't keep looking over here at you like he wants to be the one talking to you."

"He is not," I protested as my gaze slid to him and found him staring at me.

"I told you." Athena smiled. "I will never claim to be an expert in men, but I know what a person's face looks like when they're in love. I've studied it. You two are both looking for the same thing, and you've found it in each other. If there's baggage left to deal with, deal with it, but don't let him get away. I don't think either of you wants that to happen."

I smiled and nodded, knowing there was no way to argue with her. I didn't want Sebastian to get away. I walked away last time, but I didn't want to do it again. I loved him, and I loved MacKellar Cove. I wasn't sure Sebastian wanted me, but maybe I owed it to both of us to find out.

But first I needed to know I could stand on my own. I could provide for my kids without counting on someone else to do it for me like I'd done my whole life. I needed a job.

SEBASTIAN

"Can I help you this week?" Cameron asked, drawing my attention back to what we were doing. Staring at his mother was not a good idea, especially surrounded by half the town, and I needed to focus.

"Help me water everything and make sure they're all still alive?" I asked.

Cameron nodded. "This is fun. Where we live doesn't have a lot of dirt. I like dirt."

I chuckled at the honest admission. "Me, too. I've always liked dirt."

Cameron nodded thoughtfully. "I wish we lived somewhere that I could play in the dirt. Whenever it rains, my mom tells me I have to stay out of it because there are other people in our building. If I get mud and water everywhere, someone could get hurt."

"My mom was the same, but we had our own house. She just didn't like dirt."

"Girls are weird."

"Yes, yes, they are," I agreed with him, sneaking another glance at Zoey. She was still talking to the one guest who came out to help. She was smiling and looked like they were having a good conversation. I wanted to know what they were talking about, but I still didn't have the right to ask her.

"Hey, Sebastian, what do you want to do with these?" Ian asked from the other side of the garden.

He was leaning against one of the unplanted trees, one that needed to get into the ground soon. I didn't leave them for last on purpose, just got focused on getting as much done as possible.

"Let's get them in. I think everything is done except those last ones."

Ian nodded and quickly assembled a group to help. The trees were big enough that one person couldn't move them alone, but they were too small to fit more than two or three around them. They were going to be tough to work with.

Ian and Hudson rolled one of the trees out of the way and set to work digging the hole it would go into. Gavin and Colin grabbed another one. Nico clapped me on the shoulder as Rowan and James took a third.

"Give me a hand," Nico said, offering no argument.

"You sure?" I asked him. I appreciated his help, but I was also aware of the fact that Nico needed to protect his hands so he could do his job. If he couldn't treat his cancer patients because he was injured, everyone would suffer.

Nico nodded. "Absolutely. With both of you helping, I think I'll be okay." He winked at me when Cameron's chest puffed up with pride.

"I can help, too?" Cameron asked.

"Yep, we couldn't do it without you." I ruffled his hair and put my hand on his shoulder as we moved toward the closest tree.

Nico and I rolled the tree out of the way with Cameron feeling some of the weight and knowing he was helping. When it was to the side, the indentation left by the tree gave us a good view of where and how wide to dig. The three of us set to work, quickly making enough space for the root ball to fit in.

We set the shovels to the side and rolled the tree back to the edge of the hole. Nico caught my eye and nodded, understanding that Cameron wasn't willing to take a step back and needed to feel like he was important to making it all happen.

"What do you think?" Nico asked. "What's the best way to do this?"

"Can't we just roll it in?" Cameron asked.

I nodded to both of them. "Sounds good to me. It might drop off the edge so hold tight."

I stood in the hole, Nico stayed outside, and Cameron positioned himself with one foot in and one out. Nico and I lifted as much as we could and got the tree in with Cameron's help. Cameron and I stepped out of the hole and surveyed our work.

"What do you think?" Nico asked. "Does it need to be turned or positioned better?"

The tree was leaning to the side and definitely needed a better spot, but Nico wasn't asking me. He was asking Cameron.

Cameron was panting and had sweat running down his dirty face. His gloves were caked with mud. But he was grinning widely.

"I think we should make sure it stands up," Cameron said seriously. "I can do it."

Nico shook his head. "You've got the best eye. I think you need to tell us when it's good."

"Yeah?" Cameron asked, his smile broadening. He was a part of the team, a crucial part.

"Absolutely," I agreed. "Nico and I will move the tree around until you tell us when it's good. Okay?"

Cameron nodded. "Yeah, okay."

Nico tugged the tree the wrong way, letting it tilt farther. Cameron was quick to correct him. We moved it the other way, pulling it upright and twisting it just enough that it started to lean the other direction. Again, Cameron corrected us gently. He didn't get upset, and he took his task very seriously.

"That's good," he finally said, once we had the tree in the right spot. "Perfect."

Nico and I shared a smile and stepped back from the tree. "Nice work," Nico said. "It is perfect."

"We couldn't have done it without you," I told Cameron.

"We need to fill in the hole," Cameron said, still all business. He grabbed a shovel and started to add the dirt back in around the tree. Nico and I helped him out, packing in the dirt to make sure the tree was well supported. When Cameron stepped back to admire our work, Nico and I stepped back with him.

"I think it looks good," Cameron said.

"I agree. Great job. Best tree out here," Nico said.

Cameron looked around and nodded proudly. I tried not to be a little proud of him and failed. He was a damn good kid. I had nothing to do with making him that way, but I wanted to. I would forever wish things could have been different with Zoey and me, but her kids were wonderful little people whom I was happy to know.

As if on cue, Alexis came running over and plowed into my thighs. I righted myself before we both went to the ground and tried not to touch her until I realized she was covered in even more dirt than the rest of us.

"Did someone bury you like one of these trees?" I asked her.

She giggled and shook her head, sending dirt flying from her curls. "I like dirt now. This is fun."

"I can see that. So does your brother, but he just wants to play in it, not wear it," I told her.

"These two might need to get thrown into the river," Nico said. "I don't think there's any other option to get them clean."

I nodded solemnly, rubbing my beard as I looked at the kids and the water. "I think you might be right."

"No!" Alexis shrieked. "We can use the hose."

"I don't know if the hose is going to get all that dirt off of you. You're pretty covered."

"So is Amber," Alexis said, pointing to Ramsey's daughter. She was right, and the look on Ramsey's face said he was trying to figure out what to do with her, too.

"Hose?" I called out to Ramsey.

"River?" Ramsey called back.

Nico laughed. "We said the same thing."

"What did they get into?" Ramsey asked, leading Amber over to us.

I shook my head. "I wish I knew, but I hope they didn't plan to wear these clothes ever again. What do you think, Cameron? Hose or river for these two?"

Cameron grinned. "River."

The girls screamed and took off running. Cameron chased them, all three kids laughing hysterically. I stood back and watched them and tried not to let the burn of regret get to me. They would be leaving soon. I only had a few weeks left with them, and then they'd be gone again. Sure, they might come back, but when they left, I knew I needed to try to move on for real.

Or be prepared to go with them.

I looked over to where Zoey was. I was still trying to figure out how I felt about her being the one I was paired with on the app, and her not telling me about it right away, but I also knew there was a reason we were matched. We fit. We were right for each other. Even all these years later.

It hadn't escaped me that the one woman I wanted to get to know and considered spending time with after Zoey left was, in fact, Zoey. No matter what I did, I always came back to her. Back to us. And losing her again wasn't something I was ready for. It was why I was debating my options and trying to decide if I was prepared to do whatever it took to be with her.

I just needed to decide if I could let her all the way in again.

EVERY DAY for the rest of the week, Cameron was outside when I got to the garden. I told him every day what time I would be there the next day, and he was waiting for me. Ready to go and happy to help.

I showed him how to water the plants with a gentle spray so we didn't flood them but so we knew all the plants got enough water. In the morning and again in the evening, we met in the garden and watered the plants.

And talked. Cameron told me about his dad and all the hours he worked. He talked about his mom and how she made him laugh. He shared stories about his sister, and stories about the four of them together when his parents were still married.

"I'm sorry your parents aren't married anymore," I told him a few days into the week.

He nodded, looking far wiser than an eight year old. "Me, too. I don't want Mommy to be sad. She was always sad. Now, she isn't as sad, but I don't think she's happy."

"What makes you say that?"

Cameron shrugged. "She's not having fun. She doesn't

like dirt, but she likes flowers. She likes computers, too, now. She's been on the computer a lot. Maybe that makes her happy, but usually she looks like she's mad at the computer."

I smiled at him. "Maybe the computer is frustrating her. It's really nice that you care about her being happy."

"She always says we should want the people we love to be happy. If that means they can't be with us for some reason, we have to be okay with that. But no matter where people are, we should want them to be happy."

"Was she talking about your dad?"

Cameron shook his head. "No, Uncle Gavin. When he moved here, I missed him a lot. I still do. But Mommy said he's happy so I need to be happy for him."

"And are you?"

"Sometimes. I still miss him."

"Yeah, I don't think that ever goes away."

"Do you love someone who can't be near you?"

I nodded slowly, thoughtfully. He was a very intuitive kid. And smart.

"Are you happy for them?"

"If they're happy, then yes. Like your mom said, if they're happy, I'm happy."

Cameron nodded again and continued watering the flowers. It left me to wonder if it was really as simple as he said. If I could just be happy for Zoey when she left. And maybe I could be now. Maybe seeing her with her kids would give me a kind of closure I didn't have before.

I wanted to believe that, but in all reality, I knew it wasn't true. I spent years trying to get over her, and in just a few weeks, I couldn't imagine my future without her in it. I still loved her, and not only that, but I wanted her back in my life. For good.

I WAITED for Zoey to come see me, but day after day, she never showed up. I told her I would be available whenever she wanted to come over, but after I found out she knew who I was on the app, I hadn't spoken to her. Eight days was long enough.

I opened the app, almost surprised to find she was still there. My heart beat a little faster as I waited for our last conversation to load. I stared at her words and wondered what they meant. Was she moving? Did she consider it? Was I the reason she changed her mind?

I typed out a quick message asking if she was busy and if we could talk. Then I waited.

It was almost an hour of constant checking before a new message popped up.

MOMOF2

Sorry. It was bedtime. Just got my kids settled.

BETHELIGHT

Understand. Can we talk?

MOMOF2

Sure. What do you want to talk about?

BETHELIGHT

I'd like to talk in person. Can you come over?

MOMOF2

Be there soon.

I tried not to get too excited, but I was. She didn't reject me, which meant we would be able to talk. An actual conversation.

I picked up my place while I waited for her to knock on the door and had a smile ready when I heard her. It was not met with a smile from her.

"Hey."

"Hi," she said with a forced upward tilt of her lips.

I stepped back to let her in and noticed she gave me a wide berth, being careful not to touch.

"Are you okay?" I asked.

"Yeah. What did you want to talk about?"

"Before we get to that, why don't you tell me what's going on?"

"Nothing. Just talk, Sebastian."

"Something is wrong. Tell me."

She huffed a mirthless laugh and looked up at me. "I'm here. I'm ready for you to tell me you're done. I'm holding my shit together until after I leave. So just say it so I can go."

"What?"

"Just say it, Sebastian," she said, his voice barely louder than a whisper.

"I love you," I breathed, my words just as quiet as hers.

"What?"

I cleared my throat and stepped into her space, forcing her to tilt her head back to meet my gaze. "I love you, Zoey. I always have, and I always will. I was an ass when I found out you knew who I was because I felt stupid for not seeing it, but as soon as you said it, it made sense. I was falling for you online and standing in front of me, and I didn't want to love either of you, but I do. I can't deny that any longer."

"You don't love me," she said.

"I do, Zoey. I really didn't want to, but I can't help it."

"No, you told me not to make you fall in love with me. You can't love me."

"I couldn't stop myself."

"But I don't live here."

"We'll figure that part out. Right now, I just needed you to know I love you."

"I love you, too," she replied. Her brown eyes shined with tears. Her lower lip trembled before she caught it between her teeth. I cupped her jaw and brought her face up to mine.

Our lips met in a slow kiss that said all the things we hadn't gotten around to yet. There was no rush this time. Every other time we'd been together, even as kids, we rushed through it. Afraid to get caught or because we couldn't wait or because we were lying to ourselves about what it meant, but this time… This time was different. I was going to worship every inch of her body and make sure she knew how deeply I loved her.

Her tongue brushed against my lips and dipped into my mouth. I wrapped my tongue around hers and groaned. She melted in my arms, her hands clutching at my shirt in a way that made it seem like she was afraid to let go.

I slid one arm around her back and stepped closer to her, our bodies pressed tightly together from lips to knees. I hardened against her stomach, but I was in no rush to move things along. I wanted to kiss her. Needed to. I ached to know the right tilt of our heads, the right brush of our tongues, the right nip of her lips that would make her crazy for more.

Zoey sighed happily and loosened her grip on the front of my shirt. She flattened her hands and eased them up my chest and around my neck. Her fingertips toyed with the short hairs on the back of my neck, making me moan for more of her. She did it again, smiling against my lips when she earned another moan.

I bunched up her shirt until my fingers touched bare skin, then splayed my hand on her back. She moaned in reply, our kiss breaking. I trailed my lips down her throat, licking and sucking until I reached the collar of her shirt. She held on to me, letting me taste her as much as I wanted.

For the first time in years, I gave in to every last bit of desire I had for the woman in my arms. I let myself believe a future was possible for us. I stopped thinking it might end and decided I was going to enjoy whatever we had. If it ended, I would survive, but I also wasn't going to count on it ending this time. Because this time was different. This time I was going to trust her and love her and never let her go.

I dragged my lips back up her neck until our lips met once more. I wanted to dive back in, but first, I needed to say the words again.

"I love you."

20

ZOEY

earing Sebastian say those words made my knees weak. He made everything in me weak. I missed the sound of his voice saying that. Telling me with three simple words that said everything was going to be okay, and if it wasn't, he would be there with me to fix it.

"I love you," I told him, hoping he felt half the comfort I did when I said those words to him.

He hugged me closer, so close that nothing could come between us. Then he started moving us toward his bed.

We walked together, stopping to make out like we did when we were younger. His tongue teased me, making me both crazy for him and desperate to have the night last forever. Every time we started panting and our actions hurried, we slowed down, the decision made without words or thoughts. We wanted the same thing. Time.

We finally made it to the bed and were both fully clothed. His hands were under the back of my shirt, but he hadn't moved them beyond that. Our lips were glued together, neither of us willing to break our kiss again.

We eased our way onto the mattress, keeping our bodies

in contact the entire time. Sebastian settled on his back, bringing me over him. I straddled his hips, feeling both timid and brave when I felt the thick ridge of his erection between my thighs. It was like we were in a bubble. Everything was safe inside, but if we tried too hard or went too fast, it would pop and it would all be over.

Sebastian's hands slid up my sides, bringing my shirt with them. I had no choice but to lift my arms and let him remove my shirt. His eyes locked on my chest as he tossed my shirt aside. Then his hands were back on me. Fingertips glided over my bare skin, lifting goosebumps wherever he touched. He traced the cup of my bra and circled my nipple through the fabric, but he didn't try to remove it. I couldn't remember the last time I'd been touched so reverently, like he was in awe that I was there with him.

I had no idea how I ever gave him up all those years ago. I regretted it then, but sitting on top of him, the look of love in his eyes so intense it brought tears to mine, I knew not marrying him would forever be the biggest mistake of my life.

One I didn't intend to make again. Not that he asked me, but I wasn't giving him up this time.

"What are you thinking?" he asked quietly, his gentle caress on my stomach.

"That I wish I'd come back."

He understood what I meant, and instead of his gaze hardening and the memory of how I hurt him putting distance between us, he wrapped his arm around my waist and pulled my body flat on top of his. "I wish you had, too, but for whatever reason, that wasn't our time. We have to accept that and stop wishing it was different. All we have is right now."

I nodded against his chest, his words hurting more than they should. I wanted more than right now. I wanted forever.

I wanted a future. I wanted everything with him. But he was still only willing to give me right now.

As selfish as it made me, I was going to take it. I would take whatever he gave me. And if I ended up back in Pittsburgh alone, I would carry the memory of our time together and use it to heal all the pain I knew I would feel.

But I wasn't going to think of that yet. Not when we had the night. I saw Piper on my way out and told her I was going to see Sebastian. She promised they would listen for the kids and be there in the morning in case I wasn't. I laughed it off at the time, but now I was more than happy she'd offered. Because I wasn't planning to leave Sebastian's bed anytime soon.

His hands ran up and down my back in a soothing way that before long had me squirming. I turned my lips toward him and licked his throat. He groaned and tightened his hold on me. I kissed and nipped his jaw, rubbing my cheek against his beard. He unclasped my bra and pushed me up to remove it. As I slid it down my arms, he leaned up and yanked his tee off with one hand behind his head. Then he pulled me back onto him, our bare skin meeting.

"I love you, Zoey," he breathed into my hair.

"I love you, Sebastian."

He brought my lips to his again and devoured me. I felt his desire like it was inside me. We always had a connection, but this connection was different. It was twisted and wrapped together, the past and the present tangling inside me, creating something that would never let go.

My hips moved on their own, our lower halves still covered, but I could feel him hard through his shorts. The restrictions reminded me of the first time we were together. The first time he kissed me and touched me and made me come in his arms. He was always a gentle lover, passionate but concerned with making me feel good.

He rolled us, my back hitting the mattress before I really figured out what he was doing. He tore his lips from mine and kissed his way down my throat to my breasts. He took one nipple into his mouth, and I moaned at the feel of his tongue licking over it. He cupped my other breast and offered it to himself.

I watched him, the pink of his tongue darting out to lick the tip of my nipple. The soft hair of his beard tickling the side of my breast. His eyes closed in pleasure. I couldn't get enough of him.

He moved down, kissing and licking every inch of me as he went. He traced my stretch marks with his tongue and pressed a kiss to my appendix scar. He unbuttoned my shorts and licked the edge of my panties before he hooked his fingers in them and drew both down my legs. He pressed my thighs wide with his hands and just stared at me, exposed and vulnerable on his bed.

"I've missed you," he said, his eyes lifting to my face. "I never thought I'd get to have you in my bed, Zoey. And this... I love you."

I swallowed roughly and nodded. "I love you." I couldn't say anything else through the emotion in my throat, but the burning in his eyes told me he understood all of it. The pain, the regret, and the hope I had for our future.

He lowered his head and settled in between my thighs. He ran a finger through my folds, spreading my wetness around and teasing me with every brush. When he finally lowered his mouth to me, I cried out, an orgasm already pulsing in my center. The anticipation of him making it impossible to hold back.

"Don't hold back, Zoey," he said, as though he could read my thoughts. "Give me all of you."

I moaned my answer, not bothering to be quiet. Trevor never liked it when I made noise, but with Sebastian it felt good to let go. To tell him with my body and my words how good he made me feel.

He licked me again, his tongue exploring my body, but carefully avoiding where I needed him. His fingers teased my entrance but never went inside. Every move made my breath hitch and my body tighten. I knew when he finally gave me what I needed, I'd lose my mind. And I couldn't wait.

"Sebastian," I whimpered. My body was coiled tight, my breath pulsing out of me in sharp pants. I couldn't hold back much longer.

He growled against my center and speared me with his tongue. I moaned, the pleasure of it pushing me closer to the edge but not quite there. He licked his way up and sucked hard on my clit as he pressed two fingers deep inside me. And I lost it.

I screamed and cried and stopped breathing. I flailed and writhed and swore I peed a little. I couldn't control any of it. I was done, a useless puddle of orgasm on his bed.

When the fuzziness in my brain receded, his face was right there in front of me. His fingers were on my cheeks, holding me gently. I felt his hard length between my thighs, where I still quivered and pulsed from the power of the orgasm he gave me.

"You back?" he asked with a smile full of male satisfaction and pride.

I nodded, words impossible in the moment.

"You ready?"

I nodded again, spreading my thighs to accept him inside me. He pushed gently, sliding into my wet body easily. We both groaned and moved together to bring him deeper into me.

"You feel so good, Zoey."

"So do you."

"I love you."

"I love you." Tears pricked my eyes as he filled me. I held on to him, needing the connection. The love in his eyes was like nothing I'd ever seen in my life. He was it for me. This was it for me. If I died right now, I'd know I was loved.

He moved in and out in short, gentle strokes. It was the kind of sex we'd never been able to take advantage of before. Lazy, unhurried, beautiful. I stared into his eyes the entire time, and he watched me. When he got closer, I saw the change in his face and tightened around him.

"Fuck, Zoey."

I did it again, meeting his strokes with a little extra resistance. He groaned and sped up, never breaking the connection we shared. When he came, he whispered he loved me and kissed me.

We laid like that for a long moment, our bodies and heart connected. I didn't want the moment to end, but we both knew it had to. Sebastian got up and took care of the condom, then came back to his bed and laid down with me. He kissed my neck and pulled me close.

"I know you have to get back to the house, but I want to stay here with you for a little while."

"Actually, I don't have to get back right away. Piper said she'd take care of the kids if they needed anything. And would be around in the morning, too."

"Remind me to get them a really good wedding present, okay?"

I chuckled and nodded. I would be doing the same.

A FULL NIGHT in Sebastian's arms was better than I ever let myself imagine it could be. We both slept hard all night, but when morning came, we took advantage of the alone time and teased each other during naked breakfast in bed and shared shower time.

By the time I headed back to the house to change into clean clothes for the day, I knew I had to figure out a way to stay in MacKellar Cove. I just wasn't sure what I was going to do for money.

I changed quickly in the silent house and checked the job boards in Pittsburgh before I realized I needed to be checking the job postings in MacKellar Cove. There were a few places within thirty minutes that were looking for new employees, but all of them said seasonal and were likely already filled since summer was almost over.

I closed my laptop and hurried to the Inn to find my kids and check in with Piper and Gavin. And thank them for my night.

"I don't know what we can do," I heard Piper say when I walked into the Inn. "There isn't an option. I was worried this was going to happen."

"I know, and I should have listened to you," Gavin said. "Come here."

I found the two of them in a tight embrace in the foyer. Piper looked like she'd been crying, and Gavin looked like he wanted to.

"Are you guys okay?" I asked, hating to interrupt the moment.

Piper pulled back from Gavin and shook her head. My gaze went to my brother for explanation.

"Aunt Gina said she'd make us a wedding cake, but with the Inn and all the food for the wedding, now she's not sure if she can."

"Okay. What's the problem?" I asked.

"We have no cake. We never did cake tastings, and we have no backup plan. I don't know what to do," Piper whispered.

I glanced back at the kitchen where Aunt Gina had to be working. I felt bad for all of them. I was sure Aunt Gina thought she could handle everything, and she didn't want to let them down, but she was getting older and it didn't surprise me she wasn't able to do it all. But Piper and Gavin deserved a beautiful, delicious cake. Something I was not capable of providing.

"What about Cove Bakery?" I asked.

"I'm sure they're swamped," Piper said.

"What's Cove Bakery?" Gavin asked.

"It's a local bakery. I had a cake from them when I went to Melody and Ramsey's house. It was really good. Maybe they can do it," I suggested.

The front door opened, and a couple walked in. Piper pasted on a smile and went to greet them.

Gavin cupped my elbow and led me away from the guests and Piper. "She's losing it, Zo. I don't know what to do."

"Why don't you let me handle it? I've leaned on you both a lot while we've been here. I was going to take the kids into town today and just wander a little. I'll find Cove Bakery and see what I can find out. Do you have any requests?"

"No. I mean, really, we'll take anything right now. We just need something."

"What if all they can do are cupcakes? Or something not very traditional?"

Gavin snorted. "Have you met us? We're not very traditional."

I grinned. "Good point. I'll let you guys know what I find out."

"Good. And when you do, you can tell me about your night."

His grin was curious and open, but there was something in his eyes that made me think he wasn't as happy for me as I wanted him to be.

"Are you upset?"

"Upset? No. Worried about you? Always."

"Sebastian would never hurt me."

"Not on purpose."

"Not at all, Gavin. He loves me."

"He told you that?"

I nodded. "He did. And I love him."

"What does that mean?"

I shook my head. "I don't know yet, but I want it to mean things will work out. I'll let you know when I know."

Gavin smiled and pulled me in for a hug. He kissed the top of my head and said, "As long as you're happy, I'll be happy for you."

"Thanks, Gavin."

Zoey was still talking to the guests, so I went out the back and found the kids. They were up for a drive into town and a stop at a bakery for a treat.

Cove Bakery was a little more than a block away from Catherine Park, so I left the car near the park after we played a little, and we walked through town. The shop was adorable, with its pink and white striped awning and glass front windows that gave you a peek inside before you entered.

The sweet scent of sugar made my mouth water as soon as we walked into the bakery. A woman who looked close to Aunt Gina's age was behind the counter, boxing up treats for the young mom and two boys in front of us. She looked up and welcomed us when we walked in, then focused on the customers she was serving.

We walked to the case and marveled at the fudge, cupcakes, pies, cakes, and more treats than we could eat in a lifetime.

"Can I get one of each?" Alexis asked, her eyes wide. She licked her lips and pressed her hands to the glass.

"Um, no, but how about we each pick something and we can all share," I suggested instead.

"I want that cupcake," Cameron said. He pointed to a blue cupcake with a chocolate swirl on top.

"I want the chocolate," Alexis said, eyeing a chunk of fudge.

"Sounds good. I think I'm going to try a brookie. I always wanted to taste one."

"What's a brookie?" Alexis asked.

"It's part cookie, part brownie," the lady behind the counter answered for me. "It's my favorite treat."

"I want to try some, Mommy. Can I try some?"

"Of course," I told Alexis. "I said we were all going to share. Why don't you two sit at a table, and I'll bring our treats in a minute?"

They nodded and rushed to choose a table in the empty cafe. It was a beautiful day outside, and a weekday, so we had the run of the place. It was better that way since I had a favor to ask.

"So, one brookie," the woman said. "What else can I get you?"

"The blue cupcake, and a piece of the double chocolate fudge," I told her.

"Ooh, excellent choices. You guys know how to pick good stuff. Where are you visiting from?"

"Pittsburgh, but we're here for the summer."

"That's a nice trip."

I nodded. "It is. My brother lives here, and so does my aunt. Gina Holbrook?" I hoped she would recognize the name and be more willing to help.

"You're Gina's niece? Zoey?"

I nodded and felt my smile grow. "I am."

"It is so nice to finally meet you. I'm Harriett. Your aunt and I have been friends for years."

"Aunt Gina has a way of collecting people and making everyone feel welcome. You're the same."

"You're too kind. How is Gina doing? I haven't seen her much."

"She's doing okay. Slowing down some. That's actually part of the reason I came here today."

"Really? Is she okay?"

I nodded quickly, sorry to have worried Harriett. "She is. Yes. But she was supposed to bake my brother's wedding cake, and told them today she doesn't think she can do it. Is there any way you could?"

"When's the wedding?"

I winced. "A week from tomorrow."

"Ooh, man. Um, hang on. Valentina! Can you come out here, please?" Harriett slid the plates with our treats and three bottles of water across the counter. "Valentina is my baker. I've been slowing down a lot, too, and she's the one who really runs this place these days. Let me see what she thinks. Why don't you take these to the kids and we can chat?"

I nodded and carried the plates to the table and told the kids to save a few bites of each for me to try, then went back to the counter. A shorter Black woman had joined Harriett and was talking to her.

"Valentina, this is Zoey," Harriett introduced us. "Gina Holbrook is her aunt. Gina was supposed to make the cake for her brother's wedding next week but can't. Do you have time in your schedule?"

Valentina drew a deep breath and stared up at the ceiling. She winced but met my gaze with a steady, open one of her own. "How many people?"

"Fifty."

"When's the wedding?"

"Friday."

"Are they picky?"

I shook my head. "No. They will take anything. Seriously, they're just wanting to find something they can serve to guests. It doesn't have to be a cake."

Valentina thought for a minute, then nodded. "I can make it work."

"Seriously?"

"Yeah. It might be a few different things, but if they're open to that, it won't be an issue."

"No, they'll be fine with that. Thank you so much."

"You're welcome," Valentina said. She glanced behind me and chuckled. "You might need a few napkins."

I looked at my chocolate-covered kids and shook my head with a laugh. "Well, you know your stuff is good."

She smiled back. "I hope so."

21

The next week was a flurry of activity. Sebastian and I were able to steal time together in the evenings when the kids were sleeping, but it wasn't enough. Especially since I hadn't yet found a job in MacKellar Cove and knew my time was fading fast. I wanted to stay, but without a job, I couldn't afford a security deposit and first month's rent on a new place. At least in Pittsburgh, we had a home. It wasn't perfect, but it existed. If it meant I had to stay there for a year and move after the school year, I would do that, but I didn't love it. But I also didn't love moving the kids during school.

But none of that mattered when my brother's wedding was a day away. We were all so excited and ready for it to happen. I'd met with Valentina again and tasted more of her delicious treats through the week. Piper went with me one day and asked Valentina to come to the wedding. I told her she could be my date.

She laughed and finally agreed.

I was in the sitting room at the Inn, waiting for my

parents to arrive, when Piper walked in with her computer. "There you are."

"Hey. Is something wrong?" I asked, nodding to the laptop. I'd finished all the program upgrades we'd talked about and Piper was happy with the improvements, but I also assured her she could call me with any questions or issues.

"No, nothing's wrong. I just wanted to thank you again for all the work you did. And I wanted to give you something."

She pulled an envelope out and handed it to me. I opened it and gasped. It was a check. A big one. "What's this?"

Piper smiled sheepishly. "I know you said you didn't want me to pay you, but I didn't feel right about that. You did a ton of work, work that we had every intention of hiring someone to do for us. It's only right that you get paid for it."

"Piper…"

"I know. I know what you said, but you were wrong. We invited you to stay here because we love you. All three of you. We've loved having you here, and that has nothing to do with you doing all of this work for us. We didn't expect it, and it saved us a lot of time and frustration. And you earned every penny of that."

I stared at the check. It was a big one. Not big enough that I could live on forever, but big enough that I could put down a security deposit on a new place and afford to stay in MacKellar Cove for a few months and work on finding a job while living here.

But I couldn't accept it.

"I don't feel right taking this money."

"Then you're really not going to want to take the job I want to offer you," Piper said.

"What?" I blurted.

"I've thought about it, and I really want someone who can manage our computer systems. It might not be full-time work, but I think there's enough for you to do that we can stretch it to full time. It would mean moving here, but I'm hoping you're okay with that. Gavin would love to have you here, and Sebastian doesn't seem to be a reason not to come here now. So, I want you to work for us. Then you don't have to worry about anything."

I gaped at her, unsure if she was joking or not. The hopeful smile on her face made it look like she wasn't joking, but she had to be. And if she wasn't, it didn't matter because I was not going to take a pity job offer. I needed to stand on my own. I needed to know I could provide for my family. I wasn't going to count on everyone else to take care of me like I'd been doing forever. It was how I ended up married to the wrong man, and divorced with two kids.

"I—"

"Hello!" my mother shouted from the open doorway.

Piper and I turned. I hadn't even heard my parents drive up or get out of their car, but there she was. My mother dropped her bags at her feet and opened her arms. My father was only a few steps behind her, doing the same.

"It's so good to finally meet you," Piper gushed, hurrying over to my parents and letting them both pull her into warm hugs.

The noise in the front brought the kids, Gavin, and Aunt Gina out to say hello also. Hugs and kisses and smiles were exchanged by everyone while I stood back and watched. I was numb. Frozen. Hurt. Piper didn't mean to do it, but it didn't matter. She thought I needed help. She thought I wasn't capable of taking care of myself and my family. She created a position and was willing to stretch it to full time for me. It didn't get much worse than that.

"Are you going to say hello?" my mom asked after a few minutes.

I forced a smile and went over to greet my parents. They

both looked good. Happy. I was happy for them, but it stung. Everyone around me was blissful, and I was spiraling.

I spent the rest of the day in a little bit of a fog. My parents spent time with the kids and me and helped Piper and Gavin with whatever they could for the wedding. We all had dinner together at the Inn before a quick rehearsal. After the rehearsal, Gavin and Piper had dessert in the garden for us, and we all sat around and talked until the kids started falling asleep in their seats.

Piper offered to stay with them, but I waved her off and walked them up to the house. Once they were tucked in, I sent Sebastian a message that I wouldn't be over since everyone was still outside talking. He said he understood and missed me.

I tried to read a book, but the words kept spinning on the page. All I could think about was Piper's job offer. And the more I thought about it, the more bothered I was by it.

My sleep was fitful, and by morning I was even crabbier. I tried to paste on a smile all day and limited how much I talked to everyone, but it was hard since I was the Best Woman.

Piper was getting ready at the house with Sofia, so Gavin and I went to our parents' room at the Inn to get dressed. I was in the bathroom getting changed when I overheard them talking.

"Piper is lovely, Gavin. I'm so happy you found her," Mom said.

"Me, too, Mom. She's amazing."

"You two look happy," Dad said.

"We are. I never thought I'd come back here after college, but being with Piper and being here is right." His voice was quieter when he continued. "Don't say anything, but we're trying to get Zoey to move here, too."

"Really?" Mom asked. "Does she want to?"

"I think so, but she's practical. She wants everything just right. Piper created a job for her. They talked yesterday before you guys arrived, but she didn't accept it yet. We're hoping she will soon so she can move up here before the kids start school."

"That would be so nice. I've been worried about her all alone without you. She needs someone," Mom said.

I stared at the door and tried not to cry. My entire family thought I couldn't take care of myself. That I needed someone and that creating a job for me was the right move. Who did they think I was?

I sucked in a shaky breath and did what I always did. I pretended nothing was wrong and walked out.

Gavin and I posed for pictures while we waited for the ceremony to start. Whenever he said anything to me, I distracted him with the kids or the boats going by or asking if Piper was coming. I was not ready to talk to him about the job or moving or any of it. Not if I was going to make it through the wedding.

I watched as my friends found seats and chatted. Gavin walked around and said hello to people. I kept my eyes on Alexis and Cameron, after threatening both of them to not get a speck of dirt on their clothes. When the ceremony was about to start, I put the kids on chairs in the front row where my parents and Aunt Gina would sit and keep them still. I hoped.

My mom was in a tan dress that had bright flowers flowing from her waist to the hem. It looked elegant and beautiful on her. Casual enough that she wasn't out of place at the garden wedding, but formal enough for the mother of the groom.

Piper's parents didn't come to the wedding, so once my mother and Aunt Gina were seated, Gavin took his place next to me, and we waited for Sofia and Piper to walk out.

I glanced out at the crowd and found Sebastian staring at me. His gaze locked on mine and heated as he took in the pale blue dress I wore. It was one I'd had for years, but a dress I loved. Sofia was wearing a similar color for her dress, and Gavin had a matching tie on with his crisp white shirt and black pants. He opted not to wear a jacket, a look that suited him.

My own wedding was as opposite from Gavin's as it could have been. I had a massive white dress with poofs and big sleeves and an endless train. Trevor wore a tuxedo complete with cummerbund and fancy new shoes. We got married in a church and invited almost four hundred people, more than half of whom came. It was big and lavish and not at all me, but it was what Trevor wanted.

Everything was about what Trevor wanted throughout our entire marriage. He wanted to get married quickly and in a big way, so we did. He wanted me to stay home, so I did. He wanted kids right away and to live in a certain area and to have certain friends, so we did. All of it was on Trevor's terms.

And I went along with it because I felt like I owed him. Because I chose to marry him, even though I was still in love with Sebastian. I loved Trevor, but I always knew Sebastian was it for me. But I made my choice and chose to do whatever it took to make him happy for the rest of our marriage.

Except he wasn't happy either.

The minister went through the ceremony while I zoned out. I handed over the rings when it was time and smiled when Gavin dipped Piper low and kissed the hell out of her, but my mind was on everything else going on in my life. I was happy for my brother, but for the first time, maybe ever, I needed to do what was right for me. And that meant not taking the job Piper offered me.

The guests meandered through the gardens and out onto

the large grassy area between the house and the garden. Tables and chairs were set up for people to sit and eat dinner, with a section to the side for dancing.

Gavin and Piper were so happy. I could see it plainly on their faces. I hated that I would ruin that happiness for them, and that they were only trying to help, but it was time for me to make decisions that were right for me. Not ones that were right for everyone else.

Sebastian made his way over to where I was standing on the edge of the reception area and smiled. "You doing okay?"

I nodded. I wasn't ready to tell him everything either. "Yeah."

"Are you sure? Because you look like you're upset or bothered or something."

I shook my head. "It's nothing I'm going to worry about tonight."

"So there is something."

I nodded. "Yes, but—"

"Dance with me." It wasn't a request. I studied him, trying to understand what he was thinking, but I couldn't read him as well as he could obviously read me.

I slid my hand into his and let him lead me onto the dance floor. He wrapped one arm around my waist and grabbed my hand with his. He threaded his fingers into mine and brought them to his chest. He was close. Close enough that not one person there would think we were simply friends. Our bodies rubbed together, our small steps keeping us touching.

Sebastian didn't say anything while we danced, just held me. Tears formed in my eyes, but I refused to let them fall. He loved me. And he was there for me. He didn't know why, but it didn't matter to him. He was there.

As the music changed from slow to fast and back to slow, we kept dancing. Off to the side, out of the way of the people who were dancing along to the music. We just held each other and swayed, not speaking or caring about anything other than being in each other's arms.

The DJ announced that dinner would be served soon and that the food was getting set up at the buffet tables. He was going to continue playing music through the reception so people could eat when they were hungry. Piper and Gavin wanted it to feel like going to O'Kelley's for the night. Music and laughter and food whenever people wanted it. It was perfect for them.

"Come with me," Sebastian said when the DJ was done talking.

We were already off to the side, half shrouded in darkness as the sun sank deeper into the river. He waited for me to nod, then pulled me around the side of the house. He kept going until we reached the front porch. He led me up onto the porch and sat on a chair, bringing me down onto his lap.

He didn't say anything, just stared at me for a long moment. I wanted to tell him about the job offer from Piper, but I was worried he'd push me to accept it so I would move. I wanted to move, but I needed to do it on my terms. I hoped Sebastian would understand that.

He tilted my chin down to meet my gaze and smiled sadly at me when he did. I tried to return his smile, but too many things were on my mind for it to be right.

Sebastian slowly brought me to him with a hand wrapped around my neck. I went willingly, giving him everything in my kiss. I wanted him to know nothing had changed between us and that I would find a way to make it work. I needed him to know that.

His hand on my knee slid up my skirt, holding my thigh without going any farther. I was wet and ready for him, but we needed to wait. Piper and Gavin were leaving for their honeymoon so I wasn't going to have anyone at the house who could stay with the kids for a while. Which meant

Sebastian and I were on hold. With the summer coming quickly to an end.

He hardened under me, making me moan at the feel of him. I was ready to drag him inside and take advantage of the empty house when I heard Cameron's voice.

"Stop touching my mommy! What are you doing?"

Sebastian immediately withdrew, breaking our kiss and turning to see Cameron. I followed his gaze, jumping off Sebastian's lap and straightening my skirt.

"She's still in love with my daddy. She's not going to marry you. You're not allowed to kiss her!" Cameron continued.

"Cameron—" Sebastian started.

"I hate you! I hate being here. Why did we have to come here? I wish I'd never met you. I want to go home. I don't want to stay here any longer. I want to see Daddy!"

I took a step toward him, and my heel caught on the porch. I lost my balance, prompting Sebastian to reach out to me again.

"Don't touch my mommy!" Cameron shouted. He ran up the stairs and pushed Sebastian's hand off me.

"Cameron!" I scolded.

"No, Zoey, it's fine," Sebastian said. "I'll go."

Cameron dragged me to the side so Sebastian could walk away. He didn't look back before he walked around the edge of the house and disappeared. Only then did Cameron speak again.

"I hate it here. I want to go home!"

I took a breath and let it out slowly. Before I could say anything to him, he ran into the house in tears, leaving me feeling like the worst mom in the world. It was clearly not the right time to tell him I wanted MacKellar Cove to be our new home. Shit.

22

I chased Cameron up the stairs.

"I hate this place!"

"Cameron, don't say that. Let's go back to the wedding."

"No. I don't want to." He yanked off his dress shirt and threw it in the corner of the room.

"Cameron!"

He ignored me and kicked his shoes on top of his shirt, then tore the rest of his clothes off.

"What are you doing?"

"I want to go home."

Going home was not the problem. "Cameron, I thought you liked Sebastian."

"I hate him. He made you not love Daddy anymore."

"No, honey, Sebastian had nothing to do with that."

"But you were married to Daddy, and now he's kissing you. He shouldn't be allowed to kiss you."

I sighed heavily and tried to figure out a way to explain the situation to him. He always seemed to understand, but understanding and witnessing a change were different. Very different.

"Daddy and I aren't married anymore. That means we're allowed to kiss other people."

"Who else have you kissed?" he asked me accusingly.

"No one. But I want to kiss Sebastian more."

"No! He's not my dad!"

"I never said he was, or that he would be. But I love him."

"You're supposed to love Daddy. Mark Johnson in my class said his parents still love each other. They got divorced but then they got married again. You and Daddy were supposed to do that. You told me you would always love him."

I sighed and moved closer to Cameron. I kneeled in front of him and looked up at my son. He looked more and more like his father, but those eyes of his held so much wisdom for only eight years old. He'd always been the shy one, the kid who hung back and figured things out. His sister jumped in with both feet, but Cameron trusted his mind and his heart. He got that from me.

"I will always love your daddy, Cameron. Always. He's a wonderful man, and he gave me the best things ever. He gave me you and your sister. And your daddy loved me, and he took care of us, and I loved him and always will. But sometimes, love isn't the only thing that matters in a relationship. Sometimes, you need more than that."

"No."

"No?"

"No. You said love matters. You said you love Daddy. You can't marry Sebastian."

"Sebastian and I are a long way from talking about getting married."

"You can't. It's not fair. I don't want to live here. I want to see Daddy!" He burst into tears and threw himself on the bed. My heart shattered knowing there was nothing I could do to make it better. He was going to have to be okay with it eventually, if Sebastian was still willing to try. And if I found a job in MacKellar Cove.

I sat on the edge of the bed and put my hand on Cameron's back. He squirmed away from me and yelled into his pillow, "I hate you!"

His tears were nothing compared to his words. He'd never said that to me before. Cameron was not a dramatic child and never had been, but the divorce was harder on him than it was on Alexis. He missed his dad. Even though Trevor hadn't been there enough before we divorced, after was worse, and Cameron felt it.

And now he was blaming me.

I stayed there, soaking in his pain and unwilling to walk away. He was upset, but I needed him to know I would be there for him no matter what. He could say anything, and I would never leave him.

His tears slowed and finally stopped, and the snoring started up almost immediately. He'd cried himself to sleep. My poor, sweet boy. I wanted to pull his lanky form into my arms and rock him and soothe all his pains like I was able to do when he was a baby, but this couldn't be rocked away. It was bigger than that.

I sat there for a few more minutes, then eased off the bed. I was exhausted from the last two days and not in the mood to go back out to the party. I changed out of my dress and into a tee and sweatpants, then went down to the kitchen to make some tea.

I curled up on the couch and listened to the sounds of the party. People were having fun. Music was playing, laughter was abundant, and life was good. It was how it should be.

I wanted that. I wanted to feel like I was a part of something like that. I had fallen for MacKellar Cove, and Sebastian aside, I felt like it was the right place to continue raising my kids.

With the tea sitting next to me, I turned my computer on. I was not going to accept Piper's job, but it definitely made me think about some options I hadn't allowed myself to consider before. I did some research and came up with an idea.

The front door of the house opened quietly, and my parents walked in with Alexis limp in my dad's arms.

"She fell asleep right there in the chair," my dad whispered. "Do you want me to walk her up to bed?"

I nodded and rose from my seat, setting the computer aside. "That would be great. Cameron is already asleep. Thanks, Dad."

He nodded and started up the steps. Alexis whimpered, but she settled again as he talked to her on the climb.

"Are you okay, honey?" Mom asked when Dad was up the stairs.

I wanted to smile and say I was fine, but after the day I'd had, I couldn't lie. "No, actually, I'm not."

"What's going on?"

I drew a breath and debated how much I wanted to tell her. I was close to my mom growing up. We would go shopping and to the movies. She would talk to me about boys and life and the future. But somewhere along the way, a lot of that stopped. We didn't talk like we used to, and I realized there was a lot I wanted to say to her that I wasn't sure I could.

"Why don't we sit?" she suggested, gesturing to where I'd been on the couch.

I resumed my seat, and she settled across from me.

"Why did you leave the reception?" she asked.

Might as well dive in. "I left with Sebastian Parks."

"The lighthouse keeper who helps Gina?"

"Yes. I'm in love with him. I have been for as long as I can remember."

"I know. I didn't realize you still were, though."

"What do you mean, you know?"

Mom shrugged. "You were in love with him when you were a teenager. He was too old for you, but he seemed like a nice man. I figured he'd find someone his own age and that would be the end of it, but I guess he never did. Then you married Trevor. I assumed it was because Sebastian was married, but Gina said he never was."

"You knew about Sebastian and me?"

"Yes, I did. I didn't like it so I didn't ask you about him."

"Is that why you were always trying to get me to date other boys in high school?"

She sucked in a breath and nodded. "It is. Sebastian was a man when you were in high school. He was working here, and he was an adult. It would have been illegal for the two of you to be together—"

"We never did anything until I was eighteen," I protested. "He was very respectful of me, and he refused. He wanted me to be sure, and he wasn't willing to take advantage of me."

"Are you sure about that? You came home the one summer all upset and refusing to go back. I asked Gina, but we had no way of knowing if something happened."

"Is that why you took me to the gynecologist and got me on birth control?" I asked. Lies. So many lies.

She nodded. "I was worried about you."

"Why didn't you just ask me? We used to be able to talk about everything."

"You never mentioned Sebastian, so I figured you knew I wouldn't approve of him. You kept him a secret. But now you're an adult, so I can't stop you from seeing him."

"But you would? If you could stop me from seeing him, you would?"

"Your mother didn't say that," Dad said from the bottom of the stairs. "We worry about you. You're all alone in Pittsburgh now. Gavin told us Piper offered you a job, so we're happy to know you're going to be moving up here, but—"

"I'm not taking the job," I interrupted.

They exchanged a worried look.

"Why wouldn't you take the job?" Mom asked. Her voice was a little panicked.

"Because I've made too many choices based on what other people need or want, and I'm going to live my life for me."

"What does that mean?" Mom asked.

"It means I only married Trevor because you guys were worried about needing to file for bankruptcy," I blurted.

Mom and Dad looked at each other, eyes wide with fear and regret.

"How do you know that?" Dad asked softly.

"I overheard you one night. You were talking about money and how you'd lost your job, Dad, and Mom's salary wasn't enough to pay for everything. My college was expensive, and the loans for Gavin were worse, and you didn't know how you were going to manage everything. You were talking about selling the house and credit cards and… I met Trevor the following week. He had money and wasn't afraid to spend it on me. I loved him, but I would have come back here and married Sebastian if it weren't for needing to take on my student loan debt. So, I married Trevor, and he paid off my loans. We tried to make it work, but I think we both always knew that it wouldn't. I didn't love him the same way I loved Sebastian."

"Oh, Zoey, I'm so sorry you ever found out about that," Mom said. "We never wanted you or your brother to feel like you were a burden."

"But we were, Mom. Dad didn't have a job, and we had no idea things were as bad as they were. Gavin could have started paying his own loans a lot sooner, and I could have been working through school. You hid things from us that we should have known."

Mom nodded slowly, her head down. She didn't argue with me, just kept nodding.

Dad sat next to her and took her hand. "We made mistakes, Zoey. We never expected you to pay for them. We did the best we could."

"I know. And I don't blame you for my choice to marry Trevor. All I'm saying is that I married him so he would take care of me. I didn't have the confidence in myself, or Sebastian, to move here or be on my own. I had never worked a real job, and I was sure I would fail. So I made the easy choice and married Trevor when he asked. But now… I'm not doing that again. I appreciate Gavin and Piper's offer, but I can't accept it. She created the job for me. They need all their income to help keep the Inn running. To make upgrades and to turn it into whatever they want it to be. They don't need to create a job for me because they feel bad that I'm alone."

"But you are alone," Mom said.

I huffed and fought the urge to growl at my mother. "Yes, but I can handle it. And I will handle it. I don't need someone else to take care of me. I need to take care of my kids. I need to give myself the chance to be happy."

"What is going to make you happy?" Dad asked.

"Being with Sebastian. Living here."

"Then why won't you take Piper's job offer?"

"Because it isn't what I want to do."

"When family offers help, you should take it. We did," Mom said.

"What do you mean?"

"She means Gina helped us. That's how we managed to not file for bankruptcy. We listed the house, but we were able to hold on until it sold because Gina sent us money every month until I found a job and we sold the house and we were back on our feet."

"Aunt Gina? Why didn't I know this?"

"Probably because we didn't know you knew any of this."

I nodded. They were right. I overheard them talking and made my own decisions based on what I heard. I made the best decision at the time, but this new information wouldn't have changed that. It just proved my point.

I was done taking handouts and counting on others to take care of me.

"Zoey, I wish things were different when you were younger. Your father and I did the best we could. We love you and Gavin, and we tried, but we obviously fell short a lot of the time. We were scared, and you might not think it's right that we accepted money from Gina, but—"

"I think you did what you had to do."

"You're refusing a job because you think it's charity. Charity is what we accepted. You think it's wrong."

"Actually, Mom, no. You and Dad were in a position that required something drastic. You had no choice. Dad was out of work, you had a lot of debt, and you didn't know what to do. I'm not in the same situation. Trevor pays me child support and alimony. I worked last year so we would have a little extra spending money. I want to keep working because you taught me to take pride in what I do and work hard. I haven't been doing either for a few years. I loved being home with the kids, but they're in school now. I need to do something with my days. And I don't think it's fair to ask Trevor to pay for me to stay home. I always planned to work when Alexis went to school. But working at a manufactured job for my brother and his wife isn't the same thing."

"We're really proud of you, Zoey," Dad said.

"Thank you."

"We both are," Mom said.

"Thank you. I want my kids to be proud of me, too. I want to be someone they can look up to as a role model. Like I always did with both of you."

Mom wiped at her lashes, and Dad squeezed the back of her neck. They both smiled at me.

"But that means I can't accept Piper's job."

"So, what are you going to do?"

"I don't know yet, but until I figure it out, I'm going back to Pittsburgh."

23

SEBASTIAN

Zoey told me before the wedding that she planned to spend the weekend with her parents and the kids. When I didn't hear from her, I didn't think twice. Until I noticed Monday that her car was gone.

I walked into the Inn for lunch and found Gina in the kitchen. She was humming a tune and arranging a buffet for the guests who were around.

"Need any help?" I asked.

"Oh, yes, I do. It's been far too long since I've had to do all this on my own."

"It's short-lived. Why isn't Zoey here to help you?" I reached for the plate as she brushed her hands on her pink apron.

"She's gone," Gina said simply, as though it wasn't news.

Everything inside me went still. I almost dropped the plate but regained my hold just in time. I shifted it to my other hand and forced the words out. "Gone? What do you mean?"

"She went back to Pittsburgh this morning. I assumed she talked to you."

"No, she didn't." I stomped out of the kitchen with Gina calling my name, but I wasn't interested in whatever excuses she was going to make up for Zoey. The truth was she left me. Again. After she knew how I felt about her. She promised me she wouldn't make me fall in love with her, but I did, and she left.

I set the plate of food on the buffet table and went straight back out the door. I knew Gina was too busy to follow me, and I knew I was being an ass, but I needed to process what was going on.

Zoey left me. The last time I saw her was when Cameron interrupted us on the porch. She insisted it would be fine, but three days later, and with no word from her, she was gone.

There had to be an explanation, but what explanation could there be that didn't involve advanced warning? She had to have known I would find out. And she had to have known I'd expect the worst. How could I not?

I forced Zoey from my mind and went through the rest of the day on autopilot. I had a lot to do since I'd taken off Friday for the wedding and ended up relaxing for the weekend. It was a good thing because it meant I could focus on work and not on Zoey the whole time.

When I got home that night, I stared at my phone. She'd lived across the yard for months, so I never bothered to get her phone number. I went into Book Boyfriends Wanted to send her a message there, but she'd deleted her profile. She was just gone. Again.

The last time she left me, I spent the better part of a month drunk. I waited for her, but she never came, and when Gina told me she'd gotten married, I couldn't handle it.

Memories of the time we spent together over the summer assaulted me. She was in every inch of my home. The bed, the kitchen, the couch. Her scent filled the air, and her laughter taunted me. She was supposed to be there with me. We were supposed to have another week.

The desire to empty a bottle of whiskey was strong, but I wasn't going to do that again. I couldn't. She left me, but I was going to have to find a way to move on for real this time. She never made me promises about staying and never said what we had was going to keep her here. She owed me nothing. A phone call would have been nice, but I couldn't change her.

I grabbed my keys, not wanting to be home alone, and headed to O'Kelley's. It was quiet in the bar and easy for me to get a seat to the side where I could sulk in peace.

"You're not usually in here on a Monday. What's going on?" Hudson asked as he set a beer in front of me.

"Zoey left. I just didn't want to be in my house. Everything reminds me of her, and I'm not willing to fall apart again."

"She left? Just up and left? No word?"

I shook my head. "Nothing. I was going to ask her to stay. I wanted to keep seeing her. Hell, I was thinking about moving to Pittsburgh if that was the only option. But she's made it pretty clear that's not what she wants."

"You don't know that," Hudson said.

I looked up at him. He leaned back and crossed his arms over his chest. He looked at me like I was a petulant child throwing a temper tantrum.

"She left. What am I supposed to think? She was supposed to be here for another week, and now she's gone."

Hudson shrugged. "Do you love her?"

"Yes," I ground out.

"Do you want to spend the rest of your life with her? And her kids?"

"Yes."

"Then quit being a fucking dickwad and go talk to her."

"Excuse me?"

"Listen, you can sit here and have a pity party. You can act like she didn't crush you. You can do whatever the hell you want, but at the end of the day, you have no idea what's going through her head right now. Maybe she got a job offer and had to go back for an interview. Maybe her ex got hurt, and she needed to take the kids to see him before he dies. Maybe she hates you and didn't know how to tell you. But you have no fucking clue. You're making up your mind about her instead of going after your woman and telling her you want to be in her life."

"But—"

"Fuck no. No buts. Either you want her or you don't. If you do, then go get her. Her marriage was over a year ago, longer than that from the sound of things. She's not going back to him. I saw the two of you at the wedding. She's in love you with you. Why would she just leave all of a sudden?"

I thought back to the wedding and cringed. Cameron.

"What did you do?" Hudson asked, his voice steel.

"I didn't do anything. We were kissing on the porch, and Cameron caught us. He said he hated me and MacKellar Cove."

"So?"

"What do you mean, so? Her kids mean everything to her."

"And you think she's going to give up living her own life because her son had a moment?"

I sighed and considered it. Zoey would do anything for her kids. She'd give her life for them. Would she give up what we had? Yeah, she probably would.

"If you think she would, would she also do it without explaining to you what was going on?" Hudson asked more quietly.

I sucked in a breath and admitted to myself he was right.

Zoey wasn't the college girl I loved the last time she didn't come back. She was an adult. A mother. A woman with her own mind. She was different. And Hudson was right. She would give up what we had, but she would have talked to me about it.

Which left very little room for excuses. So why the hell did she leave?

"You're not being very fair to her. I get that you have issues with her since last time she promised to come back and never did, but you owe it to her to listen. If you never told her you wanted her to stay or that you were thinking about moving, you can't blame her for not knowing. Your situation sucks, dude, but don't make it worse by putting names to her actions without having a conversation."

I nodded, accepting what he said. "I'm an asshole."

Hudson shrugged. "We all have our moments. Maybe she's the asshole in this situation, but maybe not. Just find out. Ask Gina for her number if you don't have it."

"No, this isn't the kind of thing I want to talk about over the phone. Or something I want to hear from Gina. I need to see Zoey. I need her to tell me to my face what's going on."

"You're going to Pittsburgh?"

"It seems that way."

THE DRIVE to Pittsburgh was long and boring. I hated to wait, but I took off first thing in the morning so I didn't show up at her place in the middle of the night. Gina tried to talk to me when I asked for Zoey's address, but I told her whatever it was she wanted to say, I needed to hear it from Zoey myself. Gina let it go after that, but I didn't miss the smile on her face.

By the time I got to Zoey's, it was almost lunchtime. I

parked in one of the guest spots outside her weathered gray building. It didn't look horrible, but it was definitely a little rough around the edges. There was nothing to stop me from walking into the building and right up to Zoey's door without announcing myself, which made my blood boil. Her ex was an even bigger piece of shit than I thought if he was okay with his kids living in a place that wasn't more secure.

I heard voices inside her apartment before I knocked. It sounded like Zoey, but the male voice was a surprise. Whoever it was, they were going to have to tell me to my face what was going on.

Zoey opened the door a few seconds later, and her eyes grew wide when she saw me standing there. "Sebastian?"

I pushed my way inside, not letting her stop me. A man who looked too much like Cameron to not be the boy's father stood near the kitchen to the right. He smirked at me.

"Who are you?" I demanded, even though I already knew.

"Trevor Wainwright. And you are?" He was pressed and polished and as far from me as another man could get. I wouldn't have been surprised if he had a weekly appointment to get his nails done by the looks of him. His hair was cut and styled just so, and his suit was flawless. I'd never looked as magazine-worthy as him in my entire life.

If that was the kind of man Zoey wanted, she was never going to find that with me.

"Sebastian Parks," I grunted at my competition. I turned back to Zoey. She was still standing by the door, watching us.

"What are you doing here, Sebastian?"

"You disappeared without a word. I need to know why."

"Maybe we can talk in a little while. Trevor and I were in the middle of something."

My heart sank with her words. He was the priority, not me. The man who treated her like she wasn't important and put everything else above her and their kids. But he got to stay while I had to go.

"That's not going to work for me," I told her.

"Excuse me?" Zoey said while Trevor snickered.

"We need to talk. I drove here this morning to see you, after you walked away from me. I think I deserve an explanation."

"This is priceless," Trevor said.

"Trevor," Zoey warned.

"What? This is too good."

I stepped toward her, blocking her view of him so she had no choice but to look at me instead of him. "I came here to tell you I'm not letting you run away from me again. I'm not letting you get back together with him, or anyone else, and I'm not letting you go. We belong together, and this fart-nozzle is all wrong for you."

Trevor snorted. I glared at him over my shoulder, but he didn't change the smug expression on his face.

Zoey kept her gaze locked on mine while she said, "I think you should go."

My world stopped. I don't know why I thought Zoey would just accept that I wanted her back and come willingly, but I didn't think she'd throw me out either.

"Are you serious?" I asked, my tone less than friendly and more than a little pissed off.

Zoey leaned to the side and raised an eyebrow. "Trevor. You need to go."

"Do I have to? This is like being a part of a live studio audience. Except real."

"Trevor," Zoey said with a laugh.

He chuckled. "Okay, okay, I'm going. I need to get back to the office, anyway. I'll see you tonight?" He paused when he was even with me to deliver his last line.

I growled, and he had the nerve to look at me with a smirk.

"Yes," Zoey said in a whispery, sexy tone. "I'll see you tonight."

Trevor lifted an eyebrow at me in question. I would have loved to knock the son-of-a-bitch out, but I just stepped to the side and let him pass.

He closed the door behind himself, leaving Zoey and I alone.

"Where are Cameron and Alexis?" I asked.

"They're with friends for the day. I asked Trevor to come over so we could talk, and I didn't want the kids here when we did."

"So you could do more than talk?" I blurted, my jealous asshole side taking over.

Zoey looked up at me in shock. "No, but thanks for letting me know what you think of me."

"You fucking left me, Zoey. You don't get to be on the high horse today. You walked out. You didn't say a damn word to me. You closed your online profile and never gave me your number and disappeared. And I come here to find out what the hell is going on, and he's in your home. What am I supposed to think?"

Zoey didn't say anything for a long moment. I hated the pain in her eyes, but I wasn't willing to back down. I was pissed. I'd been up half the night imagining all kinds of scenarios that would have forced her to come back a week early. Then I imagined all kinds of things she'd be doing, with number one being Trevor.

"Why are you seeing him tonight?" I demanded.

"Because we have things to discuss."

"Like what?"

"Like him being a more present father for our kids and me moving to MacKellar Cove."

My brows tugged together as her words sank in. I played them again and again in my head before I finally understood. "You're moving?"

She nodded. "Well, I was planning on it. That's why I came back here. My lease is up in a week, and instead of signing a new one, I decided to let the place go and move."

"Were you going to tell me this?"

"I intended to, but I wanted to surprise you. Of course now I'm not sure it's a good idea. You clearly don't want me in your life."

"Why are you moving, Zoey?"

"Are you really asking me that?"

"I need you to say it."

She stepped closer to me. She stopped before she touched me. Her eyes lifted to mine, and she whispered. "I love you, Sebastian. And I want a life with you. I wanted a life with you. I love MacKellar Cove, and I love the crazy people, but most of all, I love you."

"But you don't anymore?" I asked, my heart beating slowly in my chest. I couldn't have fucked it up with her. Not that quickly.

She shrugged. "Obviously, I didn't handle this the right way. I thought it would be fun to surprise you, but I see now that I shouldn't have left without telling you. But if your first thought is that I'm in bed with my ex-husband, then maybe we're just not in the same place."

"Fucking hell, we are. I'm a jealous asshole. He already stole you from me once. And you disappeared. You were gone. I had no way to find out what was going on. So, yeah, I jumped to conclusions. And I acted like an asshole. I can't promise you I'm not going to get jealous when you see him or talk to him. I've never been a jealous man, but I can't seem to control myself when it comes to you."

"You don't seem to have any trouble controlling yourself right now."

I shook my head slowly. "That's not true. I'm dying here. I want you in my arms so badly, but I don't have the right to touch you. I shouldn't have said what I did and I'm sorry. I shouldn't have assumed the worst from you. I'm sorry, Zoey, and I hope you'll be able to forgive me."

"I already do, Sebastian," she breathed.

"You do?" I asked.

She nodded.

"Okay, cool, bye," I said. I turned and waved and walked toward the door.

"Are you kidding me?" she asked incredulously.

I grinned and turned back to her. "Hell, yes. Do you think I would be able to walk away from you?" I took two big steps and had her in my arms. I breathed her in, feeling like it was the first full breath I'd had in days. "I love you so fucking much," I whispered into her hair. "Don't ever leave me again."

"I won't. And I'm sorry I didn't tell you. Aunt Gina knew I was coming back, but she also knew I wanted to surprise you. I'm guessing she made things worse."

"It doesn't matter now. All that matters is you're mine."

"I've always been yours."

"Yeah, but now everyone else will know it, too. You know I'm going to marry you, right?"

She nodded. "I was kind of hoping you would."

"Soon."

She grinned and held me tighter. "How's next week?"

"Perfect."

24

ZOEY

I was still reeling from my day with Sebastian when Trevor called and offered to pick up the kids and bring them to his place before dinner. He wanted to spend time with them after not seeing them for months. It was good, for all of them, but I couldn't help but be extra grateful after Sebastian showed up at my door.

We spent the afternoon in bed, kissing and touching and making promises to each other about our future. I told him all about the conversation I had with Trevor about moving to MacKellar Cove. Trevor was more generous than I expected him to be. I apologized for not being a better wife, and Trevor apologized for knowingly keeping me from the man I truly loved.

"I loved you, too," I told Trevor.

"I know," he said. "And I loved you. I wanted it to work between us, but I could see in your eyes that you never forgot him and never forgave yourself for walking away from him. Even though I didn't know who he was or what the situation was, I knew there was someone. I want you to be happy, Zoey."

I hugged him. "Thank you. I hope you're happy, too."

He nodded. "I will be. I made a lot of mistakes with you and the kids. I want to be the man I always hoped I'd be. The dad I wanted to be. And that starts with supporting their mom."

"Thank you."

He chuckled. "Our marriage might have survived if we'd been this honest with each other all along."

I smiled, but we both knew the truth. Our marriage wouldn't have lasted. And I was getting another chance at happiness.

Sebastian wanted to go to dinner with me, but we needed a family dinner. Trevor and I were going to talk to the kids together and explain our plans to them. With the way Cameron reacted to Sebastian and I kissing, I knew it would be better if he wasn't there.

I knocked on the door to Trevor's condo and waited for him to let me in. Laughter and chatter greeted me inside.

"Hey," Trevor said, leaning in for a kiss on my cheek.

"Hi."

"Things go okay after I left?"

I nodded. "All good. Thank you for being okay with this."

"Like I said before, I want you to be happy."

I nodded again and followed him into the condo. Trevor went to the kitchen where he was finishing dinner. I headed straight for the kids. They were playing a game on the kitchen table and laughing.

"What are you guys doing?"

"Playing cards," Alexis said. "And I'm winning."

"Nuh uh. I am," Cameron argued.

"Are you guys having fun?" I asked, hoping to diffuse the tension between them.

"Yep," they said together.

"Then keep playing without worrying about who's

winning. You have your whole lives to compete. Sometimes it's nice to just play the game."

They went back to it, and I went to help Trevor in the kitchen. We got dinner on the table and settled in to talk to the kids.

"So, your mom said you guys had a great vacation. Did you guys love being in MacKellar Cove?" Trevor asked.

"Yes. It's the bestest place in the world," Alexis said. "I made a new friend, and we got dessert and played outside, and we even got to play in the dirt."

"That sounds like a lot of fun. How about you, Cameron?" Trevor prompted.

Cameron shrugged. Trevor glanced at me. We expected that response.

"I heard you met a good friend of Mommy's. Sebastian?" Trevor said.

Cameron shrugged again, but Alexis jumped in. "Sebastian is so funny. He pretends not to like me, but he always watches out for me. He shares his bacon with me and he holds my hand and he answers all my questions. He even said he is going to show me the lighthouse one day, but only if you and Mommy say it's okay."

"That sounds pretty great," Trevor said. "I bet a lighthouse would be cool."

"Yeah. I like Sebastian. He's my favorite."

Trevor smiled at me, a look of true happiness. He approved, and that made all of this so much easier.

"Mommy and Sebastian really like each other," Trevor said, keeping an eye on Cameron. "A lot."

Cameron's eyes snapped up to Trevor's and widened. "You know that?"

Trevor nodded. "I do. Sebastian makes your mommy very happy. He loves her, and she loves him."

"Are they going to get married?" Alexis asked.

"That's up to your mommy and Sebastian, but I hope they do," Trevor said.

"But she's supposed to marry you again," Cameron said, his voice trembling with emotion.

Trevor shook his head and reached over and grabbed Cameron's hand. "No, buddy, she's not. Mommy and I will always love each other because we had a life together. We have you two, and we love you. We care very much about each other, and because of that, I want your mommy to be happy. And Sebastian makes her happy."

"But I want you to make her happy," Cameron whined. A tear rolled down his cheek and broke my heart.

"I wasn't very good at that," Trevor said. "I wanted to be, but I wasn't. Sometimes people get married and then they decide they shouldn't be married. Mommy and I were very happy for a while, but now isn't the time for us to be married. Now is the time for Mommy to be with Sebastian. And I want both of you to be supportive of her. I want you guys to give Sebastian a chance."

"I hate him," Cameron whimpered.

"I don't think you do," Trevor said gently. "But I understand, bud. When Grammy and Pop got divorced, I was really unhappy. I thought they should fix it. When Pop married Nana, I was mad. I didn't like her at all. I told her I hated her and refused to talk to her. But she's an amazing person. She was there for me more times than I can count. After a while, I saw how happy she made Pop, and I decided to love her, too. She was a bonus mom for me. And I hope you'll give Sebastian a chance to be a bonus dad for you."

"But I have a dad."

Trevor nodded. "You do, and I'll always be available for you. I'm going to do better. But that's another thing Mommy and I wanted to talk to you about. Mommy is moving to MacKellar Cove. And you guys are going with her."

"What?" Cameron asked.

"Yay!" shouted Alexis.

"I'm going to miss you guys, but I'm going to come up and visit every month, and you guys will come down here some of the time. And we'll all be together for the holidays. And we'll figure out summers and everything else. But Mommy and I think it'll be good for you two to be there."

"Yay!" Alexis said again.

Cameron was suspiciously quiet. I wanted to ask him how he felt, but he wasn't really looking at me. Trevor and I agreed he would be the one who led the conversation. It was his idea so the kids knew he was on board with it. But it was hard for me not to jump in and try to soothe whatever was going on in Cameron's mind.

"Cam? What are you thinking, buddy?" Trevor asked.

"Is it okay for me to be happy?"

I nearly cried with relief. Trevor reached over and pulled Cameron into a hug. "Of course it's okay. I want you to be happy. Mommy told me about all the things you guys did and the friends you made. I know you'll be happy there. And even though you're mad at Sebastian right now, I know you really like him, too. And that's okay. I want you to like him."

"Do you like him?"

"I don't really know him, but anyone who's so good to you two and who makes your mommy happy is someone I know I will like."

Trevor's answer was not rehearsed. We hadn't talked about Cameron asking that question. Which meant Trevor was being honest. The tears I was trying to hold back rolled down my cheeks.

"I liked him a lot before I saw him kissing Mommy. It's okay for me to like him again?"

Trevor nodded. "It is, bud. It definitely is."

THE NEXT FEW days passed in a blur. Between packing up the apartment and getting all their school records transferred and making arrangements to store our things until we found a new place, it was busy.

I didn't realize how much stuff we had crammed into our little apartment. Sebastian loaded up his truck with as many boxes as possible. I piled what I could into the back of my SUV. Trevor let me store the rest all at his place until we could come back for a visit.

It amazed me how well things came together. My relationship with my parents and my relationship with Trevor felt fragile, but both were better than they'd ever been. Trevor was my partner in a way he hadn't been when we were married. He came by the morning we were leaving to see the kids and to wish us well, and he called that evening to make sure we had a good trip. He was already talking about coming up to visit in a few weeks. Once the kids were settled in at their new school.

I didn't think Sebastian would take me seriously about getting married in a week, but as soon as we got back to MacKellar Cove, he started planning.

"I've waited almost half my life to marry you. I'm not waiting another day," he said. The garden was already set up and perfect, and neither of us wanted anything big or flashy.

It was a Tuesday afternoon when we met in the garden. My brother and Piper joined us, and so did my kids and Aunt Gina. We invited Melody, Ramsey, and Amber, and Derek and Jude so Cameron had a friend. The ceremony was quick but perfect. Sebastian and I vowed to love each other for the rest of our lives and to always be honest and faithful to each other.

The best part for me was when Sebastian brought both

the kids up to the front and made vows to them. I was help-less to hold back my tears.

"I know I'm not your father, and I never want to replace him. He's a part of you both, a big part, and he's important to me because of it. But even though I'm not your father, I hope you both will always know I'm here for you and I love you. I will do the best job I possibly can to support you and love you and encourage you. I will let you steal my bacon and let you play in the dirt. I will help you with homework and help you to have fun. I will always love your mother, and I will always push you to be better people. As much as I vow today that I am marrying your mother, I also make these same vows to you. To love, cherish, and honor you both. Forever."

"Okay," Alexis said simply, as though it was no big deal.

The small crowd we gathered laughed at her easy accep-tance of Sebastian. Then we waited for Cameron to speak.

"My dad said you're like a bonus dad for us. He said he wants us to like you. Would you be okay if I called you some-thing other than Sebastian?"

I closed my eyes to keep the tears inside and swallowed roughly. When I opened my eyes again, Sebastian was on his knees in front of my son. "You can call me whatever you feel comfortable calling me."

"Can I call you BD?"

"BD?" I asked.

"Yeah. Bonus Dad," Cameron said. "I already have a dad, but I like having a Bonus Dad. But that's too long, so BD works. If that's okay."

Sebastian nodded slowly, his throat working overtime as he reached for Cameron. Cam went to him and threw his arms around Sebastian's neck. Sebastian squeezed his eyes shut as a tear leaked out. I saw his lips move as he told my son he loves him.

"I love you, too, BD," Cameron said.

Sebastian squeezed him tightly, then let go when Cameron struggled. I smiled, my heart too full.

"Can I call you that, too?" Alexis asked when Sebastian let go of Cameron.

"Of course," Sebastian told her. "I love it."

"Good. Because Sebastian is a big word. BD works." Alexis nodded sharply, the decision made.

The rest of the ceremony was quick, and before I knew it, Sebastian was sealing our union with a kiss that held all the promises of a future together.

Our small group headed back to the Inn for dinner. Aunt Gina insisted on having something for us even though we planned a reception at O'Kelley's over the weekend with the rest of our friends.

Aunt Gina and Piper arranged the dining room so everyone could sit together for dinner. They had space for the Inn guests, but for the wedding, we had our own room. Piper refused to let me help with anything and pushed Sebastian and I to talk to everyone while Piper and Gavin served dinner.

"How do you feel?" Melody asked.

I laughed. "Like I'm living in a dream."

She grinned widely. "Sounds like the perfect answer for your wedding day. This was beautiful. Thank you for inviting us."

"I'm so happy you could be here. I've never made friends easily, but you made me feel like I could be myself without having to hide the mistakes I've made."

"We've all made mistakes. And we're all going to make more. If we aren't willing to own that, we miss out on all the other good things in life."

I nodded, letting her words sink in. She was right. If I hadn't been willing to admit to my mistakes, I wouldn't have given myself a chance to do better. Talking to my parents and talking to Trevor helped me to move past the things I regretted for years. It helped me to grow and change and marry the man I've loved for most of my life.

Sebastian slid his arm around my waist and kissed my throat. "What are we talking about over here?"

"Our mistakes," Melody said with a smile.

Sebastian's brows went up quickly. "I hope you're not thinking this was a mistake."

I shook my head and turned in his arms. My hands flattened on his chest. "The mistake was not doing this years ago. You are my reward for owning up to my mistakes."

"Hmm. I like the sound of that. I'm willing to be your reward for any mistakes you make in the future, too."

I smiled at my husband. Oh, my God, my husband. Sebastian was my husband! "I love you."

"I love you. And for the record, I don't think you made a mistake. I think we just had to wait for our time. Now, we'll appreciate each other more. And appreciate all that we have together."

I nodded. "I will definitely appreciate you a lot tonight."

He grinned and slowly closed the distance between us. I felt his erection twitch. He whispered, "That appreciation will be mutually beneficial." Then he kissed me again. My husband.

The sound of glasses clinking broke us apart. Gavin was standing at one end of the room, tapping a spoon on his glass. "I'd like to make the first toast of the night. For years, I watched my sister fall for Sebastian. I saw the way he protected her and cared for her, letting her go every fall so she could live her life without him. When I first came back last year, I had a hard time blending the man he'd become with the man he used to be. But this summer, that man has returned. The one who's warm and kind and loves my sister with everything he is. I couldn't be happier for the two of you. For the love you've shared all this time and the way it brought you back together. And for the people you've become along the way. It was a long road to get here, and not always an easy one, but now you get to travel that road together. Always." Gavin paused and lifted his glass. "To Zoey and Sebastian."

"To Zoey and Sebastian," everyone repeated.

Gavin winked at me and sipped his champagne. I nodded back and sipped mine.

"He's right, you know," Sebastian said for my ears only.

"About what?"

"All of it. I was a miserable bastard. I never thought I'd love again. Then you came back. I didn't want to love you, but I couldn't stop it. You're everything to me, and I'm so happy we have another chance at a life together."

"Me, too."

"I do have one question, though."

"Oh, yeah? What's that?"

Sebastian glanced at Alexis and Cameron. "Have you ever thought about having more kids?"

I wrapped my arms around his neck and leaned in close to him. "I'm sure I can be convinced."

"Yeah?" he asked, his eyes sparkling.

I nodded. "Yeah."

"Want to start trying right now?"

I laughed. "We're at our reception. We can't leave."

Sebastian hardened against my stomach. "No one will miss us."

I snorted. "Yeah, they will."

He pouted. "Fine. But tonight, this beautiful dress is going on the floor. And I'm not letting you out of bed until we absolutely have to leave."

"I am definitely on board with that idea."

"Good. And tomorrow, we're buying a house."

"What?"

He smiled. "I've been planning to buy you a house for a decade. Tomorrow, we're making it happen. One with lots of bedrooms we can fill it with lots more children. And an office for you to start your computer consulting company."

"I love you so much."

"The feeling is mutual, Wife."

I smiled. "That's good to hear, Husband."

EPILOGUE

FINLEY

I leaned back in my seat and smiled at my friends. It was a good day. A good summer, really. It was hard to believe only two years ago our summer ended with a trip to Hawaii to get Ms. Georgia and Eddie married before cancer took Ms. Georgia from us. I wished she could be there to see how we were all doing.

"What are you thinking about?" Blake asked me quietly.

Having Blake go from my best friend to my sister was my favorite change. We'd always been close, and when she and Ian got together, it felt natural and normal and perfect.

"I was just thinking about Ms. Georgia."

"She would have loved this," Blake said. "She would have been right in the middle of all of it, offering advice and telling all of us to live life and enjoy."

I nodded, smiling at the thought. Blake was right. Ms. Georgia absolutely would have told us that. She was big on not wasting the time we had, even before she found out her own time was limited.

"I feel like I need to take that advice," I admitted.

Blake tilted her head and looked closely at me. "Is everything okay?"

I grinned, happy I could answer the question honestly. "Yes, it is. I've poured so much of myself into Book Boyfriends Unlimited, and I put off all the other things I wanted. It was my choice, and I'm happy I did it, but we're thirty-three. I hope I still have a lot of time left, but I don't want to spend all of it working my ass off."

"So, what are you going to do?" Blake asked.

I shrugged. "I don't know yet. One thing I want to do is take a vacation this winter. While it's quiet here, I want to get away. And maybe have a fling. Meet someone. Have some sex."

Blake cackled, tossing her head back and leaning into me. "Sounds like a great plan."

I nodded, liking my unconfirmed plans more and more. My store was secure for a while, and I'd been talking to Karissa about designing an app that would allow me to sell ebooks, and I was enjoying life again. I had time to relax a little. Not that I could coast, but I could slow the hustle some.

"I want what you and Ian have. What Zoey and Sebastian have. Not that I'm jealous, but especially watching Zoey and Sebastian fight their attraction all summer and end up married, it gives me hope that maybe I'll find that, too."

"You will," Blake said with a certainty I didn't feel. "You haven't been open to it in a while, but now that you are, it'll happen."

"We'll see. For now, I'm just going to focus on fun. And I think I'm going to finally reactivate my Book Boyfriends Wanted account. I've talked about it so many times but keep chickening out. I'm going to actually do it this time."

"Good for you," Blake said.

"What's good for you?" Zoey asked. She fell onto the chair next to me and picked up her water.

"Finley's going to start dating again," Blake told her.

"That is good for you. I don't feel like I ever actually dated, so I can't help you, but movies make it look fun," Zoey said.

I snorted a laugh and shook my head. "Dating sucks. How have you never dated before?"

Zoey shrugged. "I fell in love with Sebastian when I was a teenager. I had no interest in any of the boys at school because I knew Sebastian was here, so I never dated in high school. Once I was eighteen, he and I got together so I never dated anyone at college. Not that any guys were begging me to go out with them. When I met Trevor my last semester, we just started seeing each other one day and then got married a few months later, and after my marriage ended, I didn't date anyone. I signed up for Karissa's app and was paired with Sebastian, and here we are. At my wedding reception."

"I hate you," Blake said.

Zoey laughed.

"I'm with her," I agreed, pointing to Blake. "You suck."

Zoey shook her head and looked blissfully happy. "I know. I kind of hate myself, but I've also never had sex with a stranger or a one-night stand or got butterflies in my stomach wondering if a guy was going to kiss me on my porch or any number of things. And I've been divorced, so obviously my path isn't the best one out there."

Blake and I chuckled with Zoey. "But you made it all work in the end," I told her, looking at Sebastian. He was staring at Zoey, a heated look in his eyes. I'd known him for years, but he was always quiet and reserved. I barely spoke to him before a year ago, and now I considered him a friend. And I was thrilled to see him so happy.

"I'm lucky," Zoey said dreamily as she met her husband's gaze.

"Yes, you are," I told her.

"Excuse me, ladies," Zoey said a minute later. A flush worked its way up her cheeks as she stood and stared after Sebastian as he disappeared toward the bathrooms.

Blake and I looked at each other with wide eyes and surprised laughs. "Are they...?"

"I think they are," I told her.

"Damn. Good for them."

"Yep. Good for them."

"Is Rissa ready for her surgery?" Blake asked.

I drew a breath and nodded. Karissa had been planning on a preventative double mastectomy since her mom died. She finally had it scheduled in a few weeks. She was trying to enjoy life before then, but she was also adjusting to the idea that she might never have her own kids or get married. She bounced between relieved and depressed regularly.

"I think so. She's anxious."

"I would be, too. Is she going to go on vacation with you?"

"That's a good idea. I'll talk to her about it. I haven't made any plans or really thought about it other than going some-place warmer than here in the dead of winter."

Blake laughed. "It won't be too hard to find places warmer in winter."

I grinned. "True. I wonder if Rissa will be interested in going back to Hawaii. See Kiana and Sawyer and everyone."

"That would be a fun trip. Man, you make me want to go."

I laughed. "Maybe we should make it a girls' trip."

"Yeah, but you want some downtime. I won't invade your vacation."

"You'd never be invading."

Blake leaned against me. "I know. But I also know you. I can see the exhaustion in your eyes. I'm happy it's fading and that the store is doing well these days, but I know you need some real downtime. A real break."

I nodded. I thought I was hiding the truth better than I

was, but I should have known Blake would see through me. She always did. I could never hide anything from her. And I never really wanted to. She was my person, my best friend and sister, in every sense of the word. She was the only one who ever really got me, and I was lucky to have her in my life.

"I'm guessing you need the same," I told her.

Blake shrugged. "I do, but I haven't had the pressure on me that you have. And I feel like I've been neglecting our friendship since Ian and I got married."

"I promise, you have not."

Blake smiled. "Just know I'm always here for you. If you ever need anything, you can always come to me. Forever."

I laughed and hugged her. "Trust me, I've never once doubted that."

"Good. I actually wanted to tell you something, if you're up for it."

My eyes widened as she nibbled on her lip. "Oh, my God, are you pregnant?"

She shook her head quickly. "No, but we are trying. We only just started, so we're not stressing about it or anything, but I wanted you to know. Like you said, we're thirty-three."

"Oh, I'm so happy for you guys! You're going to be such amazing parents."

Blake smiled widely. "Thank you. I know we always talked about having kids together, but—"

"God, no. Don't even think about that. I'm nowhere near ready for kids. But I can't wait to be the best aunt in town."

"Without a doubt," Blake said.

THANK **you** for reading Zoey and Sebastian's story! Some of my favorite stories are second chance romances. Stories where there is hurt and regret, but also so much hope and love. I hope you enjoyed these two, and their surprise wedding!

The next book in the series is Finley and Trent's book. Finley wants to have a little fun and meets a guy on Book Boyfriends Wanted. But a little fun leaves her with more than she bargained for when two pink lines appear, and the baby daddy accuses her of trying to trap him. So much for a little fun. Start His Curvy Craving today!

Looking for more from Zoey and Sebastian? Sign up for my newsletter today and get a free, exclusive bonus epilogue of their first Christmas together! Only available to subscribers!

Love second chance romance? Daniel Dunn is a man who prides himself on his instincts. Too bad those instincts keep letting him down. He's trusted the wrong person too many times, and when his biggest regret shows up on his doorstep, he's not sure if he can trust anything she says. Or if he can trust himself to keep his hands off the woman he once loved. Get your copy of Failure now!

ABOUT THE AUTHOR

USA TODAY Bestselling Author Mary E Thompson spent most of her childhood wishing she had a few less curves. She hid in the pages of books because her favorite characters never cared what size her clothes were. Now, neither does Mary, and she writes stories that celebrate women like her. Real women who have curves, chase dreams, and find love, because we should all be happy, no matter our dress size.

Mary spends her non-writing time with her husband and two kids, watching too much TV, cheering for her home-town football team (Go Bills!), and hiding chocolate from her family.

Visit https://MaryEThompson.com/ to sign up for Mary's newsletter, **Romancing the Curves**. Subscribers get free ebooks and other fun stuff, like exclusive, members only content and giveaways, plus are the first to know about new releases and sales!